A DIAMOND TO DIE FOR

A DIAMOND TO DIE FOR

ANN BLAIR KLOMAN

Rev. date: 09/05/2013

To order additional copies of this book, contact:
Xlibris LLC
1-888-795-4274
www.Xlibris.com
Orders@Xlibris.com
140147

DEDICATION

Thanks for the patience of those of my family who read
and edited for me after the forest hid the trees.
Forgive my liberties with the family of my old friend Fred Church.
Thanks to Anne with an e for helping clear Bainbridge
Island, Washington of shellfish smugglers.
Again, forgive more manipulation of the Maine harbor to
which Isobel brings mayhem.
Thanks to Connecticut State Trooper Gary Inglis for taking
his time to correct the errors of a person of interest, and
especially for Sylvia Marsh, our writing guru.

And, as always, no harm intended.

ONE

Storms wash up strange things. On that wet afternoon with damp penetrating her bones and in haste to return to the hotel's warm comforts, Isobel's downcast eyes caught something partly buried in the sand that did not belong on this Rhode Island beach. At first glance it resembled half a large skeletal crab, but after the back run of foam subsided, she nudged aside a snarl of seaweed with her toe and abruptly jerked her foot away.

It was not a crab. It was a human hand, severed cleanly at the wrist. Above the arthritic knuckle of its ring finger, shone a large glittering diamond. Repulsed, for a long minute she could only stare down at the grisly thing. Though the bones were washed clean of flesh, the enlarged joint had fused and held the ring in place. Isobel saw that a wrap of clear fishing line must have protected it from time's battering by the sea.

Isobel had dealt with far worse sights, and hesitated only a moment before bending down to pick it up. The stone, which she guessed at several carats, stood mounted high in the prongs of an old-fashioned Victorian setting. She frowned. The ring had to be paste. But if not, and the gem on this skeletal finger was a genuine diamond, she'd found a most valuable piece of salvage.

Not that she would keep it, she argued with herself. Or should she? Isobel pursed her lips and frowned. Think about it. If she rushed into town and turned it over to the police, what would they do with it? Obviously, judging by the skeleton, this was no recent crime. Did marine salvage belong to the finder? Ought to be easy enough to check that out.

Isobel hunched forward against the wind and, despite a sudden gust that chafed her skin, removed her silk headscarf. Salty spume blown from the tops of whitecaps whipped her hair across her face. Her feet squished through the wet shingle in the thin rubber boots she'd packed and now were numb with cold.

She looked around the deserted beach, wrapped the hand of bones gently in her scarf, and headed back to the hotel.

───────────

Isobel felt sure the décor of the inn's dim foyer was designed as a spoof. In one corner of its checkered tiled entrance, stood a grey, withered relic elephant's foot filled with umbrellas. Beside it, a huge and ugly cloisonné vase held the vicious swords of a formidable *Sanseveria*— mother-in-law's tongue—prepared to launch a battery of attack spikes. Much to her relief, as Isobel passed through the empty lobby and climbed the two short flights of steps to her room, she encountered no one who might question the lumpy bundle cradled in her arm.

Safe in her second floor suite, she laid the damp package on the bathroom floor and shed her wet outer clothes. She rummaged in her baggage for her toiletry kit, and was not surprised that the bathroom, with its huge spa tub and walk-in shower, was nearly as large as the bedroom. She approved the chenille rugs that cushioned the marble floor and sniffed the soaps and lotions—all expensively herbal.

After a quick hot shower, and snug in the inn's terry cloth robe and slippers, Isobel sat at the intricately inlaid desk in the alcove overlooking the harbor and opened the earmarked page of the complementary glossy magazine she had browsed through on her arrival. She stroked the tasteful photograph, and could almost feel the soft drape of velvet caressing the emerald necklace. Isobel nipped at her lower lip and sighed at the jeweler's price. In discrete and tiny print—$280,000. Pocket change, she guessed, envious of many of the summer guests at this noveau castle. Not that Isobel didn't have the money. It was not a question of cash flow. More, she thought wistfully, a suitability issue. The exquisite bauble was designed to grace a neck decades younger.

She looked around the suite she had booked to spend her birthday on this stormy March weekend. The inn was a former Newport mansion that offered sweeping views of Jamestown and Narragansett Bay. However, upon first gazing up at its shocking architecture, she decided the original owner of this family pile had spent some of the income from that era's tax-free fortune with questionable taste.

The curved walls of her bedroom enclosed one of the old mansions many conical towers—too many and an unfortunate conceit fancied by architects of Newport's gilded age. Like the other grand estates lining the famous Ocean Drive, it echoed the era's extravagant, but often tasteless, show of wealth.

Isobel crossed the room and sank onto the pillows cushioning the vast canopied bed. Overhead, she eyed the pleated velvet tester and recalled some vague and ominous portent in Poe's tale of the victim's suffocation by its crushing, smothering descent. On either side of the bed, a pair of antique bureaus rested on a worn oriental carpet and tilted slightly leeward on the gently sloping floor.

Elegance with character. She liked that, and wondered if the owners vetted their guests. On a blustery weekend like this, she preferred her nautical quarters to be solidly anchored. Far better than being tossed about in a first class cabin at sea.

Appropriately, above the room's old and unique pieces hung paintings of yachts storming the entrance to Jamestown's harbor under full sail. On arriving, she'd read in the brochure describing the owner's nineteenth century family's history that racing yachts were the scion's major indulgence. Money better spent, she thought, than on his dubious architect. His yachts' sleek and powerful lines carving the water were more graceful in design than these fanciful turreted digs.

Isobel shifted among the bed's cushions and decided that today was one of those boring, mid-life birthdays unworthy of celebration. Her grandmother, the first Isobel, had lived past a century and she expected to do the same. But confronted by the gray, ragged waters of Narragansett Bay on this dreary anniversary, her resolve disappeared and her shoulder's sagged under a wave of melancholy. At the moment, she missed her often-annoying family and having fled them, felt suddenly too alone.

Her escape had started well. On arrival, the uniformed housemaid had settled her among these comforts and explained the gas fire that she lit with a flick of a switch. The flickering logs looked so real, Isobel expected an explosion of sparks.

"I'm Marcia," the woman said. "Anything you need, Ms. Van Dursan," nodding at the phone, "you just ring housekeeping."

Isobel got up to test the comfort of the elegant swan-backed chaise facing the bay windows and its grey view of the choppy harbor. She welcomed the fire's heat after her chill walk along the beach and, drowsy with warmth, pushed the discovery of that bizarre treasure from her mind. She nestled her cheek against the chaise's cashmere throw and considered the recent decision that had drastically changed the comfortable, but predictable security of her and her niece Jo's life.

Isobel stared down at her slim ankles. She was vain about her legs. They denied her age—after all, they had carried her still-firm body for almost sixty years. Her inner self did not feel old, but at the moment, she admitted to a touch of weariness after coping with the arduous day's flights from her Maine fishing village to the Rhode Island coast.

She missed Jo. And not just her niece's company. Their special relationship began when, at age four, Jo had climbed on Isobel's lap and insisted her aunt teach her to read. The bond established during those early cuddled hours spent spelling out the escapades of *Ant* and *Bee* and *Kind Dog* had continued into adulthood.

Last year, when Isobel abruptly chose this new career, she had convinced Jo to accompany her on that first assignment. Trial by fire and so different from those innocent adventures of dog and bee. Now Isobel realized how much she'd come to rely on her niece's help with the irritating and exhausting demands of modern travel. All that checking in and out of cabs, planes, car rentals, and then, on arrival, the tedious unpacking, hanging and stowing.

Isobel still was amazed how her current life had resulted from a whim. Last summer, she had placed an ad in *Soldier of Fortune* magazine and, as a result, accepted Malo Bellini's offer. With that decision, she exchanged her mundane existence as Frits Van Dursan's recent widow for the opportunity to live on higher plane—literally—with first class travel and all its perks included. Her employer's assignments had transformed her life—and Jo's, whom she'd enticed along as her companion.

But now, if she was to convince Jo to remain her sidekick, Isobel must seriously question how much it would compromise their integrity to continue as Malo Bellini's mercenary hit women.

After a practice run, 'accidentally' electrocuting Jo's sister Fiona's despicable husband, Eugene, her first assignment by Malo had been to dispatch one heinous criminal with poison—all evidence eliminated by a baited grizzly bear—then another international villain with just her Swiss army knife. Without complications, she'd been able to remove these two nasty men from society without much troubling her conscience. After being introduced to the malignant people inhabiting Malo's arena, she rationalized that enough evil still remained in the world to justify continuing her new career.

TWO

Isobel roused from her doze but lay nestled before the faux fire and wished that sensible Jo was here with her, and not off golfing in the south of Spain. She shook herself awake, tossed aside the throw and, tiring of her pity party, got to her feet and eyed the split of champagne chilling in its iced silver cooler. But before feeling free to indulge, her tidy nature insisted she empty her cases that the housemaid had placed on the rosewood stand beside the foyer closet.

Isobel realized that, during her very short time in Malo's employ, she'd softened to the indulgent perks her new career afforded. Her watch showed quarter past four. From the Inn's information brochure, she remembered tea was being served downstairs. Should she skip that temptation and save her appetite for dinner and the chef's renowned expertise? Isobel decided she'd unpack then go down and take only a cup of tea and maybe a piece of fruit. Good smells had wafted from the kitchen earlier and she was pleased to realize that her grim beach booty find had not diminished her appetite.

From last year's constant world's travel, she had learned to pack frugally and the room's Biedemeir's bow-front chest of drawers held everything from her cases that did not need hanging.

Next to the bureau loomed a massive armoire, large enough to hold the contents of a steamer trunk and, a century ago, it probably had. Now it stood almost empty except for her few dresses. On entering the room, she had found a tasseled brass key hanging from the keyhole in one of the wardrobe's paneled doors. Isobel had smiled. Now if she had been on a mission for Malo, upon opening it, she might have expected to find a body hanging inside—maybe several. She turned and eyed the bundle on the floor beside the desk and could no longer ignore its contents. She had removed the headscarf, re-wrapped the hand in a small towel from the bath, and placed the small parcel with its sparkly garnish on the wardrobe's top shelf.

Downstairs, ready for a cup of hot tea, Isobel paused at the foot of the staircase and regarded the lobby with its pattern of black and white diamond shaped floor tiles. A propitious omen? From this small space, probably the original entrance hall, glass paneled doors led into the tea room enclosed in yet another circular tower. On this late afternoon, she found the room empty except for one other couple. Rain continued to pelt the windows with angry gusts and it was easy to understand why so few guests had braved travel to the coast on this rough weekend.

A petite Asian woman wearing a blue and white Shibori pattern kimono bustled her to a table set for one.

"Tea, dearie," she insisted, "hot tea on a day like this."

To Isobel's dismay, the table was pre-set with a tiered plate of warm scones, sliced fruit, tea sandwiches and a tempting array of little iced cakes. When asked for her choice of tea, she selected a smoky Lapsang and was pleased when the dainty woman returned with a silver pot steeping an infuser heady with the scent of leaf tea.

Next to the fire—a real wood one—the other guests' table was angled toward her and, although the couple kept their voices muted, she sensed an unpleasant urgency in their conversation. She saw the man bend his head intently towards his companion in serious disagreement. Isobel thought them an incongruous pair. The wispy, cardiganed woman sat hunched over her plate, crumbing uneaten bits from a piece of cake. Her debonair companion, dressed in custom haute couture, certainly spent more on the weekly grooming of his perfectly styled hair than Isobel did in a year's visits to Brenda's Cut 'n Curl.

Isobel reprimanded herself, lowered her eyes and nibbled a slice of chocolate dipped mango. She knew too well the past difficulties caused by her innate curiosity, but this unquenchable weakness kept her straining to eavesdrop. The couple's words were muffled, but the intense forward lean of the man's body threatened. Isobel stared at the woman's clenched hands fighting with her napkin in her lap. When the man deliberately folded his own square of linen, Isobel summoned all her social restraint not to stare as he stood and abruptly pushed back his chair. She almost gasped aloud when he grasped the woman's wrist and pulled her rudely from her seat.

"Pack your things. We're leaving," he said. The brief smile he directed at Isobel as he urged the woman past her table was as cold as his eyes.

In the empty tearoom, Isobel inspected the candy violet topping a normally irresistible chocolate petit four and found she had lost her appetite. For the second time today, she wondered if she had made a mistake to come here alone, deliberately choosing to slip away from Elmore Harbor to avoid another traditional Van Dursan birthday ritual. Despite the season and its rigors of weather, all family anniversaries were celebrated with an outdoor lobster bake. These tiresome events took place on the lawn below Isobel's cottage where everyone dutifully huddled on the wintery slope leading down to the icy waters of Penobscot Bay. With heads covered by wooly hats and shoulders hunched in scarf wrapped parkas, they would shift from foot to foot, clutching hot toddies in mittened hands and dodge about trying to evade drifting smoke from the fire pit.

After raising toasts to their hardy souls for enduring this silly Polar Bear rite, everyone, with relief, would hurry inside. From an eclectic potluck buffet set up in Isobel's dining room, they would fill their plates. After everyone jockeyed for seats near the living room fire, they would dutifully murmur pleasure over Raybelle's, Isobel's southern daughter-in-law, inevitable quivering salads and pimento cheese spread. Later, in an alcove, on a lace-draped tea trolley, Isobel could imagine the chocolate frosted red-velvet birthday cake waiting to be served. Probably topped with a tactful symbolic candle.

But not this year.

Away from it all and alone upstairs in front of her toasty gas fire, Isobel suppressed the guilt at avoiding this ordeal. Despite the stormy day and tea shared with that sour couple, she intended to enjoy this lovely, peaceful respite and definitely consider making it a yearly habit. She yawned and, sated by too many sweets, decided a little nap was in order.

THREE

Isobel awoke refreshed and in a better mood after an hour's rest and, checking her watch, decided it was time for something stronger than tea.

Downstairs she found the tearoom now converted to a cozy cocktail lounge. The wooden panels of one wall were folded open to display shelves of jewel-like liquor bottles backlit behind a fiddle-railed mahogany bar, and the afternoon accouterments were now replaced with trays of savory hors d'oeuvres. Isobel idly wondered if the petite Asian lady had hustled home to cook up a tasty Pad Thai for her family. She found it impossible to stifle her curiosity, and sometimes unable to resist elaborating on the private life of strangers—such as this afternoon's disturbing eavesdropping. What was going on between that angry couple?

Across the room a dapper gent, looking right out of a London pub, fingered his mustache and gave her a beaver-toothed smile. She half expected him to wiggle his eyebrows. She chose a table as far away from him as possible, and the young server placed before her a generous single malt whisky.

"Courtesy of the gentleman," he announced. Annoyed, Isobel frowned at the ogler, worried that he might consider his offering of drink an invitation to join her. She ignored his eyes. The waiter's words brought a nostalgic flash of memory that returned her to the hot afternoon last summer in the dining room of her Bermuda hotel. On that tropical day, another waiter had brought her and Jo a restorative aperitif and, with British accent, spoken the same four words.

She and Jo had looked around, puzzled as they sat alone in the sun-filled patio. "By phone, madam," the waiter explained. On that tense afternoon, the offering had come from Malo Bellini—sent from his Dordogne villa in southwest France, and today, in Newport on this blustery day, the memory of his voice tingled her spirits.

"Happy birthday, Isobel."

Startled at actually hearing the familiar voice, she turned toward the entrance and a surge of pleasure swept her to her feet. As if in instant answer to her wishful memory, Malo stood grinning at her from the doorway.

He strode to her table, bent to give her a discreet kiss on the cheek, and held out a small turquoise box. She recognized the jeweler's exclusive trademark. With a cry of surprise and a hug that buried her face in his chest, she accepted the gift. Knowing his good taste, it would be unique.

Her first meeting with Malo had been a surprise for each of them. He'd expected the I. Van Dursan who had answered his inquiry for a hired mercenary to be a man, and she had expected some stereotypical gangster. They were both wrong. Malo Bellini appeared fit and slightly grey at the temples. With the blue eyes and ruddy cheeks of an Irishman, he had instantly charmed her. She had learned that, in spite of his Italian father's inherited business connections, Bellini was named after his Irish mother, neé Malone. A complete gentleman.

He warmed the large Jameson he'd ordered between his palms and she eyed the whisky and smiled.

"How did you find me?" Isobel spoke in a rush, buoyed by the unexpected pleasure of his company. "Are you staying here? Are you on a holiday, or," she asked warily, "have you come on business?"

He smiled and kissed her hands. "My dear Isobel, yes, yes, and no. I'm in one of those tower suites next to yours and, believe me, though there's plenty of work for you if you want it, I've come for a weekend of relaxation, good food, and some off-season tourist gawking at the lifestyles of those American once rich and famous. I've never visited this nautical city and, from what I hear of its wicked history, it's a far cry from your tranquil Maine harbor." He paused, puzzled. "Why choose to travel alone and so far for your birthday?"

"Malo," she leaned toward him, "need I remind you that last summer, in our 'tranquil' harbor, your wife tried to kill me? Trapped me in my wreck of a car and tried to suffocate me with dry ice!"

Malo grinned. "Of course, how could I forget? However, fortunately, in spite of her attempt, both you and the ice-packed lobsters survived. And, you have to admit, her plan for your demise was ingenious. Worthy of your own invention."

"I'm sorry, but I found that near-death experience too close a call."

"Don't worry," he said and patted her hand. "I assure you that the wretched woman has since been certified mad and is now discretely tended by watchful eyes. Most important, my dear, you lived, and your life is all that matters to me." He pointed to the gift resting on the table between them. "Open your present."

Isobel pulled at the satin ribbons and lifted the lid of the small box. Under folds of delicate tissue nestled an original Fabergé brooch. The treasure was exquisite and she felt a huge relief that, after today's discovery on the beach, he'd not chosen a gemstone.

"This is beautiful, Malo, and so special," she said. "Thank you very much." She pinned the enameled piece to her blouse, and admired its oval luster.

"To answer your question as to why I'm here," she said, "Newport's wicked history appealed to me." She frowned. "But after today's strange events, it may have been a bad idea to have come alone." She smiled at him across the table. "I am so glad to see you and, right now, nothing sounds better than spending the rest of this odd weekend relaxing together." He lowered his eyes at her. "What do you mean strange?" Isobel twisted the length of satin ribbon between her fingers. "Something rather unusual came up at teatime."

Malo took a large swallow of whisky and massaged his forehead. "Isobel—what now?"

She ignored his question and looked down at her watch. Plenty of time before dinner to explain, she thought, but not here. She nodded toward the door. He understood and, leaving a generous tip, followed her across the lobby and upstairs.

Inside her room, she hesitated before the paneled wardrobe. He watched her unwrap the hand and, when she held it out to him on the square of toweling, he said nothing, just shook his head.

"I found it this afternoon on the beach," she said.

He stared at her. "You found it?"

"The storm washed it up," she said. "It's obviously been sloshing about the harbor for ages and held intact by this wrap of fishing line. Could the stone be real? Can I keep it? Should I concern myself with the legalities of Admiralty Law and all those boring rules of salvage and Laws of Find?" Malo ignored her rush of concerns and inspected the skeletal hand.

"Forget all that," he said. "This item is hardly your usual flotsam or jetsam."

"From the small size of the bones and the fancy setting," said Isobel, "let's assume it belonged to a woman." She pointed to the severed wrist bones, still held fused by hardened cartilage. "Don't you think the clean cut suggests she must have bled to death? And no accident. Probably murdered? Knowing the scandalous history of this town, I'd like to make a few inquiries. Maybe find out where we can find records of some violent episode involving a murder by dismemberment? A crime involving a missing diamond?" Maybe visit the local Historical Society? She paused in her rush of questions. "Admit it, if someone killed this woman, it was not something easily swept under the carpet—or out to sea— even in that more lenient era. That is a huge diamond and if it's genuine we are not dealing with poor people."

Malo lay back among her bed pillows, his arms behind his neck, cushioning his head.

"Isobel," he spoke firmly. "We are not about to deal with people. Please, as we agreed, let's both take a break from work. Curb your ghoulish enthusiasm and together just enjoy a vacation from mayhem."

He watched Isobel scowl and chafe with impatience. Resigned, he sat up and acknowledged defeat. "But knowing you," he said, "you'll ignore my advice to turn the whole matter, including that distasteful extremity, over to the authorities." He leaned towards her. "Besides, I'm sorry to deflate your notions of some romantic crime committed in the glory days of nineteenth-century Newport society, but that hand, unless encased in Artic ice, belonged to a much more recent victim."

Isobel, subdued by this reality, sank down beside him.

"I knew something was wrong. And you are so right," she said, "about both the impossible survival of that hand intact and us needing a vacation from mayhem." She gave him a wicked smile. "At least for the moment." Isobel rewrapped the bejeweled piece of skeleton in the face towel and returned it to the armoire.

"Let's go down to dinner," she said. "There's another little matter bothering me. It's the odd conversation I overheard at tea this afternoon."

FOUR

Darkness came early on this March evening and beyond the surround of windows encircling the inn's dining room, lines of channel marker lights twinkled across the harbor. The storm had blown through and gusting rain pelting against the glass no longer competed with the room's candlelit ambience.

Isobel anticipated with bliss the dozen plump oysters nestled before her on a cushion of ice. She savored each one, slipping them into her mouth from their nacreous shell. They were followed by a tiny scoop of mint-flecked citrus granité that primed them for their entrée of perfectly pink lamb medallions. Avoiding any mention of her day's unpleasant events, they concentrated on dinner and agreed that the chef's creations had definitely proved his reputation. Isobel sat back, satisfied by the perfect birthday meal, and regarded the elegant room. She no longer felt guilty for deciding this evening a great improvement over Raybelle's family buffet.

To Isobel's embarrassed delight, at the end of the meal, a single candle adorned the lemon soufflé brought to their table with ceremonial hush and discreet applause from the few other guests. Malo, true to form, remembered her dislike of frosted cakes and she was charmed by his sensitive gesture. None of Raybelle's dense double chocolate layers tonight.

Irish coffees and truffles ended her special birthday feast. Malo relaxed back in his chair, peeled the gold foil from a circle of Belgian chocolate, and prompted her with a nod.

"So now, my birthday girl, what about this other matter bothering you?"

"I came down after a little nap for a cup of tea," she began, studying the plate of sweets, "in the same room where we had drinks. This angry couple sat near enough for me to overhear their conversation."

"Naturally you heard every word."

"Well, not every word. But I could tell from his fierce attitude that the man—an unctuous, possessive sort—threatened his companion. The poor woman looked his complete contrast, a mousy soul and obviously cowed by him. Suddenly he stood up, grabbed the woman's arm, and bullied her from the room. 'Pack your things,' he said in a nasty voice. 'We're leaving at once.'"

Malo leaned forward. "Isobel, perhaps your imagination . . ."

"I know," she admitted. "And it sounds in my telling that it might have been a simple marital spat. But I am not imagining the man's venomous tone. Humor me, and perhaps we can manage a peek at the guest register before we go upstairs?"

They lingered over their coffee and were the last to leave the dining room. The foyer was empty, and when Isobel saw the hotel register lying open on the dimly lit reception desk, she cocked an eye at Malo.

"Why not?" she pointed.

She paged through the ledger and ran her finger down the recent entries. With the holiday season ended and summer still months away, the Inn's only draw was the low rates offered for its off-season specials. Their reasonably priced promise of a winter escape had attracted her, but few others. Among the guests, she noted two single women with the same last name, probably sisters, and an "Esq." from London who must have been the man in the bar with the elaborate mustache who had leered at her over his Pimms. Her finger ran down the page then stopped on the line above her own name. A Mr. and Mrs. Foley, and daughter, had signed in yesterday from Hartford, Connecticut.

"That must be them," she said. She indicated their entry. "They've booked three separate rooms. I must have been right about their hostile relationship. Look, two adjoining rooms and another for their child." She smiled up at Malo. "That doesn't sound friendly. And just because they weren't in the dining room tonight doesn't mean they've left. There are good places to eat in Newport, even off-season. The weather earlier stayed nasty and if the Foleys were that couple, and he really meant 'at once,' then maybe they did leave. But then," she paused, "if they had to drive far, they may have decided to wait until skies cleared in the morning. She ran her finger across their entry and noticed that the Foley's had left no confirmed check out date. "Maybe they haven't left," she said.

Malo pushed aside the ledger and pulled Isobel against him.

"Forget them," he said and kissed her ear. "One way or another, the Foley problem is out of your hands." He pointed to the stairs. "Let's go up and properly celebrate your birthday. And there's plenty of time tomorrow to decide what to do with that item stashed in your closet."

Isobel nestled her head against his chest. She did not want to think about that item upstairs in her closet.

"Actually," she said, as they climbed the stairs to the second floor, "I read that this hotel's owner made his money from some invention connected with the weather. I'm holding steady in Gentle Breezes, and I saw in the register that you are next to me in Fair Winds. The Foley's are directly above us in Force Three and Force Five. Their kid is in the Crow's Nest." On the second floor landing Malo stopped and smiled.

"I like our innkeeper's sense of humor," he said. "Perhaps he can feel a guest's aura and, in the Foley's case, his intuition cast them into storms."

"I'm fine with Gentle Breezes," said Isobel. "Being prone to mal de mer, the tilt of the floor in my tower suite is enough nautical reality."

"If those gale force rooms are in the same tower and directly above us," said Malo, "why don't you just pop up and listen at their doors? I'm sure your shell-like ears can detect a fart in a gale."

Isobel climbed the narrow circular staircase leading up to the Foley's rooms and wondered how they passed today's building code. On the third floor landing she stopped for breath in an area only large enough to swing the proverbial cat. She pressed her ear to each door, but heard no noises from either Force Three or Five. Above, on the topmost floor, the sound of canned laughter came from inside the Crow's Nest. If anyone emerged suddenly from this room, Isobel would have a hard time explaining her lurking about.

From a niche carved into the landing's mahogany paneling, the beveled glass of an old ship's lantern reflected dim prisms of light on the conical roof of this aerie turret. She reminded herself that the pricey pleasure of staying in these upscale digs meant that such treasures as the inn's antique furnishings, its displays of China Trade porcelains, and the guest room's fine paintings were not nailed to the walls. She wondered if ever a guest had departed with one of these rare pieces tucked in his luggage?

Isobel turned to leave and, with one foot resting on the top step, the door behind her abruptly opened and a young girl appeared—as startled as she.

"I'm sorry," Isobel gasped. "I'm Mrs. Van Dursan staying in the room below and thought I heard someone fall. Are you all right? The desperate lie sounded ridiculous, but the girl, perhaps in her mid-teens, only blinked and shook her close-cropped blond curls. For a moment she peered suspiciously at Isobel, then smiled and held out a hand.

"Hi. I'm Allyce." She pronounced it Aleece. She had an edginess about her that Isobel thought a little out of place for her young age—as if she'd already seen more than her share of rough times—and perhaps should be wary of strangers lurking in hallways. She also bore no resemblance to the odd couple Isobel had watched at tea earlier in the day.

"No, I'm fine." The girl smiled at Isobel and seemed relieved that someone would care. "Thanks though for asking."

Oh dear, thought Isobel. Her intuition had often proved right, and something felt odd here. With a wave of her hand, she apologized again for her curiosity. Allyce shrugged, "No problem." An artificial burst of laughter blared from the room's television before the girl gave a little bye-bye wiggle of her fingers and shut the door. Winding her way back down the short flight of spiral stairs, she wondered whether to mention the encounter to Malo. Allyce—really, what has happened to all the plain Janes—seemed edgy though unthreatened. Malo would find it highly unlikely that they had stumbled on the victim of white slavers from Hartford, Connecticut.

The next morning she awoke to sunlight flooding her room and had just finished dressing when Malo's soft knock at her door reminded her they'd agreed to meet for breakfast. Downstairs, along with a menu that included every possible choice, their waitress placed small coupes of something pale orange and creamy she called a mango smoothie in front of them.

"Tones the palate," the girl announced with a smile.

Isobel's palate never needed toning. Breakfast was her favorite meal, and often unusual.

"A delicious organic sausage with sauerkraut, a chicken enchilada con queso, and crisp bacon with mustard on rye toast," she ordered. "That would be perfect." The well-trained waitress only nodded. Malo winced.

When Isobel saw that he'd drunk enough coffee to allow communication, she commanded his attention.

"We've got to take another look at the guest log. They usually make note of your license when you sign in and we need to know more about the Foley's." Malo looked at her across the table with resignation.

"Why?"

"I think the young girl with them may not be their daughter—if they're even a 'couple' at all. I'd say she's about sixteen. That's probably the reason for the separate rooms, and I'd like to check them out. There's something odd that I just can't put my finger on. Maybe we can learn more about them from tracing their license plate." She was relieved when Malo did not accuse her of too vivid imaginings. He just stared at her, leaned back in his chair and pianoed his fingers along the tablecloth.

She knew his history of association with corrupt people. Those same sort who promise success in whatever guise kids crave and prey on those who are desperate to escape their dead-end lives. Isobel had sadly discovered in the short time working for Malo how much tragedy flourished below the surface of apparently humdrum normality. She sat silent, staring at her empty plate, and recalled her first assignment at the five-star dude ranch in Montana where she had dispatched the benign, bonsai-loving Mr. Akuratzu and ended his offshore human organ farm industry.

"Before we assume the worst," she said appealing to his skepticism, "we should simply check them out." She patted her belly. "But before we do any serious tracking of these Foleys, let's begin this beautiful day with some touristy bits on foot."

"I hate to remind you on a full stomach," said Malo, eyeing her middle, "but we must soon deal with the item stowed in your cupboard. It's hard to ignore."

"Don't worry," she said. "My salvage won't deteriorate much further while we do some exploring."

Downstairs, the hotel's reception desk was busy with morning departures and left them no privacy to check the Foley's auto license.

"Let's get out into the sunshine," Malo insisted. "I've rented a fancy car. We'll put the top down, drive around town, and stop somewhere on the waterfront for lunch. No business talk, no body parts, no talk of Danni Asker."

"Who is Danny Asker?"

Malo turned the ignition, and the Maserati engine rumbled to life. Typically, he had not found this auto at Avis. Isobel thought of her recent VW beater, its tenuous outer parts held together with duct tape. It now rested on blocks in her Maine garage, and reminded her of the day she had almost lost her life. After the success of her first assignment, as a bonus, Malo had replaced it with a sleek new hybrid. A bright red convertible and symbol of what she loved most about her new life—indulgence in practical but not excessive luxury. "Danny Asker," she repeated the name. "Who is he?"

"She," he answered, "and spelled with an i, is the first lady of teen porn. She began her career decades ago as a club lap dancer and, being a savvy businesswoman, quickly realized the potential of internet pornography. Danni became the CEO of an enterprise that, in a short time, netted her over $8 million."

Isobel scowled. "Do you think this has something to do with Allyce and the Foley's? I imagine that, to a girl her age, this kind of thing sounds an appealing lure, and she seems pretty enough."

"I'm sure she is," said Malo. "These kids all are young and pretty—and easily enticed." He raised an eye in disgust. "And not just girls. The new breed of persuaders involves kids in little films at first, very soft porn—even Danni had her limits. She insisted on no penetration, no violence against women, no grossly explicit sex." He gave the car's wheel a savage slap with his palm. "How times have changed. Today you can order up snuff films at the click of a mouse."

"Snuff films?"

"Isobel my dear, this ugly conversation is over. I hope your Allyce proves an innocent relation of the Foleys and all of them have set out on some banal destination."

The low-slung car hugged the curving drive along the mansion-lined avenues above the ocean, normally clogged with tourists. They passed the post office and Isobel insisted he stop at the drive thru Fed-Ex drop. She pulled a padded mailer from her oversize handbag and dropped it through the pull-down opening.

"What was that," said Malo.

"A gift for Jo," she answered.

They drove on, gazing in awe like most tourists, at the empty estates just visible behind high guarding brick walls. Stark trees silhouetted against the sky stood bare of leaves. A landscape so different from summer, when carefully tended gardens softened the grounds of these massive stone homes. Malo gestured at the rambling wings of an estate covering at least an acre of barren lawn.

"Take a look at that massive pile of bricks," he said. "What would we do with twenty-seven bedrooms, tout en suite?"

"First thing," she answered, "employ two dozen servants."

FIVE

"Stop!"

At Isobel's abrupt command Malo jammed on the brakes, gripped the wheel and swore. Luckily no one back-ended them.

"There it is," she pointed. "That colonial building across the street. And with a parking space in front. Now isn't that a good omen?"

The carved granite lintel over the building's entrance read: "Newport Historical Society."

Inside its somber interior, a Jack Spratt and his wife combo looked up from behind an antique ball and claw foot desk. Newport was known for it history of fine furniture and Isobel had done her research. She recognized that its delicate fan-front panel had been carved by the nineteenth-century cabinetmaker Edmund Townsend. The walls of the room portrayed a gallery of murals evolving the early history of Newport and Jamestown, and Isobel was subdued by that particular hushed and socially prim aura evoked by old museums.

The gentleman, gaunt framed but dapper in blue pinstripe, peered at her over his spectacles. Isobel could not help staring at the elaborate and complicated fold of the cravat at his neck. The buxom matron seated beside him looked corseted so tightly that her bosoms bulged from her blouse like melons. Isobel turned to Malo, suddenly hesitant to inquire of dismembered bodies before this austere couple. Should they have gone instead to the police, or chosen more subtle research? Beside her, Malo avoided her eye. Isobel gathered her wits.

"Have I come to the right place to research information on past local . . . ." What to say? She paused and fumbled for an acceptable phrase. Crimes? Cold cases? Isobel leaned toward them and whispered, "Old unsolved murders?" She reddened, embarrassed, as if personally guilty of some conspiracy. She turned to Malo for support and saw he had deserted her. He strolled, hands clasped at his back, along the walls of the room studying the panoramic murals dedicated to the historic town's past century. Too overly intent, she thought, on the island's pictorial history.

Hearing her request, the two elderly docents looked at each other and, to Isobel's astonishment, burst into laughter. Their stuffy demeanor vanished as they nudged each other and shook with amusement.

"Now that's a new one, right Amber," he said. Amber, as in *Forever,* Isobel wondered? Images of Kathleen Winsor's fictional lusty wench flashed through her head as the amply endowed woman behind the antique desk wiped tears from her flushed face with a handful of tissues.

"Everyone's heard the infamous stories of the town's scandalous element," said the female docent, immediately resuming her dignity and whose discreet nametag indeed read 'Amber'. "And yes, we have several books on 'ye olde wicked Newport' in our library upstairs. People love to read about that wealthy realm of last century's society and their atrocious behavior. Believe me, our Ocean Drive tours exposing the history of its residents are as fully booked as those Los Angeles routes among the homes of the stars. Everyone loves a celebrity scandal."

She dabbed at her eyes and, in serious docent mode, continued her talk. "With great fortunes at stake, there are always crimes, and knowing how many unfortunate arranged marriages during that era involved huge sums of money, you must expect—she leaned forward—crimes of passion." She narrowed her eyes. Are you are interested in some particular inquiry other than our more gossipy disgraces?"

Mr. Latham—Isobel noted his nameplate—spoke up. "If you are looking into last century's actual police records," he said, in the cultured voice of someone who came easily to such an elaborate cravat, "I'm not sure how far back they're kept on file. If you're researching a specific case, I suggest you visit our police headquarters." She had not noticed that Malo had silently returned to her side and was startled by the slight pressure of his hand at her elbow. He pointed to a lighted display case in a corner of the room.

"Come over there and look at the collection of photographs of those elite society parties," he said. "There's one of a woman decked out in ball gown and jewels that will interest you," he raised an eyebrow, "especially her ring."

He led Isobel to a glass-topped case holding a tableau of photos taken when party times in those massive mansions indulged their guests with elaborate, tax-free excess. He tapped on the case above one particular image.

Isobel stared at the faded daguerreotype displaying a fancy affair in the Breaker's ballroom. Its label noted the assorted Astors, Vanderbilts, Dukes and their kin, all captured in full regalia. The guests gathered around a laden buffet towered over by a five-foot carved ice swan. Malo pointed to a trio of stiffly posed women gowned in their jet-beaded and elegantly jeweled costumes. He indicated the largest of the photographs.

"Check out the arrogant *grand dame* in the middle of those three ladies. The one with the head full of spit curls." Isobel examined the beautiful woman. A peacock feather sprouted from the headache band circling her brow, but unfortunately, a pleated fan modestly hid her face.

"Take a close look at the ring finger."

"Oh my."

The young woman wore the exact ring Isobel had found on the skeletal hand washed up on the beach. She turned to Malo and whispered.

"Do you think it's our severed salvage?"

"Who knows," he said. "But don't you think it's highly unlikely there are two such identical rings?" They looked up and saw the docents, across the room, eyeing them curiously. Malo shifted uneasily. "Let's get out of here." Isobel glanced at him, wondering why his sudden impulse to leave, but without question, returned with him to the desk.

"Thank you both," she said to the docents. "We apologize for taking your time with our odd request but will do as you suggest and visit the police station. They may have kept old records." Mr. Latham took out his thick-barreled, important fountain pen, wrote the Broadway Street address of police headquarters on his card, and handed it to Malo.

"Regardless," Isobel smiled at the eccentric pair, "we're enjoying late winter in Newport. It's a lovely time to visit without the usual crush of tourists." She fidgeted under their amused scrutiny. "Again, so sorry for the bother."

"No trouble at all," repeated Amber. "Please sign our visitor's ledger." She pushed the leather book towards them and Latham handed her his fountain pen. "Believe me, my dear, you've made our day. You can't imagine how dull this job is during the off season." They heard the couple chuckling as they left.

Outside, they squinted against the bright sun that glinted off the harbor where only a few masts spiked the clear sky above Bannister's Wharf. In March, even at mid-day, no one waited for restaurant seating. Isobel checked her watch and decided that one o'clock was time for lunch and they needed a place to sit and discuss this fascinating business they'd uncovered regarding the mysterious lady and her ring.

"Now that we've worked all that breakfast off with our traipsing around," Isobel said, "perhaps something light for lunch?"

They were seated immediately at a sunny table overlooking the harbor, impossible during the summer in this popular wharf-side fish house. The only other diners in the normally packed room were an elderly couple with matching three-prong canes hooked over the back of their chairs, and a leathery skinned, watch-capped dock man sitting alone at the table across from them. They ordered Campari and soda aperitifs.

The waitress brought them lunch of soft sourdough rolls encasing fillets of fresh caught flounder. Isobel watched Malo douse the skins of his potato wedges with malt vinegar and sympathized with his poor regard of Americans who drowned everything fried in catsup.

They ate without hurry and when Malo wiped his lips and pushed back his empty plate, he patted his lean stomach, and sighed with pleasure.

"Delicious."

"Agreed." She looked at her watch and anxiously prompted. "Shall we call on the police?"

"Are you asking my advice? Because, if we do, there is no way to make such an inquiry without raising awkward questions. And," he insisted, "awkward does not begin to cover the problem."

"That ring's size and setting are unique and could be on record and recognized if I tried to sell it," Isobel said. "You must admit it's a lovely piece and though I want to keep it, maybe we should check the laws of salvage before just handing it over to the police. Besides," she reasoned, "what will they do with it? They might not take the trouble to trace its original owner after all this time— especially with no body attached."

"Especially that." said Malo. The irony in his voice at his experience with official corruption made her smile. "Believe me Isobel, I understand your argument. I've dealt with many unscrupulous police."

Isobel focused on her nails. "Whatever we decide, I'm afraid the matter is moot."

"Moot?"

"We've no evidence of foul play to bring them," she said.

"Isobel," said Malo. She heard the impatience in his voice. "Forget foul play. You are not Sherlock. Where is the ring?"

"Remember when I insisted we stop at the post office this morning? The package I mailed was not a gift for Jo. I posted the whole thing to myself in Maine. I couldn't get the ring off and I'm not about to cart a severed hand and diamond around in my luggage." Malo sighed and signaled for the bill.

"I think that our first order of business, once you are safely returned to Elmore Harbor," he added, "is to research the feathered lady in the photo we saw at that Breaker's gala and find out more about her while she was still attached to her hand."

The young waitress standing behind them, ready to offer their bill, gasped. When Isobel turned and saw the girl's wide-eyed alarm, she patted her arm.

"We're discussing a movie script, my dear. Only fiction."

Malo left her a large tip.

SIX

Thirty thousand feet above the New England coastline, Jo peered through the scratched Perspex at ominous banks of fog below. Asleep beside her, Pen twisted in his seat and stretched his long legs outside of the seat in front, threatening to trip the incessant aisle roamers. Jo saw his lids twitch, entrapped by some unpleasant dream, and thought his regular features handsome enough to model for a sportsman's magazine. She nudged him gently awake.

"We're almost home. Prepare yourself for return to real life."

Pen blinked awake and stiff with cramp, tried to hold onto the warm, muddled dream of Spanish golf greens—Cádiz, 70 degrees and the gentle breeze ruffling his hair.

"Home? Real life?" Groggy, he realized that the breeze hissing from the jet nozzle above his seat was aimed at his face and chilling him with stale air. He sat up and stared blankly at Jo, stretched and mumbled something rude but inaudible. "Where and what are you calling real?"

"The coast of Maine below us is genuine and it doesn't look good," Jo said. As if on cue, the captain's voice filled the cabin.

"Ladies and gentlemen, thanks to the jet stream and my skill as your pilot, we have enjoyed a smooth and fast flight from Madrid. I wish it would end as well, but we have word that heavy fog over our scheduled airport will prevent our landing." Murmurs of discontent swelled from the passengers.

"Not the worst news," his upbeat voice continued. "We have received confirmation to land at the nearest open airport, only a short distance away in clear and semi-sunny Providence, Rhode Island. Remember, your safety is our primary concern and as your captain and father of six adorable children, it is also mine. Ground transportation will be provided to your ticketed destination."

The rumblings of discontent quieted as the pilot's genial voice soothed most of the savage beasts trapped on board. Jo fumbled for her cell phone.

"I'm calling Isobel as soon as we land. She'll be worried when we don't arrive in the harbor on time for her birthday celebration and, if I remember, they were planning the family do on the boathouse lawn, no matter how frigid the weather."

"Praise the lord and his benevolent fog," muttered Pen. "You've been saved from another Van Dursan Polar Bear Birthday Rite."

As soon as they were safely landed, Jo placed a call to Isobel's cell, but crackling into the phone at her ear, instead of her aunt, came the unexpected voice of Malo Bellini. Alarmed, she blurted out rudely.

"Where's Isobel? Is anything wrong?"

"Nothing's wrong Jo," Malo spoke patiently. "Why does the sound of my voice over the phone set off sirens? I answered because Isobel insisted on driving and, besides being illegal, I won't allow her to maneuver the loops of this ring road around Providence while talking on one of these mobiles."

"Providence? What are you doing in Rhode Island? Isobel's supposed to be in Maine—making nice at the frosty birthday duty."

"We know, but, on a whim, your aunt decided to escape that scene this year and enjoy her anniversary without forcing everyone to freeze to death. The smart woman booked into a fancy inn—some nineteenth-century baron's ersatz castle overlooking Newport's Narragansett Bay where we enjoyed a private celebration. I sussed her out from abroad and managed to arrive in time—long story—to share her birthday dinner minus the obligatory *gateau* à la Raybelle. We just left Newport and are now driving downeast to Elmore Harbor where we'll make proper amends to your family for missing the ritual."

Jo's voice broke up and Malo shook the folding phone. He hated them, and this one was much too small for his hand. "You are fading away. Are you with Penfield—calling from Spain?"

"Yes, no—both. We couldn't land as scheduled in Boston due to fog. They diverted us to Providence where we've just landed. If you haven't gone too far, could you ask Isobel to pull a U-ey and head back to the airport? Actually, this diversion from Boston is so fortuitous it's eerie. If you can return and meet our plane, it would save us the trouble of renting a car and we could travel to the harbor together."

"We're on our way," assured Malo. "Call when you're through customs and we'll pick you up outside your airline's arrivals." He snapped the phone closed and grinned at Isobel. "Jo commands that you pull a U-ey."

Isobel dared take her eyes from the rush of traffic for only a moment.

"What's going on? There is no way I can reverse on this highway." Malo wiggled the phone.

"Your niece is with Penfield and their flight from Madrid has just landed. Because of fog they couldn't put down in Boston, as scheduled, and want us to divert our progress east—do the U-ey—and return to pick them up at the Providence airport." Isobel nodded and without question slowed for the next exit.

"Now don't you find that odd?" she asked. "Almost portentous."

SEVEN

"You have arrived at your destination safely. You are a very good driver."

The chirpy smugness of the GPS automaton's congratulations as they entered the road leading into the airport made them laugh. Isobel's abrasive relationship with the device had often prompted impolite retorts, but today she was thankful the woman had navigated them back to the airport. More amazing, Malo spotted Jo and Penfield waiting outside their airline's arrivals, luggage in hand. Without needing to circle or the harassment of impatient honking, they stowed their bags in the trunk and, within minutes, Isobel had threaded them through the maze leading to the exit.

She couldn't help glancing at Jo's ring finger and, secretly relieved, saw it remained naked of significant jewelry. The concentration needed to navigate their way out of the busy terminal gave her no time to pry, but Jo had caught her aunt's quick dart of eye and they exchanged conspiratorial smiles. Jo, in turn, raised her brows and nodded from Malo towards Isobel who shook her head but grinned. Jo looked puzzled. Good grief, Isobel thought, they were mind texting like teenagers.

She navigated them safely onto the ramp leading onto the interstate before anyone spoke.

"I understand your motives auntie, and I'm glad you had the gumption to evade the family's arcane rite," said Jo. "Those picnics are fine for our summer birthdays, but not yours in March. Maybe a year at a time, we each could make it a habit."

"My escape began cold and wet, but ended well," said Isobel. "Rain howled around the day I arrived, but the place was luxuriously cozy and after the surprise of Malo's arrival, my spirits rose and the weather cleared." She looked back across the seat at Jo. "I have something to tell you. While walking the beach, I uncovered—literally—something most unusual." She paused. "I am now in possession of a very large diamond." Jo leaned forward and rested her hand on Malo's shoulder.

"How romantic," Jo said. Malo turned and raised his arms.

"No. Sorry my dear, that was your aunt's attempt at drama. The ring is not mine."

"Unfortunately," Isobel said, "it's still attached to another woman's severed hand."

Pen sat up and grinned with amusement.

"Jesus, Isobel, talk about drama—these things only happen to you. Explain." She did.

Hours later, after driving the tedious two-lane coastal Route One along the coast of Maine, the GPS robot spoke again.

"I'm sorry, there is no such destination."

This time the lady spoke sadly. Isobel ignored the dismayed woman's warning, and they bumped through the icy puddles rutting the drive leading down to her cottage overlooking Elmore Harbor. Opening onto Penobscot Bay and the Atlantic Ocean, throughout summer and fall, the protected harbor is a haven for cruising sailors. During the warmer months, hundreds of buoys floating above their lobster pots challenge sailors navigating its entrance. Now, in March, beyond the inner harbor stretched a desolate and empty passage leading out past Southern Island lighthouse to the sea.

The four sat in travel numb silence. They needed a minute to gather themselves, after the long drive home, before entering the musty, cold house. Pen rolled down his window and looked wistfully out at the ocean.

"It's hard to believe it's almost a straight shot across to Spain where Jo and I soaked up the sun only yesterday." He shook his head. "First thing," he said, "we'll build a huge fire and cheer the place up."

Malo looked at his watch. "And I'll make something to cheer us up too." He raised his eyes to the star-studded sky. "Fortunately, the sun is well under the yardarm."

"Well under," they agreed in unison.

Pen lit the logs left ready in the stone fireplace that took up almost one wall and, while the fire crackled and raised their spirits along with the temperature, they dulled their appetite with drinks, cheese and crackers. In the pantry off the kitchen, Isobel and Jo foraged in the freezer for dinner and they were soon spooning up fish chowder and crunching on toasted garlic bread. Satisfied, Isobel set aside her empty bowl. Jo gave a huge yawn that set off a contagion.

"We're all dead tired," she said. "Pen and I began the day in Spain hours before you, and my body says it's already early morning." She pointed at the phone on the roll-top desk across the room. "I'm sorry Isobel, but I'm compulsive about unanswered messages and that red blinking light on your answering machine is driving me crazy."

Isobel struggled to rise. She hadn't noticed the silent signal, but Malo, less comatose than the others, got up and pushed the message button. He hit speakerphone. They heard the anxiety in the voice on the machine that, at first, sounded anxious, then hesitant, and finally pleading. Isobel, who knew her grandson Tom as the most cocky and cheerful of her kin, recognized his distress and immediately sensed something wrong.

———————

"Gran, its me. I'm in some trouble." Tom's voice, three thousand miles away, echoed through the room. "I hate to bother you—hey, Happy Birthday—but could you give me a call? If Malo's around he might help. Don't worry, I'm okay, so please don't call Mom. Just give me a call, here's my cell number. I'm in Seattle, sort of."

They looked at each other over the disconnected hum after the message clicked off. Isobel stared, first at the phone and then at her watch.

"It's still early on the west coast. Should I call now? Tom sounded upset. It's unlike him." She looked at Malo. "You know Tom and his weakness for the ladies. Do you think this trouble is just another woman thing?"

"If you want a good night's sleep," said Malo, "and we all need it, don't call him tonight. Whatever mess he's in, he said not to worry. There's nothing we can do that won't wait until morning." He put his arm around her shoulders. "Jo's right. It's been a long, tiring day and we're all ready for bed."

The drafty room chilled as the fire settled and died to orange and black embers. Gusts of mean rain rattled the windows and a wailing wind echoed in the chimney and encouraged their escape upstairs and a layer of down duvets. They exchanged good nights and convinced Isobel that, whatever Tom's dilemma, it would wait until tomorrow.

The next morning, because of jet lag, Jo was first up and stood at the range stirring a pot of Irish oatmeal. Overnight the rain had stopped, but no sun broke through the fog and all the lights were on in the big kitchen. She drained thick strips of bacon on a brown paper bag and listened while Isobel, phone tucked between chin and shoulder, struggled to keep her temper as a series of robotic voices confirmed possible flights to Seattle. After minutes of being prompted to push more buttons, her aunt turned and raised a hand in victory.

"Finally, a human being," she said. "Why do airlines make it so hard to suffer their indignities?" While Jo ladled them out hot cereal, she heard her confirm a flight for two arriving at Sea-Tac the next day. Jo frowned at her aunt.

"I take it you and Malo are determined to fly across the country and rescue Tom from this latest disaster? By now, we all know his problem with women and, believe me, I bet this trouble involves a new one."

"Actually," said Isobel. "This time I don't think so. He didn't sound like himself. I heard none of the casual 'no problem' in his voice. And as far as traveling three thousand miles, maybe I'm just being selfish." She shivered and wrapped her arms around her middle over two layers of sweaters. "I really can't bear this dreary time of year in Maine. Even most of the natives go south and join the snowbird migration. And don't roll your eyes at me, young lady. I know what you're thinking. Seattle in March is no garden spot, but at least it's green, wet and soggy, not leafless, brown and frozen."

"A minimal difference," suggested Pen, looking out at the white caps roughing the harbor. "But not if you're desperate," he agreed. "After you and Malo leave, I plan to find the nearest palm-shaded golf course and entice Jo to snowbird it with me."

"Aunt Isobel, why Seattle in March?" argued Jo. "You promised that the whole purpose of your new life style is to pamper yourself. Enjoy all those great perks. And honestly," Jo admitted, "this past year, traveling with you, I've also become disgustingly spoiled by them."

"I have no intention of giving up my new comforts," said Isobel. "We're not exactly planning to head into the wilderness. Malo and I will stay somewhere very pampering—outdoor hot tubs, roaring fires, endless plates of ice-nestled Olympia oysters. I know it's wrong to admit favorites, but Tom is special to me, despite his endless bad judgment regarding females. In fact, I think most of his difficulties result from this act he projects of helplessness. Tom is wily as a fox and I know it."

"Those blond curls and blue-eyed innocent charm doesn't hurt either," said Jo.

"So you've noticed," said Isobel, and has used it to full effect since he learned to talk. But the tone of his voice on that call last night concerns me and my offer to help him out of this new dilemma gives me a good excuse to escape Maine." She pointed out the kitchen window at her dismal landscape of her winter garden. "That brown tangled bracken depresses me. The sight out this window every morning was another reason I flew down to Newport rather than spend another winter birthday here. Much as I love Elmore Harbor, I realize that until some serious sun returns to warm my bones, I need to get away."

"But do you really need Malo with you on this trip?" And why not, thought Isobel. Did she detect a small nose out of joint?

"Yes Jo, I really do." Jo passed the platter of bacon.

"Ah bacon," Malo exclaimed, sensing an uneasy silence as he entered the kitchen. He rubbed his palms together and poured himself a mug of coffee. "Crispy American bacon, nothing so tasty. Not like those salty, flabby English rashers. And yes Jo, I'm traveling with Isobel. Don't worry. Since I hired her, your aunt's safety is my utmost concern—especially after last summer's debacle. Rest assured, I will make sure she risks no more gambles with lowlife."

Pen, having declined the oatmeal and with a spoonful of Cocoa Crispies halfway to his mouth, was unaware of the brown milk dripping into his lap. Malo offered his napkin.

"I feel fully responsible for the risks she encountered last year," he continued. "We don't know, until we talk to him, the nature of Tom's newest difficulty, but we are all aware of your aunt's predilection for rash decisions. Over that, I have little control."

Isobel poured fat-free cream over her steaming oats then covered them with a layer of brown sugar. "Listen, all of you," she said firmly. "Please understand that last summer I agreed to those risks after Malo hired me, and I accepted them as part of the job. The disposals he assigned me did not seem unreasonable. I regret that I grew quite fond of poor Mr. Akuratsu. We shared our knowledge of bonsai and a mutual love of and esthetics of Japanese gardening."

"Really, Aunt Isobel," said Jo. "We understand he was an unique person—like many despots—but, admit it, basically the man had the morals of the mass murderer he was." Isobel pursed her lips. "I can't deny I felt terrible about it. The way I so efficiently poisoned him."

"Ah," Pen broke in, "if I remember, in your usual hands-off manner, you elaborately arranged that a grizzly bear actually killed him. One of God's more natural predators."

"Enough," Isobel said, exasperated. "That first disposal remains in the past and I don't want to discuss it over breakfast. I appreciate your concern for my safety, but here I am alive, and ready to accept more risks in exchange for my perks. I prefer this new way of life, and pale at the thought of my friends so satisfied with their benign routines. God help me from dying at the bridge table. Besides, I'm taking this trip to help Tom on my own and not one of Malo's assignments." Her good humor returned. "I'll even pay for my own treats."

"I applaud that you're going," said Pen, who swiped at his milk-stained lap with Malo's napkin before helping himself to the rest of the bacon.

They finished their breakfast and Jo carried their dishes to the sink, edging Pen aside from his inept attempts to load the dishwasher.

"I confess I'm still worried about Tom," Isobel said. "And Jo, be glad Malo's coming with me. Before you all came down this morning, I called his cell and got no answer. I know it's much too early on the West Coast to expect him awake, so I left word that Malo and I will arrive in Seattle as soon as any airline makes it possible."

She looked up at the wall clock, a plastic cat whose rolling eyes and two-foot pendulum tail ticked time away in hypnotic rhythm. Someone's joke gift from Harry's Olde Antique Shoppe, an adjunct of the town dump and everyone's source of unusual, trashy treasures. She frowned and made a mental addition to her list of things to do: recycle cat.

Malo looked at Pen, then Jo, and massaged his temples.

"By now," he said, "we know that when Isobel makes up her mind, it's a given. And Pen's right about getting away until spring." He turned to Jo. "If you have any more leave from your job in the city, close up this cottage until we return. If you will drive Isobel and me down to the Portland airport tomorrow, you can keep the Maserati rental for as long as you need. Book yourselves into somewhere warmer, preferably with aqua water and a palm tree lined golf course. Soak up a few more weeks of sun."

"Excellent idea," agreed Pen. "Cadiz was perfect and maybe I can convince Jo to enjoy more of the same." Jo looked like she needed no forcing. "However," she added, "please, if Tom's trouble is serious and we can help, call. We can fly west and make it a family rescue."

Isobel hesitated before facing her niece.

"Can I ask you a favor before we leave?"

"Of course," said Jo.

"There's a package being held for me at the post office in the village. Could you drive in tomorrow and collect it? Don't bother to open it. It's a surprise. Just leave it in the drawer of the front hall desk and I'll deal with it when we get back."

Isobel caught Malo's quizzical look.

"That little souvenir," she explained. "I found on the beach in Newport."

EIGHT

The *Wenatchee's* powerful engines reversed with a roar that churned green water against the massive pilings of the Bainbridge Island ferry landing. They squealed, yielded, and then resisted the momentum of the huge boat, forcing it into its slip. Chains rattled and the ferry's landing plate slid forward onto the concrete ramp. On the lower decks, car engines revved to life and within minutes the ferrymen began flagging the lanes of cars ashore in ship-balancing order. Above decks, walk-on passengers streamed out through the long covered corridor leading into downtown Winslow.

Isobel and Malo were among the last to leave. The half-hour trip across from Seattle's Elliot Bay Ferry Terminal to Bainbridge Island had been so scenically grand, they were reluctant to debark. The morning had dawned with a brilliant sunrise and promised one of those special days when Mt. Rainier's glory shone south beyond the city to make its famous snow-capped landmark proud.

Tom stood waiting for them at the foot of the terminal's exit ramp and led them to a wreck of a car that he saw gave his grandmother doubts. He diverted her with a smothering bear hug, and offered Malo a solemn handshake. As if reading her mind, Tom thumped the hood of their transportation.

"Don't worry, Gran. I rarely average more than five miles a day." He regarded their luggage. "Sorry guys, the trunk won't open." He gave Isobel a wry smile and winked at Malo. "Never has, and I've not a clue, or want to know, what might rest inside. Stow your stuff on the floor in back and use it as a footrest. It will be a squeeze but no problem, the skiff out to my temp squat is right around the corner."

Isobel thought his cheery welcome a little forced, but stifled her impulse to pry and kept quiet.

True to his word, within minutes he parked on a side street by the public landing above Heron Harbor. Malo raised an eye when Tom hung a 'Rector on Visit' permit on the rearview mirror.

"I'll schlep your stuff down to the landing and we'll go out in Jay's Zodiac." They followed Tom to the end of the dock where he stowed their gear aboard and gave his grandmother a hand into the rubber dingy. His passengers settled themselves gingerly while Tom untied the inflatable from the landing's iron cleat.

"You live on a boat?" asked Malo.

"It's become complicated," said Tom. "It's better than it sounds. My new pad is a small tugboat, but I'll explain when we get on board."

On the way out to Tom's 'squat', they took in the forested mainland. Tall firs spiked the sky and reflected below in the green water. Isobel breathed deeply of the retsina-scented air. "It smells sharp and briny," she said. "Like Maine on a foggy day."

"But very different," said Malo and gestured at the horizon. "Your western coast is wilder with its surround of real mountains, new ones, not the glacial moraine remnants poking above Penobscot Bay." Despite his wounding stab at her Maine loyalty, Isobel admitted that the jagged snow covered peaks of the Olympics and Cascades were more dramatic than the softly rounded and aged Camden Hills.

With an expertise acquired by living most of his life near the water, Tom settled them aboard the 'liveaboard' he shared with his new friend. He explained that Jay's vessel was not one of the controversial derelicts, squatting without permission in the front yard of pricey Heron Harbor, but a well-maintained mini-tug, a houseboat with comfortable quarters and surprising privacy below.

"You're welcome to stay with me on board," said Tom as he stowed Malo and Isobel's gear on a spacious double berth forward, "but I think you'd be more comfortable with the perks of the inn ashore. Whatever you decide, I can take you back to shore after we talk." He gestured at the head. "Use the facilities if you want and then come back up on deck and I'll tell you my tale of woe."

Tale of woe. Isobel sighed and eyed Tom with resignation. He had graduated two years ago from Yale with honors and she'd hoped that by now the boy—no, young man—would have found a more productive career than working as his brother's sous-chef at the Bearfoot Lodge, a five star Montana resort and scene of Malo's first assignment. At Tom's last report, they'd heard all was well. What trouble had sent him north to Seattle?

Above, on the rear deck, Tom wiped the morning dew from the plastic cushions with a chamois and gestured for them to sit. He saw Isobel shiver in her down vest.

"I made coffee," he said. "Better idea, let's go below where there's a nice little heater. Jay restored this vessel with mucho mod con comforts. There's a gimbaled stove with an oven in the galley, cabins with bunk berths, roomy salon, and a decent head with shower. Not bad for a forty foot bachelor pad."

"Sounds too good to be true," said Malo. He had looked at the homes above the surrounding shoreline as they came on board. "This harbor looks like pricey real estate. How do those people living up on Heron Hill feel about your friend mooring free in their front yard?"

"That's the problem. The current issue here is the rights of the flotilla of 'liveaboards'. Some of these boats are derelicts, not only neglected eyesores, but they flaunt sanitation safety. Heron Harbor bottom is a lucrative fishing area and shellfish are very sensitive to the slightest pollution. The bad guys who ignore the DNR—Department of Natural Resources—rules are not popular. No violence yet, but a lot of rumbling in the wings. Jay keeps this little tug up to code. He pays his fees, and is only fighting for his right to a mooring."

Isobel looked around at the Harbor's early activity and inhaled deeply of the tangy evergreen forest and shale beaches that surrounded them.

"It's too nice a day to go below," she insisted. "Let's stay up on deck. Maybe Tom will warm us with some of that famous Seattle coffee. I'd offer to help but would only get in your way." Tom climbed down the hatchway and Malo and Isobel leaned back against the rail. Malo pulled the wool cap off his head and raised his face toward the wintry sun.

"I think we can assume," he said when they were alone, "that Tom did not ask us to come three thousand miles to discuss his friend's real estate issues."

"I agree," said Isobel. "And who and where is this absent friend Jay? I'm sure there is something more serious bothering Tom, and I intend to find out over this reputed coffee."

Tom came up on deck balancing a tray with a large thermos, mugs, a small carton of cream, and sugar packets. Isobel agreed it was delicious coffee and Isobel felt the gentle urge of Malo's toe against her leg as Tom refilled her mug.

"Tom," she said, "this is a very idyllic way to spend our first morning in your new digs, but your call sounded urgent. What exactly is this worrisome tale of woe? Why are we here."

"Not woe yet, I hope," began Tom, "but something that worries me enough to want your advice. Yesterday, when I returned to the boat from the market in Winslow, Jay had gone. I figured he was off somewhere doing errands in the harbor until I realized that was impossible. He would have taken the dinghy and I found it still tied to the stern when I got back."

Both Isobel and Malo saw Tom's face pinch with anxiety as he hunched forward against a chill gust of wind.

"Anyway, by late afternoon when he hadn't returned, I really got worried. Jay's a mellow fellow, not the impulsive type. He wouldn't disappear for this long without leaving a note, you know? And in what? There's no yacht club around here with launch service. Did someone come by and pick him up?"

"Tom," said Isobel, "we don't know anything about your friend. Who is Jay and where did you meet him? And more important to me, when and why did you suddenly move from Montana to the Pacific Northwest? I thought everything was *simpatico* at that fancy resort—helping your brother in the kitchen on that roaring Vulcan range."

Tom set down his mug and shrugged. "It was, it was. Working as bro Will's *sous chef* was great—while it lasted—then I had this little problem with a lady guest who came on strong and—"

"Please," interrupted Isobel. "No details. Just the facts."

"Yes, ma'am." Tom grinned and she saw Malo repress a smile as he guessed that another of Tom's 'no problems' had backfired.

"First," she asked, "where did you meet Jay?"

Tom bent forward, his hands clasped between his knees. "Can I ask a favor, please," he begged. "Can we keep this between us until I find out what's happened to him? Mom and Dad think I'm still in Montana and I told Will I'd found a job making big money as a deckhand on an Alaskan trawler. I don't want worries from either camp."

"Well obviously," said Malo, "you have worries, so here we are and what can we do?"

Tom raised his shoulders. "I don't know where to begin, and don't want to call the police—yet. I only met Jay at the Blackfoot Lodge a few weeks ago. I haven't known him long, but I don't buy that he got a ride to shore and has suddenly gone off and done some kind of walkabout." He raked his hand through his hair. "I have this bad feeling something's happened to the guy. Anyway, I understand that the police won't do much about a missing adult for the first forty-eight hours. I've met the Harbormaster, and she seems a sensible lady. I'd rather talk to her first."

Malo and Isobel looked at each other and their unspoken thoughts were evident. That they could expect the lady Harbormaster was a blond Nordic beauty. As they expected, Tom's fair skin betrayed him with a blush. He shrugged. "Yeah Gran, she's a stunner. Anyway, small world department. It seems that Jay's an actor friend of Pen—remember the nutty guy Jo hooked up with at the Blackfoot?" He looked at Isobel. "Didn't they go off together after your near death meltdown last fall in that VW coffin you drove? I hear Jo really got into golf—and probably him," he added, under his breath. "Sorry Gran," Tom grinned. "No really, I like Pen. He's great. I think his job with the CIA and all that undercover stuff serves as some kind of sublim for a lost acting career. You can tell he's definitely a frustrated actor surviving his day job with the CIA—crazy, that man." He turned to Malo. "Wasn't there also something going on between Jo and your son Michello? What happened there?"

Malo raised his palms. "For the moment it seems Pen has won out," he said. "But, knowing Michello, my son will persist."

All this talk of last year's events reminded Isobel how her association with Malo had altered their lives. Too much many changes too fast. By recruiting Jo as her companion, Isobel worried she may have undermined her niece's ethics. How responsible she for Jo's metamorphosis from a benign and contented freelance journalist into a world-traveling assistant to a mercenary? If she and Malo found themselves involved in Tom's friend's ominous disappearance, would she now entangle her grandson? The tug rocked on a gentle breeze, and she shivered. Not entirely from cold. Tom noticed.

"Let's go below and warm up," he said to his aunt. "It's nice and cozy down there." As they climbed down the hatch into the main cabin, Isobel saw what Tom meant by comfort. The tug's wide beam afforded a bright, cozy sitting space with brass lanterns hung on gimbals between large circular ports. A comfortable settee formed an ell around a folding table that opened its full width for meals. Isobel admired the snug little craft's well-designed galley opposite its navigation desk. The dials and switches on the wall above provided the full compliment of instruments necessary to function safely at sea. A length of bookcases filled the space over the storage lockers with enough tempting reads for a month in the doldrums. High-end speakers provided the surround sound system. As they settled themselves against the cushions, she admitted that Jay's ship-shape vessel was far from derelict. She had been invited out on many small yachts visiting the harbor and failed to share their owner's enthusiasm for camping out in a phone booth. In comparison, this little craft seemed a palace at sea.

"When Jay first arrived at the Lodge," resumed Tom, "we got on right away. Jay had impressive acting credits, and he had come to the Blackfoot to meet with some big name director. This famous Hollywood honcho wanted him for the lead in a film being produced this fall. We got talking in the bar one night and Jay sympathized with my problem. He understood that I wanted to get out of my bro's hair, and offered to share his space on this great little tug while I looked for some new and lucrative employ. The next day Jay clinched the deal with the director and, as prices at the Lodge are not exactly el cheapo, we flew to Seattle and landed amidst this heated up harbor brouhaha with the liveaboards vs. the Department of Natural Resources."

"I understand your need to 'get out of town'—again—," said Isobel. Her impatient frown, however, clearly showed him she did not. "But twice in one year, Tom? You seem to repeat these difficulties with the ladies. When are you going to learn some lessons in self control?" She shuddered to think of Raybelle, his proper southern mother's reaction to this news, and she understood and would respect his plea for silence. Tom raised innocent arms.

"I have, I have," he promised. Malo, looked unconvinced, rested back against the cushions and clasped his hands behind his head.

"I swear," Tom pleaded. "I've reformed. Never again will I be led astray by a beautiful bod."

NINE

"So here we sit aboard this snug little tug," said Malo, "and you asked us here to help find your friend." It was a statement, not a question, and Tom nodded.

"Yeah, and that's what's worrying me. Not many places Jay could hang out for this long without taking the dinghy. Unless he did get a lift to shore and took off somewhere." He shrugged. "But as I said, not likely. And leaving all his gear behind? Besides, he loves this boat." Tom looked at his watch. "It's almost noon. You hungry?" He got up and moved into the galley. "There's stuff here for sandwiches and plenty to drink."

"Thank you, Tom," said Isobel. "I think we'll take your suggestion and call that inn in Winslow you recommended. And I would guess there are outdoor places in a small town like this where folks gather to sit and gossip," she said. "Maybe someone's seen your friend."

Malo edged out of the settee, but Tom motioned him back.

"Wait, I haven't told you what really worries me about Jay going missing. And Gran, that's why I asked that Malo come with you. It's kind of up his alley. I'm afraid there's another, more deadly issue than the liveaboard squats here in Heron Harbor. The sea bottom below us is home to this repulsive looking bivalve called a geoduck. Locals call them gueys. It's a bivalve that burrows down in the bottom muck so fast they're a challenge to chase and catch. The guey has this six to eight inch neck," he glanced at his grandmother and blushed. "Honestly, it looks like a huge grey penis. The Asian elite gourmets prize these two-plus pound longneck clams—a big one's three footer is a pricey banquet number and prized for its briny sweetness. I personally think it tastes like fishy rubber. But this native shellfish phenom has become the new Asian delicacy and the Chinese mafia was quick to take advantage of soaring prices and begin illegal harvesting. Their poacher's scuba divers go down at night and, using spray hoses to flush them out of the mud, bring up their hauls in net bags. They pack them in coolers, and truck them to the nearest airport to be flown out that morning. A single pair can fetch enough for a high price Seattle dinner, and three crates bought by a Shanghai restaurant would pay for a year's tuition at UDub. Jay said he's heard of transactions bringing up to a hundred grand for one night's drop. The Asians pay over $150 a pound, and have ready cash money."

"Are you're afraid there is some connection with your friend's disappearance and this local smuggling?" Isobel asked. She thought it ominously ironic that the Chinese mafia had brought her to the Blackfoot Lodge in Montana last year for her first meeting with Malo. The Lodge was also where she had first meet Penfield on that fateful trail ride.

"Yes," admitted Tom. "Aside from his acting talent, Jay's a huge champion of causes. Maybe it's his public fights for gay rights that get him involved in these volatile issues." He pointed at Malo. "Gran says you know from personal experience that these mafia crews don't tolerate interference. That's why I called you for help. I'm seriously worried that if Jay's trying to expose their smuggling divers caught with their loot, he might be courting a cement sandwich."

Tom returned them in the dinghy to the Winslow landing and the three hiked the short distance into town. He toted their duffels to the local inn and waited while they checked in. Upon inspection, Isobel saw that Jo would have approved of the Harborside Inn. Embroidered linens, heated towel rack, and the promise of impeccable service. To gild the lily, a sunny atrium overlooked an enclosed garden fitted out with tables for breakfast and tea buffets. Best of all, noticed Malo, a well-stocked honor-system bar. More than enough pampering amenities to satisfy the most demanding guest.

Settled upstairs in their room, Isobel rested against the pillows and pulled the bedside phone to her lap.

"I'm going to call Jo," she said, "wherever they've got to. I've her cell number and want to leave a message that we've arrived."

"Good, you promised to do that," said Malo, "but let's keep things peaceful and just tell her Tom's problem is not personal this time and, so far, everything's under control. They can't help by coming out here, so lets not involve more family than necessary." Isobel agreed and, when no one answered, put them off with a reassuring message. She looked at Malo skeptically.

"You're right not to entangle them with Tom's new woe, but can we honestly say that whatever's going on here is under control?"

She picked up a copy of *The History of Bainbridge Island* from her bedside table. On their trek through town, they had spotted an enticing display of books in the window of the Heron Harbor Bookstore. Isobel, acknowledged herself as a hard copy book-aholic and immediately knew such stores that remained were a precious and vanishing species. Despite the new electronic age and its plastic readers, some still cherished the scent and sensual feel of paper. She had argued with her committed e-book friends how impossible it would be to read *Pat The Bunny* or a scratch 'n sniff book to a toddler on an electronic tablet.

After unpacking, they left the Harborside to return to the bookstore for an unhurried browse. Almost an hour later, lugging a bag full of books, Isobel and Malo strolled down to the village green. On their way through town earlier, Tom had nodded toward a rhododendron and azalea enclosed oasis that Jay had told him was the best spot to sit and suss out info from the locals.

"When I first arrived," Tom said. "Jay gave me the tour and showed me this sweet little park where the town gossips hang. It's the best spot for you to ask questions."

Tom was right. The town green was a garden within a garden. At this time of year its brick paths, edged with yellow and white daffodils, blossomed in contrast to the dark green rhododendrons, heavy with globes of bloom.

In one corner, they spotted several men hunched over stone tables set with games of chess. Isobel paused, put her hand on Malo's arm, and gave him a mock serious frown. She leaned toward him and murmured.

"If Tom's concern for his friend leads us to any of your old buddies, am I now on working time? With my usual retainers?" Malo conceded, amused.

"If you've decided to continue as my employee—of course."

He peered over Isobel's shoulder as she stood above a pair of men intent on their moves. She understood the strategy of chess and politely waited for a pause in their game.

"Excuse me," she interrupted during a lull. A fiercely bearded Ahab, who could have strode right off the whaler *Pequot,* raised his head. "My friend lives on a tugboat in Heron Harbor and asked us to meet him here, but we must have missed him." She described Jay from Tom's account. "Have any of you seen this young man around town?" It was such a strange query from a dotty old lady that she hoped they might think her story true.

The bearded Ahab's opponent swept his bishop diagonally across the board and captured a rook. Ahab scowled, annoyed by his error. Distracted, he looked up at Isobel and ran his fingers through his beard.

"That sounds like the kid from the market who helps me carry my groceries out to the car," he said. "He's one of the liveaboards, but a good one. We hear he keeps that sweet little tug of his real shipshape. Legal too."

"That's him," said Isobel. "Jay lives aboard a refitted tugboat."

"Well, I'm sorry ma'am. We know your friend, and he's a decent sort, but I've not seen him for a couple of days. He's a regular checker at the town market, and I miss him 'cause when my arthritis kicks up, he's always ready to help me tote and carry." He chuckled and turned to his chess buddies at the next table. "Anyone seen the kid around lately?"

"Sorry," they mumbled in unison. The men bent their heads over their stone boards and were immediately absorbed in the game.

Isobel and Malo strolled back through town to the inn where he swiped his keycard through the door slot and held it open while she entered. Isobel crossed the room to the window that overlooked the view of an active working harbor. Unlike Elmore, Penobscot Bay's summer yachtsman's haven, the year-round town of Winslow offered a more spectacular horizon. Back in Maine, when Isobel had crossed her frozen lawn in winter and stood at the end of the dock, her view stretched over a bleak and not always friendly span of ocean.

The message light blinked red and she heard Tom's voice with directions to meet them for dinner. She dropped onto the bed and heard the shower running in the bath, thankful it was large and not carved out of a closet space, the bane of too many village inns.

Malo emerged from the steam with a towel tucked around his trim waist. An arousing sight, she mused. Her handsome employer had proved one of the most agreeable amenities of her new job.

"Tom left a message while we were out," she said, "and asked to meet us for a special sushi dinner here in town. He suggested his favorite place and said it's just around the corner. He promises us it serves the freshest fish and has an imaginative sushi-san. I wrote down the address." Isobel rolled over and pulled open the bedside drawer. She felt around for the paper with the name of the restaurant. When they went out together, Malo always covered their expenses so she had left her purse in the drawer and clearly remembered placing it beneath the requisite Gideon's before they had left for the bookstore.

Though out of sight, she knew it was an obvious hiding spot if someone really planned a theft. Alarmed, she sat up. She hadn't noticed before while copying Tom's directions, but her purse had been pushed to the back of the drawer and was not under the Bible where she'd left it. She pulled it out and quickly checked its contents. Her money, credit cards, a squashy old piece of gum, and all the gritty debris women's purses collect despite regular tossing. Nothing missing.

"Malo, someone's been in our room."

TEN

Concerned by Isobel's discovery, Malo opened his bureau drawers and found that no attempt made to hide that his clothing also had been shifted about. He ran his hand over his freshly shaven chin.

"You are right. Someone poked around our room while we were out this afternoon." He sat on the bed and rested his elbows on his knees. "It is obvious that whoever searched us meant it only as a warning." He got up and checked through the piles of clothes in his side of the double bureau. "Like your purse, things are out of place, but nothing taken."

"I'm afraid," sighed Isobel, "that despite rumors of your retirement, some suspicious soldier of one of the Capo family still finds you a threat. Your past connections still continue to haunt you and one of them might be determined to destroy anyone," she pointed at Malo, "foolish enough to interfere with his climb to the top." Bellini shrugged and shook his head.

"I'm afraid that's true and, if so, I'd guess he's associated with this shellfish smuggling here in the harbor. Entering and riffling our room is their threat to intimidate me." Isobel was not surprised that Malo did not seem concerned. Much of his past would always be a mystery to her. They both preferred it this way.

He selected a tie and held it up for her inspection. She recognized the design of the Celtic Knot on the dark green silk as belonging to Trinity College, Dublin—a tribute to his Irish roots—and nodded her approval.

While Isobel took her turn before the bathroom mirror, she was pleased at how easily she could still plait her hair into a smart French twist. She wound a length of cream Hermés silk under the collar of her blouse and secured it with her Fabergé brooch. Malo came in and stood behind her to perfect the knot of his tie. He nuzzled her neck.

"If I remember," she turned to remind him, "the Chinese mafia wasn't happy with our eliminating their kingpin Akuratzu. Your exposure of yet another of the Triad's illegal scams might seem suspiciously co-incidental. Perhaps they find you treading too closely on their toes?"

"At Tom's plea, we've come a long way to help," he said. "But, believe me, if I find that my past dealings with the Triad Society have aroused their ire, I insist that we leave. I won't risk your life again. These are violent men and not meant to be threatened. Believe me, Isobel, I have witnessed the results of their anger at the slightest interference and watched with horror their immediate and vicious revenge."

Subdued, they walked the short distance to the restaurant and where they found Tom waiting outside. The dainty kimono clad waitress that led them to their table in a private alcove greeted Tom with a bow and a smile. She returned within minutes carrying bamboo baskets holding steamy cloths. This slim young beauty reminded Isobel of the petite woman in the beautiful Shibori who had served her tea on that stormy afternoon back in Newport. While the men talked, her mind drifted for a moment and slipped into an invention from the past. She imagined both women as geishas ready at the whim of some wealthy emperor's call. At the young waitress returned to their table, Isobel returned to reality.

Malo asked Tom to chose their meal from the sushi-san's iced display and, while the chef prepared their plates, they sipped from small wooden boxes of gold-flecked sake. A tourist conceit, Isobel thought, and awkward to drink from, but so elegant. The three toasted their health.

"Kanpai! And long may it last," said Tom.

While they sampled the chef's unusual array of delicacies, as beautifully plated as delicious, they told Tom of their intruder.

"Nothing was taken and we doubt theft was their intent. Whoever rifled our things meant it as a warning," said Malo. "However, I'm afraid it adds to our concern for your missing friend."

"There's no sign Jay's been back to the boat," said Tom, "and he's not been seen around town. The harbormaster is making inquiries, but she said nothing suspicious has occurred on the water, at least during the day. No sighting of monitor boats or signs of illegal diving. Though she admits that, without lights, activity may have gone unobserved at night. Dive bags full of shellfish brought to the surface are often secured under a boat's hull for later pickup. She said they haven't the manpower to patrol the entire harbor, so while illegal diving may be risky, it's obviously going on."

It was a dark and starry night when they left the restaurant. Not a drop of rain since they had arrived.

"Give me a call in the morning, and I'll pick you up at the landing," Tom said. "The national weather service promises another beautiful day. I'll cook you up a gourmet breakfast and, though I can't promise anything so great as that," he nodded back at the restaurant, "remember, I'm an ex-professional sous-chef."

NOAA's forecast proved right. Next morning, on their way out to the tug, the harbor's water sparkled in the morning sun although the air remained cool enough for Isobel to zip up her fleece jacket.

Back on board, the three of them sat up on deck around the hatch-top table and soon were devouring Tom's *huevos rancheros con queso* smothered in fresh salsa verde, rounds of Canadian bacon, and buttered sourdough toast. Tastebud bliss, they agreed.

"Tom," said Malo, accepting more coffee, "it's sad that your peccadilloes sent you packing. I think the Blackfoot Lodge is short a fine chef."

Tom raised his hands in protest. "Hey, I'm reformed. The Seattle area is famous for excellent restaurants and as soon as this mystery over Jay is cleared up, I'm going to make the rounds. Probably have to start at the bottom as prep serf, but that's my price to pay for playing Romeo." He raised a brow at Malo. "Exactly define me a peccadillo?"

Isobel waved the banter aside and took her coffee to sit on the stern seat while the men cleared away. The sky had dawned clear, and in the distance, across the sound, *both* Mt. Rainier and Mt. Baker jutted their snow-capped peaks toward heaven. She leaned over the rail to watch the water lap against the tug's sides and breathed in that sharp, tangy brine and envisioned plates of plump

Olympia, Pacific, and Kumamoto oysters nestled in a bed of crushed ice.

"Good grief," she admonished aloud, "I'm stuffed with breakfast and already thinking of lunch." That's when she noticed the steady rise of bubbles from beneath the hull.

She crossed the deck and called down the open hatch. "Tom, come up and look over the side. Something is leaking from the bilge.

ELEVEN

A half-moon slid from behind a ragged band of clouds and, for a moment, light glinted off a pair of night vision lenses. From the dive boat, Yuri Virtenën caught the brief flash and froze. Again the watcher's glasses reflected the moon's light, but higher, as if he had risen to his feet. Like an owl, only Yuri's head turned on his neck as he focused across the water to the light's source.

Back in Russia, Yuri had reached his full height of just over five feet by age sixteen. Too many brutal encounters as a street child had proved that bravado didn't work as defense against bullies, and by twenty, having survived his teens and self-trained in the martial arts, he learned to use his taut, wiry strength to advantage.

Unfortunately, along with his skill as a black belt that enabled him to toss a man twice his size to the ground, Yuri's genetic inheritance also included an innate, amoral meanness. He experienced an intense, almost sexual high when he delivered that single killing blow.

Tonight, he crouched on the deck of the dive boat and felt the familiar burning at the back of his neck that alarmed him to danger. He relied on this premonition—his extra sense—that many times had reliably saved his life. It had warned him the night he sensed that he and his diving partner had been watched. Tonight he would take care of that complication. Invisible in his black neoprene suit, Yuri rested one hand on his dive belt and waited motionless to refocus on the next glimpse of the moon's reflection.

When his eye caught the flash from the watcher's lens, Yuri dropped to the deck and crept aft on his hands and knees. Reassured by the touch of the knife at his thigh, and slick as an eel, he eased his body over the side into the icy water.

The tide was running out, and Yuri raised his head above the surface for only a moment to correct his course against the current. He swiped his hand to clear his night vision mask and set aim for the eerie shape of the figure standing in the inflatable a few hundred feet from shore.

Jay didn't expect the apparition that rose suddenly from the water and when he felt the lurch of his dinghy, bent to grab at its side. He'd been wrong to think he'd been lucky. His last bit of luck was that, before losing sight of the smuggler's dive boat, he'd filmed its registration number. Without warning, the unstable craft, under Yuri's sudden weight, tipped violently and toppled Jay into the frigid water. His camera flew from his hand and sank below the surface. Struggling in the dark water, Jay felt a powerful arm grasp his neck and hold him under. With a final rush of adrenalin, he fought against the strength of his wiry killer until Yuri's sharp, gutting knife ripped into his belly.

The moon disappeared behind a curtain of cloud, and a fine rain began to fall. No one witnessed the empty dinghy moving by an invisible tow through the water or the trail of blood streaming from the entangled body dragging in its wake. No one saw the diver tie the dinghy to the stern of the tug.

Harbormaster Swenson pulled her aluminum skiff along side Jay's tugboat, disturbing the quiet morning with the raucous cackle of her cockpit radio.

"Hey, Tom," she called. "What's up?"

Isobel directed a suspicious glance at her grandson. The young harbor officer, in spite of unflattering mufti, was indeed a gorgeous Nordic blonde.

"My gran," Tom nodded at Isobel, "was relaxing on deck with her coffee and noticed these bubbles rising from beneath the tug. I'm not about to jump into this freezing water," he said, "but something's leaking from below, and I've no knowledge of the inner workings of tugs."

"Any word of Jay yet?" Swenson asked.

Tom shook his head. "We've asked around town and checked out his usual haunts, but no one's seen him."

Isobel caught Malo's eye and they communicated a mutual premonition of a connection between the gaseous percolations from under the hull and Jay's disappearance. For the next five minutes they watched Swenson's unsuccessful efforts to probe under the tug's stern with her gaff.

"I'm afraid I'll need an assist here," she conceded. "This gaff's too short. I need to call my partner to suit up and come out to help." She bit her lip. "I haven't had a lot of experience with drowning's, but this doesn't look good. You'd better gather your belongings and be ready to come ashore if there's a problem."

A problem? Tacitly, the three shared Swenson's morbid suspicions and climbed below to collect their gear. Isobel remembered that classic film where the yacht's owner, confident he had gotten away with murder, tossed his victim overboard then unknowingly dragged the body, entangled under the hull, all the way home. No, no, she hoped. Please, not another murder. Malo saw her knuckles whiten on the rail. He put his arm around her shoulders and pulled her gently against him while Tom stood at the rail with his shoulders slumped and hands thrust deep in his pockets.

"I'm sorry Gran," he said. "When I called you, I never thought we would uncover this kind of trouble."

"I'm sure you didn't," said Isobel and squeezed his shoulder against her. "But after your remarks about your friend's championing of lost causes, I think Jay was unwise to interfere with these men. Our recent experience with the Chinese Triad Society was not pleasant." She shuddered and recalled Akuratsu's body-processing vessel moored off the coast of Indonesia. "I became involved with them in a far worse kind of smuggling."

A short while later, their premonition proved true. From the tug's deck they watched Harbormaster Swenson's co-diver arrive and pull the bloated body of Tom's friend to the surface. It was obvious from the state of his corpse, that Jay had been lashed to the underside of the tug for several days. As they lifted his body into Swenson's skiff, they were repulsed and shocked by the sight of Jay's arms lashed across his chest. Both hands severed at the wrists.

Isobel closed her eyes and felt her knees buckle. Tom reached over to steady her. As she sank onto the hatch cover, the scene brought to her mind was too familiar—the clean cut wrist bones of that skeletal hand on the beach in Newport with its jeweled watery memento. A gruesome coincidence?

During her initiation by Malo into the grim side of organized crime, she'd never viewed the end results of any of his assignments and carefully arranged to be off-stage during the actual disposal. And what of the intruder who had rummaged their room? Nothing taken, but a look at her driver's license in her purse would confirm her identity and all kinds of personal information could be gained from it. Because of her association with Malo, was she also being watched?

They left the tugboat wrapped with yellow tape, as Tom's 'problem' became an official crime scene. A somber Swenson ferried the three of them and their gear back to the town dock and escorted them on the short walk to the police station.

"You are not under arrest," she assured them, "and if you object, you will not be detained for questioning. However," Swenson gave Tom a guileless smile, and in her Scandinavian lilt, said, "it would be helpful to our inquiries and we'd be grateful if you could take the time to tell us anything you know about your friend, our victim. Its vicious nature suggests a revenge murder, and I'm curious why. Jay was one of the quiet, law-abiding liveaboards. He never caused trouble and complied with all DNR regulations."

They stopped in front of the Police Headquarters and Isobel and Malo viewed its flat-roofed façade.

"It was built in '69 as the Town Hall," the harbormaster said. "It was never designed as a police facility. The town's sentimentalists think it's cool and retro, but it's honestly claimed by the police who must work there to be totally outdated. Entirely unsuitable and never intended to house modern law enforcement."

Inside the building, Isobel repressed a grin as a sallow, gaunt officer slid the cone of his nose mask over his head and crossed the room to greet them.

"Sorry," he said, wheezing and blowing into a large wad of tissues. "I'm Detective Björnson. Rather not shake your hand, too many germs here already. My body can't cope." He gestured around the fluorescent-lit room. "Walls here are full of mold and asbestos. Toxic poisons we shouldn't breathe."

His miserable whine reminded Isobel of Martha Grimes' sidekick to her Inspector Jury—Detective Sgt. Wiggins and his constant hypochondriac laments.

"It's sadly true," admitted Swenson. "Detective Björnson is one of the asthmatics and allergic types working in this building who complain their health suffers."

"Yeah, and I'm one of the worst, for sure," griped the sniffing, nose-daubing detective. "There've been some make-shift solutions," Björnson went on, "but the place is still contaminated. The Chief promises to fix things, but only—and I quote from his last report—'after an intensive assessment of the totality of the city's portfolio and its assets.' Now if that isn't political speak for never . . ."

"Bear with it, Björnson," said Swenson and led Malo, Tom, and Isobel down the hall to a decent sized corner office. "I'm leaving you in the capable hands of our First Detective, Sam Rodgers." They saw Swenson and Rodgers exchange familiar glances. "Sam here is an old buddy of mine," she said. "Literally, Sam will get to the bottom of this if anyone can."

Isobel thought Detective Rodgers as cool and laid—back retro as the building he worked from. Tall and husky, he came around his desk to shake their hands and motioned them to three orange molded plastic chairs. Isobel recalled the décor of that era and was thankful they were not those triangular metal-framed hammocks she'd needed to be hauled from.

"This kind of ugly murder is pretty unusual for us. We average about four homicides a year and, in my memory, nothing so vicious. But then again," Rodgers paused, "we have never dealt with the Mafia before."

He spoke softly, but directed individual concern to each of them in turn as he eased his muscular bulk into an oak swivel chair. Its sturdy frame squealed under his weight and they saw him jot WD-40 on a note pad. The desk's surface was buried under a jumble of pens, fasteners, piles of papers, and framed photos of dogs held in the laps of gap-toothed children. Isobel decided it looked more like a dumped litterbin than work surface. She guessed Sam was one of those people who operated mostly from inside his head. He leaned forward, and they all winced as the chair protested.

"Your friend's body will be sent to the Kitsap Coroner in Port Orchard to be autopsied. Again, the explanation for this kind of brutal killing is the typical reaction of the organization. A grim warning to not interfere with the Chinese Triad." After Rodgers updated them on Tom's earlier report of the current shellfish smuggling in the area, Isobel broke in.

"Tom says that Jay's a determined protester and must have tried to take threating action. We are sure that this young man's death was a warning—a terrible retaliation."

Detective Rodgers eyed Isobel sharply and doodled a noosed hangman on his deck blotter. "Personally, I regret we're not officially on top of this operation." Sam expelled a heavy sigh and met Tom's eye. "I'm sorry if your friend got too curious and interfered in some way. This ugly incident is their clear warning for us to lay off." He rolled back the recalcitrant chair. "Don't worry, we don't intend to."

Isobel felt tempted to mention her past solution to an equally nasty operation, but looked at Sam's doodled noose and kept quiet.

Rodgers shrugged and shook his head.

"It's going to be hard and take a lot of time to prosecute this one. These organizations have too many tentacles. I'd like to vindicate your friend as fast as possible, but despite our best efforts, so far they've proved powerful in the past at getting away with—well, murder. I promise we'll do our best to keep this one out of the cold case file."

Before they left, a clerk brought in a box of maple glazed crullers, hot milk, and a carafe of coffee.

"Don't laugh," said Sam as he bit into a sweet, airy rectangle. "Donuts and policemen. But these are special and above any donut you will ever sink your teeth into. Help yourself. They come from a bakery over in Poulsbo." Sam wiped flakey crumbs from his tie. "Luckily, though, you've missed another specialty of Poulsbo. You wont believe what the Scandia natives there do to our lovely codfish. In a special Lutefisk festival, during the season before Christmas, they soak fresh cod in lye—the same poisonous stuff used to unclog drains. Believe me, it tastes—ah, to be polite, badly spoiled."

Malo and Isobel helped devour the lattes and pastry and spent another half hour explaining their presence on the island and Tom's history with Jay. Isobel did not elaborate on why her grandson had called her for help, but realized that, if this gang of thieves stymied the police, she would revenge Jay's death in her own signature way.

While Tom was denied access to the tug as a crime scene, Isobel booked him a room at the inn in Winslow and left him to set up restaurant interviews within the driving limits of his decrepit transportation. Malo disappeared for the day on some unexplained errand. This going off on their own was a mutual arrangement as they both relished independence and agreed that not needing to be entertained by each other or live in each other's pockets was the key to their relationship. This compatible ease had evolved into the mutual concern and protection essential to their line of work.

Isobel brewed a cup of tea at the suite's coffee buffet and emptied into it a bottle of *fino* sherry from the mini-bar. The combination would either send her to sleep or stimulate some solution for her next disposal—the diver responsible for Jay's death. Sam Rodger's prophecy of it languishing as a dead-end cold case would not do. She planned to make sure the assassin who strapped Jay's body beneath the tugboat's hull would pay for his murder.

It must be simple. Most undetected murders are. She rummaged in her handbag and found her Swiss army knife. The most efficient arsenal of weaponry ever designed by a peace-touting nation. The sharp little blade had done its job before. Why not again? In this case, Jay's severed hands seemed synonymous with the severing of a diver's air hose—his lifeline.

The scene unfolding in her mind needed only a few touches to encourage a verdict of an accidental death.

Something nudged at Isobel's memory, but its importance flew from her head at the sound of the Malo's key card swiping the door. He strode into the room and, obviously pleased with his day's booty, emptied a huge shopping bag onto the bed. The carrier bore the logo of the bookstore they had browsed through the day before. She eagerly examined the titles of the half-dozen books he'd tumbled onto the spread.

"How lovely. You know that print books are my favorite possessions," she exclaimed, caressing their glossy jackets. "But so many! How can I read them all before we leave?"

"What's our hurry?" he said. "I like this place. We've come so far. Why not spend some time and explore?" He unrolled a band-wrapped cylinder from a cardboard tube. "Look at these nautical charts I found of Puget Sound and the Straits. There are twenty-two ferry routes that travel the area. It reminds me of the Swedish archipelago. We could spend an entire month exploring these northwest islands."

Isobel was amused by his fervor. This was not the reserved and taciturn man she had known over the past year. Standing before her, brandishing an armful of charts, Malo unrolled one and pointed to a large yellow area amidst wandering expanses of depth notated blue.

"And the mainland includes this entire Olympic Peninsula—see this big wedge jutting into the ocean?" He pointed. "It sounds foggy and wild. And you wanted primeval moss! They say the Peninsula's rain forests are legendary. Massive miles of moss. Weren't the tracks of the mythical northwestern Yeti—the giant Sasquatch sighted there?"

"Good grief, Malo."

He laughed at himself. "Well, rarely sighted."

"That sounds like a wonderful adventure," she agreed, then hesitated and added. "Rainy, but—a challenge." She pulled him down gently onto the bed beside her, but for once he was not distracted.

"America's huge compared to my France," he went on. "You could get lost here—disappear from the world."

Isobel, though still amused by his excitement, was distracted by his words. She lay back against her pillows and idly picked up the little red knife she'd placed on the bedside table. She weighed it in the palm of her hand. Disappear, she mused. If her plan to dispose of the diver failed, she thought, she might just have to.

TWELVE

That evening Malo and Isobel strolled Winslow's main street and found, posted beside the entrance to a hole-in-the-wall restaurant, a menu claiming to have the Northwest's best Dungeness crab salad. She grabbed Malo's arm.

"Let's have dinner here. I suddenly crave mounds of Dungeness slathered with Thousand Island dressing. It's the sweetest tasting crab in the world. An ugly crustacean, big as a dinner plate, with a rock hard shell that, I admit, takes effort, but offers up meat that is absolutely delicious." She edged him towards the door.

"Isobel, do you always think about food? I recall you insisted your Maine harbor's hand picked crab was the best in the world."

"That's when I'm in Maine."

As usual, her logic defeated him. Seated inside and soothed by excellent dry martinis, Isobel diverted him with her plan for disposing of the diver responsible for Jay's death. Malo's wary reaction made her realize this was the first time in their partnership she'd taken the initiative. Before this business with Jay, he had always assigned the target. Someone, they both agreed, who well deserved to be better off dead.

"I appreciate your zeal," he admitted. "But though your efficient Swiss knife did the deed in Sweden," he paused, "what do you really know of diving operations? Because I don't think scuba gear includes air-hoses. The acronym means Self-Contained Underwater Breathing Apparatus." Isobel's fork stopped halfway to her mouth.

"Oh my," she sighed. "I knew something about the plan bothered me. I guess I've relied on too many shark attack movies."

"Actually, it's a good idea," Malo said, motioning to the waiter for the check. "First, let's do the necessary research. We'll find a local dive shop and ask some questions. Have you ever spent time underwater?"

She laughed. "I've never 'spent time' as you phrase it, anywhere—yet. Brief vacation snorkeling in the Caymans," she recalled. "But never, ever, above my knees in our freezing Maine Atlantic. For years I've watched the local divers set and pull moorings in Elmore Harbor, but never paid attention. I guess I should have." She smiled ruefully. "That was before my new career and the need for these special skills."

Lajala and Daughters, Divers. The shop on Winslow Way smelled of rubber and neoprene. Its walls were hung with hoses, goggles, regulators, and every other kind of apparatus needed for functioning below the water's surface. Isobel stood mesmerized before a huge screen showing a continuous underwater adventure video featuring close-ups of divers, their faces squeezed gargoyles behind masks, bubbles streaming, making hand signals indicating all was well and beckoning for her to join them. The scene looked tempting, but she could not imagine herself struggling into the black body suit necessary to keep warm at those depths. Another day. She planned to manage this diver's disposal from dry land.

The helpful young owner, another silvery blond Nordic with Anni stitched on her vest, offered help.

"How does the underwater breathing system work?" asked Isobel. She gestured at the walls. "All this gear looks so cumbersome."

"It is," said the girl. "But only for the short time until you fall back over the rail into the water. Below the surface you are buoyant, even with tanks on your back."

"What's in the tanks? What do I breathe and how?"

Anni led her to the tank storage area. "Divers drop their empty cylinders off at the fill station where the attendants attach the valves so the tanks can be filled at the compressor with the correct mixture needed for their particular operation." She showed Isobel the regulator and how to fit the mouthpiece and facemask. "And believe me," Anni laughed. "Rolling yourself into the neoprene bodysuit is easier than wiggling into tight skinny jeans on a hot day."

Isobel did not say that her days of tight, skinny jeans were past. She left the shop with an enticing brochure full of all the information needed to become a human fish.

With the tug still impounded, Tom borrowed from a friend of a friend, a Seasport—a comfortable small craft with a protected forward cabin. They didn't have to wait long for a cloudy night. The next evening, starting at dusk, the three of them rowed out to the Seasport in Jay's dinghy and began watch sessions, each taking four-hour turns with night vision glasses to scout the area for signs of activity.

Isobel was first to spot two men arrive in an unlighted skiff and be dropped off at the dive boat anchored in a nearby cove. As the divers began suiting up, she scanned the water but reported no watching monitor boat.

"I'm not surprised," said Tom. "Swenson said the harbor patrol has been keeping their eye on this particular dive boat but the operator's been careful." Despite Isobel's protests, Tom and Malo, both dressed in black jeans and sweaters, insisted she remain behind.

Tom untied Jay's dinghy and quietly rowed them close enough for Malo, using infrared film, to record the dive boat's registration numbers. Tom held the dinghy steady while Malo, adjusting the night vision glasses, watched two men appear on deck. One of them helped the other adjust his weight belt and attach his collecting bags.

After several hours' surveillance, while the diver worked the bottom, Malo and Tom felt satisfied by what they'd recorded. Confident their observations had been unnoticed, and after the smugglers left with their haul, they rowed back to the Seasport and told an impatient Isobel what they'd accomplished.

"With the dive boat's registration and tonight's illegal haul recorded on film, let's hope it's enough evidence for Detective Rodgers to close this case.

Isobel said nothing. Though they probably had enough proof to indict the diver, she knew the Triad's skills at subversion and was determined not to leave things to chance.

"I did some research this afternoon and it wasn't hard to trace the diver," said Tom. "He's an illegal immigrant.

A Russian Finn named Yuri Virtenën, and if things go as usual, he'll drop off his empty tanks tonight to be refilled at the local station." Tom turned to Isobel. "From here on, we'll follow your plan."

Before dawn, with no lights and under a starless black sky, they followed Yuri in Tom's wreck of a car to the filling station where the diver unloaded his tanks. The night remained moonless and they waited out of sight until Yuri's red taillights disappeared down the road. Isobel removed a coil of hose from the rear seat.

"Gentlemen," she announced, "we are about to maim the Mafia's local shellfish racket."

Malo got them inside the fill station using the time-proven piece of plastic. Isobel followed and, insisting that the results of their tampering not kill some innocent diver, carefully checked the identifying markings on Yuri's tanks.

Outside, Tom backed his heap up to the compressor while Malo attached Isobel's length of hose from the rusty tailpipe to the machine's intake pads. He looked at Isobel. "How much?" She shrugged.

"I can only guess. Top it off so he first breathes enough carbon monoxide to fall unconscious, drop his mouthpiece and drown. Weighted with dive belts, by the time his accomplice on deck begins to worry, poor Yuri will be long gone."

THIRTEEN

The breakfast special at the Harborside Inn was a Hangtown Fry, and Isobel forked up a creamy mouthful of oysters and eggs. Malo and Tom watched her shake large dollops of hot sauce onto the remaining mound.

"This is best eaten with cold beer," she admitted. "But maybe not at breakfast."

Malo held up his newspaper. "Listen to this," he said and read aloud the one-inch headline emblazing the front page of the *Bainbridge Review:* "Drowned Body of Diver Found in Harbor."

Tom and Isobel exchanged satisfied glances. Malo continued reading.

"Harbor police found the body of a diver believed to be a member of a gang of shellfish smugglers raiding the waters off our Island. The body of the illegal harvester, identified as Yuri Virtenën, a Russian immigrant, was brought to the surface by dredgers working off Blakeby Cove. Pending further inquiries, authorities found no evidence of foul play."

"How interesting," said Tom. Malo handed over the paper.

"I'd guess that when his dive mate discovered Yuri drowned," said Malo, "he figured he'd suffered a heart attack. I doubt there's much allegiance among these sangfroid killers. I expect he cut and ran, literally, and left Yuri to the fishes."

"I'm sorry your friend Jay is gone," said Isobel, "but at least you have the consolation that so is his murderer." "Uhmm," murmured Tom. The three finished their breakfast in silence.

Malo broke their solemn mood. He turned to Tom.

"Your grandmother and I are taking off today to explore more of this Northwest corner. We want to start with the hydrofoil to Victoria on Vancouver Island. You're welcome to stay as our guest here at the inn for as long as you need to find work and get settled."

"Thanks, guys," said Tom and gave his grandmother the thumbs up sign. "For everything, understand?" Outside on the sunny sidewalk, he paused before they parted.

"Hey, I've some good news. A hot new restaurant in Ballard wants to hire me. The Blackfoot gave me a pretty generous reference and, thanks to my brother, they even praised my kitchen skills." He grinned at Malo. "No mention of any peccadilloes."

Nearby, at the Bainbridge Police Headquarters, Detective Sgt. Björnson brewed a fresh pot of herbal tea and covered it with a double-knit cozy he'd made himself. An anonymous manila envelope lay on the desk before him.

Björnson slit it open and pulled out several enlarged photographs of a fishing boat with clearly visible registration numbers and the un-masked face of a diver, his hands laden with bulging bait sacks. The Detective Sgt. swiped at his nose, sniffed, and gave a satisfied smile. Gotcha. He slid the pictures back into the envelope and carried them into Rodgers office.

In their room the next morning after breakfast, Isobel spent an hour on the phone navigating her extensive list of garden club connections. Finally, through a docent friend living on Bainbridge, she had permission to spend a mystical, serene afternoon walking the Zen gardens located within the Island's famous Bloedell Reserve.

Malo did not share her joy at this achievement or understand her passion for garden tours.

"I'm not wasting the day traipsing through other peoples' yards."

"But like your rainforest, this garden's special for its primeval moss," Isobel insisted.

She watched him gather up his precious rolls of charts. Tension developed. "I'm sorry," he announced firmly, "but I plan to spend the day travelling about on ferries. You go walk the moss."

The next morning, Malo joined Isobel at breakfast. Previous ill will forgotten, they kissed over orange juice and apologized for their mutual stubbornness. Lessons learned, they agreed their day apart had been a pleasant and welcome break from each other's company.

Back in their room, after an austere meal of poached eggs on toast, Malo spread his charts on the bed and suggested they rent a car and follow a route by ferry among some of the San Juan Islands that he promised would interest them both.

"I've even included a stop in Victoria so you can indulge yourself traipsing those famous Butchart Gardens and we can stay at that grand hotel," he said. "Their brochure says that, since the Queen's Jubilee, Victoria, they mean, they've updated the chain-pull toilets."

Isobel looked over his shoulder at the inked lines he drawn snaking across the waters of Puget Sound. "That island is special for more than the gardens," she said. "I don't understand those crowds of tourists who mill about those tedious bedding plants, exclaiming over patterned plots of puce begonias. All replanted for each season and tended by dozens of hired minions. They bear no relation to dirt gardeners like me."

Malo sighed with silent relief.

The bellman had collected their bags and Malo was on his knees checking under the beds for a lost sock when he saw the phone light blinking red. Message waiting. Neither had noticed it while packing.

He cast a surreptitious glance at Isobel and casually covered the phone's display buttons with the message pad. If possible, he'd divert her attention and get them out of here on time. Too late. She crossed the room to collect their keycards from the desk and brushed the notepad aside.

"There's a phone message," she accused him.

"Isobel, please don't. Let's just get on our way."

"You know I can't do that," she said sharply. "I'd be miserable. What if it's an emergency?" Malo squeezed his eyes shut and she softened her voice.

"I'm sorry to be such a worrywart, but let me take one moment and find out who called."

Malo formed a little church and steeple with his thumb and fingers while she connected with the front desk.

"It was Jo," said Isobel and replaced the receiver. "She left a message to call her as soon as possible."

"Fine." He checked his watch. "But let's not miss the ferry. You can return her call in the car from your cell." Without a word, he gathered their coats and propelled her towards the door.

The luxury hybrid Malo rented indulged them with all the newest bells and whistles that make modern car journeys a pleasure. Isobel nestled into the cushioned leather passenger seat and dialed Jo's cell number. Her niece answered after two rings.

"Malo didn't want to miss the boat," explained Isobel, "so I'm calling from the ferry on our way across Puget Sound to Seattle. From there we're taking off for a week to explore the Pacific Northwest. Are you and Pen staying someplace warmer than Maine? You sounded worried. Is everything okay?"

"Aunt Isobel, whoa. First of all, did you solve Tom's problem?"

"Well, yes," Isobel paused. "More or less. There were a few unexpected difficulties. We'll talk about it when we get home." To Isobel's relief, her niece sounded too absorbed by her own worries to question Tom's latest issue. "You said to call back right away. What's up?"

Jo's voice, when she answered, sounded suspiciously nonchalant.

"While Pen and I were closing up your Maine cottage after you left, I got a call from Fiona. She knew we'd returned from Spain so I brought her up to date—including your plans to visit Tom in Seattle."

"Speaking of past issues," interrupted Isobel, "we all miss her, but your sister was wise to leave Elmore Harbor. Bad memories are more easily forgotten in new surroundings. I've heard she is doing well, found a nice gatehouse cottage and made new friends. Is something wrong?"

Still vivid in her memory, Isobel recalled how, last summer, the entire family had watched helplessly while Fiona, her younger and more delicate niece barely survived her husband's control. Eugene's timely demise—Isobel's practice disposal, had been nasty electrical "accident." Eugene had not been much mourned, but Isobel had not yet wiped his grim death from her conscience. By fall, the gossip surrounding Eugene had ebbed and the entire village no longer speculated—at least aloud—over his unpleasant end.

Fiona's friends knew her as a sweet and gentle person until she floundered under her husband's thumb, and though they would miss her, were happy she had left the harbor's mean associations behind. The last word was that Fiona had settled comfortably in a small art colony on the coast of Connecticut's Long Island Sound.

Isobel glanced up and returned to the present by Malo, glowering at her over his hand-formed T-sign to get off the phone.

"Jo, I'll call back, we're getting in line to board the ferry."

"Wait just one minute," pleaded Jo. There was a catch in her voice. "Let me explain why I called. I know when my sister's upset and Fiona sounded stressed. It seems one of her new art association friends is in serious trouble." Isobel shut her eyes and sighed. Thankful Malo was diverted for the moment with maneuvering into boarding lanes. She bit her lip and imagined his displeasure if another family difficulty aborted their vacation. She turned toward the window and muffled her voice with her hand.

"Jo," said Isobel, "we all know your sister is a talented poet and a lovely person, but hopeless at dealing with difficult situations. Quick, Malo's giving me the evil eye. What is this trouble?"

"When I told her that Pen and I were leaving Maine to hole up somewhere warmer, she asked if we'd stop here on our way south. Of course I said yes. Then she asked if I thought you and Malo might come and help."

"Help with what?"

"It seems that Fiona's new friend Piet—I think he sounds closer than a friend—has been accused of murder.

Isobel looked over at Malo and knew this was not a good time to probe Jo's alarming news. She hastily promised to return her niece's call as soon as their ferry docked in Seattle. She closed her phone and smiled as Malo stopped his impatient tapping on the console between them. From his frown, Isobel knew she'd been wise to make no hasty commitment to rush east.

Chocked into place at the head of the ferry and, determined to ease his testy mood, Isobel shrugged into her down vest and zipped it to the neck.

"Let's go up top and sit outside," she said. She waited, steel deck plates vibrating under foot, as Malo locked the car and, deafened by the roar of the *Tacoma's* thunderous diesels, they climbed the tiers of metal steps to the uppermost deck.

Fortified with sausage rolls and steaming lattes from the café, they went forward and stood at the rail and let the breezes off the Sound toss their hair. Only the squalling, soaring gulls and the long rush of wake under the bows broke the peace. Mid-channel, the ferry gained speed and they sought escape from the wind on a slatted bench in the lee of the pilothouse. With their faces turned to bask in the cool morning sun, they left Bainbridge Island behind.

As Seattle's skyscape loomed ahead, Malo finished his second coffee and looked over at Isobel beside him. She lay back, resting her neck against the curved seatback, her eyes closed. During the past year, he had become more sensitive to her feelings and regretted his impatience at the tone of her muffled responses to Jo's call. If life with the Van Dursans augured true to form, he'd best be resigned to some new family drama.

He knew he'd been sharp with her since they left the inn that morning, but hoped she knew by now that he needed time to change a lifetime of independent habits. For too many years, no one but himself had suffered from his actions. He now realized that, if he wanted his comfortable relationship with Isobel to continue, he'd have to make some compromises. But then, he decided, so should she.

They left the serenity of the brief water journey behind in their wake as they returned below to their car and heard the engines slow as they approached the bustle of Seattle's ferry terminal. Immediately after they disembarked, the sun disappeared and the sky, grey as a pewter lid, lowered down on them. Adding to the gloomy morning, they were told at the terminal that they must drive two hours north to Anacortes to book passage for Orcas, the first of their San Juan island destinations. As Malo navigated the traffic thundering under the viaduct along Alaska Way, he studied Isobel, sitting quietly beside him. She had curled her legs beneath her and ran her fingers idly over the cell phone in her lap. The frowns furrowing her forehead told him she still worried over Jo's call. A sure bet they were due for more problems and, naturally, three thousand miles away. Resigned to the inevitable, he reached across her knees and shoved their vacation ferry schedule itinerary into the glove box.

FOURTEEN

Six hours and a continent east of the grey, damp coast of Washington, the Connecticut sun emitted its first pale intimations of spring. By late afternoon, and travel weary, the cab left them in front of Fiona's cottage. Still barren trees cast spiny shadows along its gabled roof. The landscape here remained a depressing dun color and she missed the Northwest's reliable green canopy of evergreens.

Isobel rang the bell, and Malo waited patiently behind her with their cases. From inside, they heard the echo of hurried footsteps along hardwood floor and, when the door flew open, Fiona let out a cry of surprise. Waves of nostalgia overwhelmed Isobel at the urgent fling of her niece's arms around her neck and she realized how much she had missed this fragile young woman since Fiona had moved here from Maine.

"Aunt Isobel, I knew you would come."

"Of course I did. What's three thousand miles when my favorite niece needs me." It had long been a family joke that the child closest at the moment was the favorite. Fiona let go of her aunt's neck, clasped Malo's arm, and gave him a hug. Isobel felt pleased to see that, after a startled moment, he lost the stiff expression he'd worn since boarding the plane for their journey back east. She saw Malo relax and return Fiona's embrace.

"Come in, come in," the young woman urged. "Pen and Jo arrived yesterday and you must meet my friend Piet Sonders. Piet's the reason I was so anxious you come as soon as possible. He's been through such trouble—accused of murder by stabbing a man through the eyeball with a sharpened paintbrush!"

Before they could react to this astonishing statement, Jo and Pen came into the hall from the sitting room. Malo stood aside, still stunned by Fiona's outburst. The Van Dursan's embraced and began a rapid exchange of family gossip. While the women talked, he moved away into the central hall and stared along its length through the glass-paneled door at its end.

As he stood alone and watched, the sun sank in sherbet layers of pink, orange, and violet below the horizon of Long Island Sound. He wondered if the dramatic display was an omen. The flaming sky reminded him of the spectacular religious calendars favored by his Italian aunts. Malo pressed his lips together and recalled the two old lady's pious belief that the benevolent outstretched arms of the Lord would rise above the waters to bestow his benediction on the faithful. Could this evening sky's apparition be a favorable portent for Isobel's newest complication? Doubtful. The horizon fast faded to the color of lead and, grateful for those kind but overly religious aunts who had cared for his young son during his absences, stifled his irreverent amusement. He drew a deep breath and returned to join Isobel and her family's newest trauma in the sitting room.

While they gathered around the huge stone hearth, Fiona introduced Malo to her friend, Piet Sonders. Malo shook the hand of a tall, slim, soft-spoken man as fair and blond as his Scandinavian ancestors. At this time of year, dusk turned quickly to dark and Fiona put a match to the fire and lit table lamps. By some tacit agreement among the women, there was no further mention of Piet's dilemma. Fiona urged them to sit and asked Isobel about their week in Seattle and the state of Tom's love life. "More women trouble?" she asked.

Isobel remembered that Fiona and Tom, first cousins, once removed, had been close friends growing up. They both joked about the removed part—could never figure out what it meant.

Over drinks, Isobel related the dire details of their trip west.

As she told them their tale, Malo relaxed into the cushions, savoring his excellent martini, and let her words flow over him. On the long plane trip east from Seattle, up front of course, they'd had time to talk, and he hoped she'd been mollified by his amicable acceptance of their abrupt change of plans. By now, Isobel must know that he understood her innate need to help yet another family member out of yet another family crisis. He was charmed by her fervent promise to finish their adventure as soon as Fiona was sorted out and agreed that the northwest rainforest would wait for their return. Isobel finished the saga of their exploits and, relieved to see Malo enjoying himself, hoped she had soothed the issue and passed him a bowl of roasted almonds. She turned to Fiona.

"I promised Malo that, after things are settled here, we will return to the Pacific Northwest, board every ferry, and explore all twenty-two islands. By the time we return to Maine, our skin, under raingear, will be covered with fungus from weeks without sun."

"Nonsense," said Fiona. "She laughed and patted Malo's knee, "and I predict, Mr. Bellini, that when you return to the northwest you will enjoy endless days of perfect weather. Believe me, I've heard all that bad hype is promoted by the natives who use it as a ploy to keep people away."

Isobel popped a chicken liver wrapped in bacon into her mouth—she loved these retro canapés—and controlled her urge to argue that those damp grey winter days were not all hype. She was pleased and amazed at the metamorphosis of her youngest niece. Since Eugene's death, Fiona had emerged from an unnatural and melancholy sufferance and re-gained her spontaneous humor.

Isobel recalled how, as children, Fiona was the child who had suffered most from their professorial parent's immersion in academic life. Isobel's self-absorbed brother and his thesis-obsessed wife had left their two young daughters emotional orphans, and Isobel had done her best to rescue the girls whenever possible from their parents' neglect. They were not intentionally cruel, only obliviously out of touch.

Perhaps Isobel's closer attachment to Jo stemmed from her older niece's resilience and stubborn independence. Traits she recognized in herself. Jo had been the sister to rebel, with folded arms and uncompromising glares, against the succession of frustrated nannies and housekeepers.

After graduating from Bates College, Jo took her degree and literary talents to New York where she began a successful career as a freelance journalist. She proved good enough at the job to pick and chose her assignments.

In contrast to her sister's success, friends and family sympathized while watching Fiona, imprisoned in the web of her early and unfortunate marriage, barely survive Eugene's damage.

Isobel shook away these old emotional injuries incurred during that unpleasant year and relaxed before the warmth of the fire. After finishing the account of Tom's involvement with the Asian Mafia smugglers, Isobel had suddenly felt exhausted from their long day and unwisely accepted a second martini. Pleasantly numbed by good vodka, she watched Fiona charm Malo out of any remaining grumps.

"Piet and I regret interrupting your vacation," said Fiona, "but believe me, we are so grateful you came east to help us solve this mess. Knowing the past results of your combined talents, I'm sure you and Malo will find a way to prove him innocent" She gave him her most engaging smile. "Before you know it, you'll be back on those ferries and cruising, shirtless, among the islands."

At dinner that evening, the six of them sat close around Fiona's table. These colonial cottages along the shore, with their head bruising lintels, were built three hundred years ago for smaller bodies. But tonight, the flickering warmth of the fire Piet had lit in the dining room's smaller hearth warded off the drafts endemic to its age.

On their arrival, Fiona apologized for her lack of bedrooms but their guests were quick to agree that her quaint cottage was too authentically original for their spoiled dependence on modern comforts.

At Jo and Pen's suggestion, Isobel and Malo booked rooms adjoining theirs at the Bell and Whistle Tavern—a charming, but thoughtfully renovated, eighteenth century inn at the center of town. Here, the close-built old houses, fronting the cobbled historic Main Street, both look and are genuine. The town records suggest the village was settled by immigrants from Lyme Regis, Dorset, England, in the sixteen hundreds.

From the candle lit sideboard, they served themselves bowls of coconut chicken curry spooned over saffron scented couscous. Fiona had enhanced the gently spiced buffet with a tasty array of condiments and baskets of puffy, lentil poppadums.

Isobel chose to sit next to Fiona's accused friend. On first being introduced to Piet, her matchmaking agenda assumed that, after they'd sorted out this strange business, her niece, like any fairy tale princess, would wed her prince and produce beautiful blond heirs. Isobel discarded this romantic happily-ever-after fantasy, and forced her mind to return to their current problem. She recalled that, before the happy ending, most fairy tales involved witches, ogres, ovens and wolves, and were pretty grim reading.

Isobel took stock of the man seated beside her. First of all, this gentle Swede did not look capable of stabbing anyone through the eye with a sharpened paintbrush. However alarming and unlikely these facts, after Fiona's disclosure of Piet's arrest, they managed to enjoy their dinner without further comment on the room's silent elephant.

However enjoyable the evening and pleasant the conversation, Isobel could not help wonder if Fiona had succumbed to the charms of yet another dubious man and they were dining with a murderer.

FIFTEEN

"Someone please tell us," asked Malo, as they lingered over coffee, "the name and importance of this violently murdered person?" Across the table, Fiona spooned up the last bits of ethereal flan and pushed aside her plate.

"Jason Church Faraday," she began, "is—oh dear, was—a descendant, actually the great grandson, of one of the Hudson Valley School of artists established here in the 1800s. These prestigious painters were hosted, in her boarding house salon by our own Florence Griswold, this town's most influential and charismatic woman. Flo established a coterie of impassioned American impressionists, august painters who came from all over— Childe Hassam, among them—and lived under both the lady's roof and spell."

Isobel could no longer contain her curiosity. She nodded from Fiona to Piet.

"And why would your friend here want this Church descendent dead?"

"He didn't," said Fiona. "But unfortunately, this year Jason Faraday vied with Piet as the Art Association's most serious contender for their juried grand prize awarded at the closing of the current show. The honor is worth more for its prestige and enhancement of the chosen artist's reputation than the modest prize money. The day after the judge's announcement to the committee that Jason had won, Piet was found standing over Jason's ravaged body in his basement studio of the Art Association with the bloody paintbrush clutched in his hand."

They sat in embarrassed silence as Fiona covered her face with her hands. Uneasy attention focused on Piet who pushed back his chair and pulled a folded piece of newsprint from his pocket.

"Let me explain how it began," he said, and slid an announcement clipped from the *Shoreline Times* next to Isobel's plate. "Please, read it aloud," he asked. She did.

> "Join us tonight at Memorial Hall to celebrate our town's three chosen stars. Poet—Fiona Van Dursan. Painter—Piet Sonders. Dancer—Tricia Black.
> Each of these artists represents the jury's choice for excellence in their field and the coveted $10,000 prize."

"Rumor says there's a good chance Piet will win that prize money if he's cleared of Jason's murder," said Fiona. "That's why he's here tonight and not in jail. It's the exact amount the lenient judge set for Piet's release on bail. The bondsman who posted the money knows Piet and also doubts he is guilty. Piet is rather a favorite among the association painters." She turned to her aunt. "Of course Piet's innocent and we know you and Malo will somehow prove it."

"There are further complications—another lucky reason I'm not in a cell," Piet added, bitterly.

"There's what the police call an ongoing investigation into ugly rumors of fraud and forgery," explained Fiona. "One of the most prominent of the accredited judges and present chairman of the Association became suspicious of Jason's entry. After Piet was implicated in his murder, the board decided to pend their award decision. However, there are rumblings among the judges that the prize should go to Piet if he's acquitted. I know, it sounds unorthodox, but the Association is well known for its independent and volatile members who maintain a huge influence over an artist's prestige in our corner of the art world. Unfortunately, included among our many fine and reputable painters, is a jealous nest of vipers." After her little speech, Fiona composed herself, stood and pressed her palms on the table. "One of them is guilty of Faraday's murder."

Isobel frowned and tried to catch Malo's attention, but he kept his eyes intent on the dregs of his coffee. Pen folded his napkin, looked up at Fiona and dramatically raised an eyebrow.

"If this investigation proves the judge's suspicions of fraud are founded," he said, "depending on the value of the painting, we could be talking of grand larceny along with murder." He sat back and stretched his legs. "Outside Indiana Jones territory, I've never met a nest of vipers."

"I disagree," said Jo. She turned to him with a wry smile. "Some of the people I've met in your company slithered as genuine lowlife."

"Unfortunately," Pen answered, with a theatrical wave of his hand, "one of the hazards of my employ is the quality of my associates. Unfortunately, I can't resist acting the devil's advocate and, like Jones, I enjoy

Ann Blair Kloman

prodding vipers. Do any of these Association contesters live in this area?"

Fiona fixed her serious grey eyes on Pen.

"Most of our active members live near enough," she said. "Many of the towns lining the shoreline are only minutes apart, but vary greatly in income. There are an amazing number of artists of all genres living in the area, some poor and others definitely nowhere close to starving. Our town is also home to an excellent Art Academy famous for its talented graduates." She turned to her aunt. "Aside from helping Piet out of this mire, another reason I wanted you and Malo here so soon is that Flo's grandniece, the town's venerable dame Maude, is celebrating her ninetieth birthday this weekend. It's going to be a grand party at the family home, Eagles Crest, overlooking the Sound. Many of the 'vipers' as well as some of the most interesting and curious people in town are invited. And to make the occasion more special," she tempted, "Maude's being honored by the nephew of her old artist friend, the bird painter and naturalist Roger Tory Peterson."

She paused for effect. "Townspeople say the rambling old place deserves its haunted reputation. Wait until you see it. The huge shingled barn of a house is a warren of rooms full of Dickensian atmosphere, and home to an eclectic but casual jumble of valuable antiques. It's rumored that some of Maude's treasures, many stowed away for years in empty rooms, are priceless."

"Even the Crest's workings are unique," added Piet. "A circular dumbwaiter rises from the old basement kitchen to the second level pantry off the dining room. Apparently it's her great grandchildren's favorite form of travel. Maude insists her Mum, when she lived with them, considered any hint of cooking odors rising above stairs offensive." Piet, amused, shook his head. "What a shame the days of all those servants are gone. It's marvelous how the formidable old gal manages to run the house with an iron hand and does most of the cooking for the family from scratch. Maude turns out several loaves of bread or muffins every day, but she's best loved for her Christmas tradition, treasured by special friends, of delivering dozens of baskets full of frosted and exquisitely hand painted cookies. They're delicious but almost too beautiful to eat. Those blessed receivers are expected to return the empty baskets—which they do—hopeful she'll live to fill them another year. A truly fascinating woman."

"An amazing family," said Fiona. "The house is structurally bizarre but solid. It survived the hurricane of thirty-eight, and despite heavy damage from other storms along the northeastern coast, still reigns intact on the hill above the shore. One's first sight on arriving, after winding up the long drive, is eerie enough. The shingles have darkened with age and there's a conical eighteen thousand gallon water tank rising over one corner of the roof like a giant witch's hat."

Her guests exchanged smiles.

"Fiona, if you can get us invited," said Isobel, "you bet we'll be there."

SIXTEEN

The evening of Maude's birthday gala stayed mild enough for Fiona, Isobel and Jo to leave behind the scarves and coats often needed in New England to cover spring dresses. When the six of them drove up under the *porte cochere* in Piet's old station wagon, the young parking hire gave the wood-paneled vintage an appraising eye and, after briefly puzzling over its central stick shift, whisked the antique motor back down the shrub-shrouded drive.

They stood on the drive for a minute to stare up at the foreboding tower looming darkly gothic against the evening dusk.

"Definitely an awesome feature," said Pen. They had arrived at the gala neither early or late, and a cheery, rather lubricated young relation greeted them at the open door with champagne bottle waving in his hand. "Welcome, welcome, whoever you are."

Behind him, the hum of voices and flickering lights from dozens of candelabra, greeted them. Isobel felt relieved to find no table stacked with birthday gifts in the foyer, as they had arrived empty handed. Earlier, they had questioned what might be an appropriate present for a ninety-year-old woman and agreed that Maude needed one less item for the family to discard when her sell-by date came due. Their discussion reminded Isobel to recycle her own valuables while still alive.

"This place recalls," said Malo, helping himself from the bar to a generous inch of their host's good whisky, "a fateful weekend I endured at the late Count Von Drago's Transylvanian castle."

Beside him, pouring himself an iced Stoli, Pen returned Malo's somber gaze. They bowed heads and touched glasses.

Jo and Isobel observed this wry exchange, accepted flutes of Moët from the barman, and ignored their silly ritual. Privately, both women believed that, knowing his history, Malo's recall was probably true.

They moved through the house with their drinks, impressed as most first-time guests. Eagles Crest's downstairs rooms more than verified Fiona's description as a museum. Glass-fronted cabinets held eclectic collections of curios—intricately carved Asian ivories and shelves of delicate Japanese Netsuke. Period sideboards, that Amber and Latham would have coveted, stood laden with brown-edged Georgian silver services whose gracefully fluted pieces desperately needed polishing by some phantom butler. Confronted by so grand an array of *objects d'art* made Isobel's head swim.

The walls of every room were covered by paintings of all sizes and genres. It would take an expert hand to access their value, as many were obscure with the film of age and in dire need of a conservator's attention.

Isobel sipped her excellent champagne and dabbed a smile from her lips, awed by this hodgepodge collection. She wondered how many guests noticed the economy of an occasional thumbtack holding up strips of loosened wallpaper? This simple solution to the ravages of time recalled the frantic mornings when she had repaired her school uniform's loosened hem with lengths of sticky tape.

Isobel maneuvered through the party, exchanging appropriate social noises with unfamiliar faces. Eagles Crest indeed housed a surfeit of valuables and—evil thought—a light-fingered guest's delight. She wondered about security for the evening. Were hidden cameras surveying them from dim ceiling corners?

Isobel's wanderings led her away from the main rooms full of guests and she found herself in a long empty hallway. She hesitated, then making sure she was alone, slipped through a half-open door into a dim, high-ceilinged room she guessed was one of many in this wing used to store unneeded furniture and paintings. Like an uneasy ghost, she wandered among the sheet-draped forms. Lighter squares on yellowed walls suggested spaces where frames had once hung. Where were they now? Perhaps the more valuable pieces had been shifted into the limelight for tonight's gala.

Isobel lifted the corner of a sheet and gasped with delight. Underneath the drapery stood an exquisite parquetry harpsichord. She ran her hand over the keyboard's stained ivory surface. Fingering a chord, she shuddered at the discordant plunk of unturned, dead strings. Again, nostalgia for imagined past phantoms of drawing room musicals evoked a sadness that made her shiver. No doubt her penalty for prying into the closets of other people's lives. The moment's melancholy brought to mind by these echoes of the past, hastened her need to escape and return to the gaiety of the party.

She left the storeroom door ajar, as she'd found it, and found herself facing a steep flight of stairs leading up into darkness. Above her, the reputed maze of dark paneled hallways Fiona said separated seventeen bedrooms. The spooky old place must have been the delight of children's hide-and-seek games. The chill in this unheated part of the house made her realize she'd wandered too far.

Out of sight, a burst of laughter from one of the guests aroused more guilt at having crossed even her limits of snooping. The cold curbed her of any temptation to explore further and, led by the noise of conversation, she found her way back to the party.

"Ah, you must be Mrs. Van Dursan," trilled the exuberant voice of a twittery young man advancing on her with both hands outstretched.

"How wonderful of you to come. I've heard so much about you from your lovely niece Fiona. I'm Johann Peterson. Come and meet my intrepid, and aged auntie Maude, our birthday girl." Isobel could not suppress a smile. The gay young dandy almost danced across the room with pleasure.

Their host, Johann's reputed auntie Maude, reigned like a queen on her dais from a high backed chair at the end of the drawing room. Despite the warmth of a fire in the grate behind her, a cashmere shawl wrapped the ancient lady's upright body and held closed over her chest by a diamond brooch so large Isobel assumed it must be paste. However, after having viewed Maude's collection of eccentric possessions, it might be the largest genuine gem she'd ever seen except at the cleavage of Hollywood royalty.

Impressed, Isobel drained her champagne and deposited the empty glass on a passing tray. The sight of that diamond reminded her of the unpleasant Newport find resting in the desk drawer of her Maine cottage.

In Maude's lap, her gnarly fingers rested on an illustrated quarto volume of Audubon prints and, convenient on either side of her cushioned wingchair, stood small tables covered with a clutter of writing tablets, pots of pens and pencils, half-worked pages of a book of logic problems and last Sunday's *Times* crossword done messily in ink. Party or not, like her dozen bright colored finches twitting in their wicker cage, across the room, it seems Maude would not budge from her comfortable nest.

"Aunt Maude," gushed Johann, "this is Isobel Van Dursan, our young friend Fiona's Aunt. She and her family are visiting from Maine." He noticed the book in her lap. "I see you've opened my present. Lovely, lovely pictures, don't you think? As fine as any painted by you."

Maude lowered her chin into her lace collar and scowled. "Such nonsense, Johann. Your uncle and I spent endless hours painting together *en plein air,* but we all know Tory's precise and authoritative work remains a class far above my daubs."

If the vibrant, watercolor paintings signed with her initials that Isobel had admired were daubs, Maude underrated her talent.

"Maybe you're not as famous as my uncle," Johann conceded, turning to Isobel, "but Maude is too modest and at ninety no less, remains a fine artist and still an accredited member of the Art Association. In fact, for years she was one of our most respected judges."

Another admirer arrived to offer birthday wishes and Malo rescued Isobel by the elbow and steered her away to a quieter corner.

"Where have you been? This place is a bloody warehouse of treasures," he swore. "And I bet," he said under his breath, "nothing's been moved for a century."

"Or dusted," said a waif of a girl who appeared at their side, offering a tray of crab stuffed mushrooms.

"Gran and I made them. Try one, they're tasty. I'm Phoebe." They were indeed delicious and Malo reached for another before the barefoot Phoebe wafted away. They watched Pen weave among the guests to chase her down and return with his mouth full. He swallowed.

"She looks like a Phoebe," he said, licking his fingers. Jo joined them carrying a plate of cheese puffs and meaty bits on toothpicks.

"I wonder, if in honor of her friend Peterson, Maude named all the girls in this family after birds?" she said. "I snatched these goodies from a child called Wren."

Jo popped the puff in her mouth and nodded over her shoulder at a tall, thin woman dressed in black.

"Now check her out. I'm told she's Jason's newly widowed Frances Faraday. Do you suppose she's one of the vipers?"

Isobel's instant impression of the woman suggested more middle-aged Goth. Dark smudged eyes, straight black hair that brushed her shoulders, and a calf-length black dress that skimmed slim ankles wrapped with strappy pumps. Pen, with a lecherous smile, tipped his glass in the lady's direction.

"Despite the mournful duds, I'd say the wife of the late Jason Faraday is a looker."

"Definitely," agreed Jo, but a little scary. If we stick with bird analogy, something predatory."

"So was Jason," said Fiona. "A little scary, I mean. He kept mostly to his basement studio at the Art

Association, a definite recluse. When his wife forced him to venture out, he affected strange outfits—capes and wide brimmed hats that hid his face. But aside from the clothing dramatics, he never flaunted himself as an artist. Regardless of Frances's attempts to prod him, he kept shy of society and remained a reluctant loner.

You can imagine, in a small town like this, how people speculated on what glue held their odd marriage together. Frances acted as his agent but lately with small success. We members were aware that he refused to cooperate. Some of us were embarrassed at her enthusiasm promoting him as a sudden new mover and shaker."

Fiona shrugged. "Somehow their relationship worked and, from outward appearances—at least in public, Jason doted on her."

"Gossip flourished among Association members that his recent work had lost its edge," said Piet. "Personally I agreed. His newest paintings, at least those he showed me, weren't selling. Then, to everyone's surprise, he roused from his slump and entered this brilliant piece in the show."

"No dispute, it was a fine work," said Fiona. "He had painted this small landscape with amazing skill. It showed a brightness that, in art talk, truly captured the luminous, romantic aura reminiscent of his great grandfather Frederic Church. When the judges awarded Jason the coveted first prize, there were congratulations from most members of the Art Association. Huge hoopla over his revitalized talent."

"Before the investigation began, almost everyone agreed he deserved the award," said Piet. "And, much as I hate to admit, I did too. He'd shown an amazing reversal of talent with this new piece."

Fiona scowled. "Too amazing. In fact, and one of the judge's suspicions began the inquiries into fraud."

Fiona snagged another glass of wine from a passing tray and raised it as if in a toast. "Of course when the judges announced him as the winner, Frances acted ecstatic. Jason seemed stunned, and I was—honestly—doubtful. Piet's work is consistently good and I'd expected him to win. So sure, in fact, that we'd bought airline tickets to celebrate. A two-week jaunt to Florence."

SEVENTEEN

The birthday party wound down and they thanked their hosts, said their goodbyes and left, full of canapés, but not quite ready to end the evening. While they waited outside in the chill for Piet's car, Malo decided he needed a large Jameson and something sweet. Isobel checked her watch.

"Piet and Fiona, come back to the inn with us," she suggested. "We can sit in front of the fire, have a cup of hot soup and a slice of the innkeeper Marta's amazing key lime pie. Malo can finish off with an Irish nightcap.

"Sounds good," said Piet. "The landlady there has quite the reputation as a baker." He winked at Fiona. "She promised me a piece of her apple crumb cake if I came by some morning for breakfast." Fiona knuckled his ribs as he slid into the seat beside her.

"Honey," she said, "from what I've heard of her reputation, she'll offer you more than a piece of her crumby cake." Fiona lay back against the cold leather seat, shivered, and hugged her arms across her chest. "I can't believe Marta signed up for your chiaroscuro workshop. Have you noticed how often she just happens to drop by the Association when you're downstairs in your studio? Can she even draw?"

"Egad, do I know this jealous woman?" Piet squeezed Fiona's knee. "Don't worry Fi. You are sweeter to me than any of her pies. Our landlady is an excellent baker and attractive, but a little too eager. Not my type."

"Attractive! Her face has been tweaked so much that those beady eyes are mere slits. And that platinum hair—well, I doubt if the curtain matches the rug."

"Fiona!"

"Sorry, Aunt Isobel.

Jo giggled. "Let's go. I've yet to meet our *femme fatale* landlady."

Back at the Bell and Whistle, Malo carried his whisky from the bar and joined them in front of the lounge's stone fireplace. They were the only guests on this off-season evening, and Pen had knelt to revive the fire's dying embers. Shoes off, Isobel curled her legs to make room for Malo on the sofa beside her. She sighed with pleasure as he kneaded her toes.

"Speaking of workshops, Piet," said Fiona, your studio downstairs is next to Jason's and I hear the police have taped off the entire Art Association as a crime scene. How long before things return to normal? The director says the guest artists scheduled to teach this month are as impatient to get on with classes as their students. Everyone is losing time and money."

Piet shrugged. "Who knows?" he said. "It's been almost a week since, Mrs. Ely, the docent on duty that morning opened the building and sensed something wrong. The poor woman saw lights on in studios downstairs that should have been empty that early. Those of us who rent space there have our own keys and, if we come in early to work or prepare for a class, use the upper front doors and leave them unlocked so the docent knows someone's in the building. Both Jason and I had heavy materials to carry that morning and entered through the lower entrance. Mrs. Ely is an elderly volunteer—our docents are all volunteers—and she came downstairs to investigate. She screamed when she saw me standing over Jason's body with that paintbrush in my fist. Of course, now I realize I should not have pulled it out of his eye, but to leave it— my, god, way too awful. I acted on impulse."

"We can imagine," said Isobel wryly.

"Poor Jason was murdered and, however unfeeling to complain," said Fiona. "I agree with the Association that closing off the entire building, including profits from visitors to the gallery, is costing them much needed income."

"I sympathize, Fiona," said Isobel. "But I've found the police have their routines and there's nothing you can do about it. I can understand the Association's financial concerns, but we're not going to bed until you explain how Piet got his bail money after the judges awarded Jason first prize? What happened? Fiona looked at her watch. "It's a long story," she said, "so make yourselves comfortable."

"The judge's suspicions proved right. Jason did not paint the winning piece," Fiona began. "His great grandfather Frederic Church painted it—probably around 1840. Jason was prompted to remove F.E. Church's initials and paint over them with his own."

"Prompted?" Jo gave her a quizzical look. "Explain prompted."

"Like that judge, Piet and I had our own doubts and neither of us believe Jason chose to risk such blatant fraud on his own volition. He was not that unethical or gutsy enough, and I can't believe his conscience would allow him to devalue his uncle's original work."

"One of old Church's large River School landscapes was catalogued recently at Christie's for more than eight million," said Piet. "Not a shabby price, even for one of today's less than scrupulous collectors. What is most appalling is that the forged painting Jason presented as his own has proved to be a genuine 'lost' work and too valuable to consider defacing. I thought I knew the man, and can't imagine that kind of blatant act resting lightly on Jason's conscience."

"Investigation began," said Fiona, "after the award ceremony—about a week before his murder. One of the sharper-eyed judges had doubts about the authenticity of the piece and discreetly brought the painting down to our local dealer. It's a small gallery housed in an old colonial on Main Street, but, despite its modest site, this is a sophisticated town and its owner, Talmadge Cook, has wide connections in the art world and a respected reputation."

"Granted, his works can run a bit pricey," added in Piet, "but Tal evidently has enough well-heeled patrons to afford him that hot red Ferrari he drives around town."

"Hey," said Fiona. "Tal's an attractive bachelor with expensive lady friends and he happens to enjoy his toys." She sighed. "I would die to own some of his stuff."

"Don't call it stuff, love," said Piet. "He would suck in his cheeks."

"Sorry," said Fiona. "But I saw Tal's face when he unwrapped that painting, and he did more than suck in his cheeks. He practically fainted. From the minute he held the canvas, Tal knew he was viewing a masterpiece. So much for Jason's sudden spurt of brilliance."

"Tal hustled the work—a small canvas, about ten by twelve—upstairs and, under his black light, saw the piece revealed clear evidence of new paint applied over the original signer's initials," explained Piet. "Evidently the paint Jason used to forge his own signature contained none of the chemical elements consistent with nineteenth-century pigments."

"That's the first thing they'd look for. Why would Jason chance such an easily discoverable risk?" said Fiona.

Malo shrugged. "As Piet said, perhaps it was subconscious guilt over defacing a valuable work. Maybe he wanted to be caught."

"Now for the good news," said Piet. "Tal said repairing the forged initials was a minor problem. F.E. Church often signed his landscapes within the texture of foliage or trees. The real crime lay in identity theft. The gallery called in an expert who took the work apart. They removed the frame and backing and examined the canvas—all those processes undertaken by any good conservator. The piece is now authenticated as a previously unknown, original work and doubtless of huge value."

Fiona grimaced. "Believe me, when word of finding an original F.E. Church gets around, deals will be made. This canvas will be snapped up at once by an eager private collector."

"But only if it is available for sale," cautioned Piet. "Talmadge will insist on impeccable provenance. Fortunately, most dealers are as honest. Their reputations rely on being trusted purveyors of their artist's work. Tal represents mine and I value his opinion. He's one that appreciates a fine piece for more than its monetary worth. When he learned of its questionable ownership, he immediately realized the work was not his to sell."

"Jason's fraud unraveled further when Maude heard of the commotion over the award and subsequent investigation into its origins. Her identification of the work is a romantic tale. Though stashed away in one of the storerooms and long forgotten, she recognized the little painting as a gift—a love token given to her mother over a century ago. Maude's mother was a much sought after beauty in her day, and F.E. Church, while painting at the Griswold salon that summer, became smitten and, being rather a ladies man, doted on her."

"Quite a valuable love token," said Jo.

"Understandably, the discovery that the painting was a sentimental treasure and belonged to Maude deflated Tal like a jostled soufflé," said Fiona. "He realized Jason Faraday was not only a forger, but a thief."

EIGHTEEN

Alice glanced in the diner's washroom mirror and was startled by the stranger looking back at her. Her tangle of blond curls were now dyed a mousey brown and the familiar old Alice was gone. She'd get used to her new reflection. Escaping from the Foleys—and now hiding out in this small Connecticut town—the more she changed, the better. Though at fifteen, Alice couldn't hide her youthful prettiness, the less notice she attracted, the safer she felt.

During these past weeks she had curbed the urge to run from any stranger's approach. The fake ID and social security card, surprisingly easy to obtain, lay heavier on her conscience than in her wallet, but she avoided testing her new identity by inviting curious questions. She was Alice Perkins, but not the original Alice Perkins. May that dead girl rest in peace.

It hadn't been hard to look older than her age. The strain and fatigue of being sought as a runaway made smudged hollows beneath her eyes and the slump of her shoulders added years. Sometimes she'd wake up in the night and forget who she really was.

After their trip together from California to Newport, the escape from her guardians had begun easy enough. The Foleys had treated her okay and their promises of a new life sounded totally reasonable. Anything sounded better than the strict confines of her foster home and, at first, the adventure offered no threat. Mr. Foley came on as a hale and hearty type with a huge laugh that rocked the room. His wife, in odd contrast, followed his bidding like a harmless old grannie. The woman cowed under his thumb and called him hubbie—a tag Alice found totally disgusting. At his suggestion that she travel as their daughter, the three crossed the country without a hitch.

Curiosity made her ask questions, but whenever she pried into their past, Mrs. Foley would fold into herself and dab her eyes with a wadded tissue. She wondered why Mr. Foley made no effort to comfort his wife.

"I'm sorry, Alice," was his explanation, "but this past year has been a difficult time we are trying hard to forget." Alice decided it best not to ask what kind of sorrow had caused them such pain.

Their trip east passed far too quickly. No cheap motels or fast food joints; they always stopped for the night at fancy digs, like that cool castle place in Newport. She had never eaten in such great restaurants. The Foley's insisted Alice possessed a natural beauty and, with their connections, they would easily find her film work. Studying her image in the mirror, innate vanity told her this was true. She knew she had the looks and talent for acting. Her whole life had been pretend. Why not get paid for it?

These thoughts circled her mind like the damp cloth in her hand, dreamily wiping and rewiping the countertop of the Village Pizza Boutique. She stacked the menus by the side of the register and smiled at the name on their plastic covers. A born California girl, Alice had never believed a quaint New England town like this existed except on post cards. She was surprised the place wasn't named Ye Olde Village Pizza. Achilles, the pot-bellied owner, who obviously sampled too much of his own cooking, was a good cook but no Italian.

The string of bells that jangled whenever the door opened jarred her. Their noise got on her nerves, but business was slow today and when the customer entered, she gave him her best fake smile. Then the smile changed to real. The guy was good looking and young—rare in this town full of wrinklies. Maybe a little old for her, but since she'd arrived, she'd felt fifteen going on thirty.

"Take out?" she asked.

He looked around the empty diner and shook his head. Alice started to lead him a booth by the window, but he put up his hand and slung one leg over a counter stool. She shrugged, smiled, and handed him a menu. On purpose, she'd been careful to make no friends here but she liked contact with people and the loneliness was getting to her. What she missed most was not any romance thing, but time spent just talking to guys, and this cutie looked safe.

"The cook here is Greek," she said, "and his gyros are better than the pizza." He liked that she correctly pronounced it "yeeros."

"Sounds good," he said. "Heavy on the tzatziki sauce."

Alice gave the order to the cook and because her only customer seemed cool and she needed company, she began with harmless stranger's small talk.

"You an artist?"

"No. Just visiting my family," he said. "Staying at the local inn and tired of too much good food."

"Hey, the food's good here. Really."

Pen blushed. "I'm sorry," he checked her name tag, "Alice. That came out wrong. I mean the food at the inn is sometimes too fancy for me. All those napkin covered wire cones filled with artisanal breads and dishes of reduced balsamic with extra virgin olive oil when all you crave is a soft roll and slab of butter."

Alice laughed. "No linens here. Gyros are a mess to eat and need a handful of paper napkins." She poured him a cup of the local farm roast coffee. He took a swallow and gave her a thumbs up. When she turned to the pass-through to collect his plate, she glanced in the small wall mirror placed for the servers to check their appearance. Achilles insisted his girls look sharp. Behind her reflection, she saw the guy staring at her back, a puzzled frown on his face. When he'd first come in, Alice had watched him checking out her chest, and not just her nametag. But she was used to that. She had great breasts. Two of the perkiest.

She wanted to ask him more questions but saw him struggling with shreds of lettuce, onions, and drippy sauce spilling from the soft wrap of pita, and knew he wouldn't appreciate conversation. He did not accept a coffee refill, nor could she tempt him with dessert. Worse, after she tallied his bill, he paid in cash. As he left, the echo of the doorbells jangled in the empty room and she shrugged off disappointment. But maybe just as well. She had hoped to get his name from his credit card. Find some excuse to drop by the inn where he said he was staying and check him out. She thought again. Not a good idea.

————————

Back at the Bell and Whistle and breathing garlicky lunch, Pen booted up his computer and entered the elaborate identification safeguards required by the Agency to access coded information. In this case, file data from the National Center for Missing and Exploited Children. It didn't take long to confirm what he suspected.

He took the stairs two at a time and knocked on Isobel's door. It opened a crack and Malo stood running his hand over his face.

"Pen," he muttered, groggy with sleep. "Come in, we've been having a little snooze. Too much rich food. Lost our discipline. Need some exercise." Isobel came from the bathroom, combed and tidy.

"Pen, what's up? Come in and sit." He did. "How about some tea?"

"Thanks, but there's no time for tea. Remember that girl you told me about in Newport—Alice? I've just come from lunch where I think I saw her. Look at this." He handed Isobel the single sheet he'd pulled from the printer. "Like Malo said, I needed a break from all our haute cuisine, so I took a walk through town and came upon the village pizzeria. Only it's better than your usual pie shop. The cook's a Greek named Achilles, and I've just eaten one of the best gyros outside of Athens. Anyway, the place was empty and the only server was a young girl with Alice printed on her nametag. It rested above the swell of her lovely chest."

"Really Pen," said Isobel, frowning. "You sound like Tom." Malo looked amused.

"How young?" he asked. "Are you suggesting your waitress was the same Alice accompanying the Foley's?

The girl Isobel met in the room above hers at the Castle Inn?"

"I'm not just suggesting. I remember Isobel said that the Foleys had registered with Connecticut plates. I've checked the missing children data and Alice's latest foster parents in California were concerned enough to call the state police there and report her a missing minor. She still calls herself Alice. She was born to John and Doris Gowan, druggies who overdosed on meth and left the girl orphaned at twelve. The real Alice Perkins, whose identification she stole, also age fifteen, died with her entire family in a house fire two year's ago."

Isobel read the printout and handed it to Malo. "Read this. It sounds like Pen's found her."

"We don't want to scare the girl off," said Isobel. "I pose no threat to her, and she probably won't remember our brief conversation outside her door that night in the tower. I 'll find some way to identify her without her recognizing me." Isobel gnawed her lip. "Poor Alice. She seemed such a naive, young person. I'd guess the Foley's plans for her life in films must have gone awry and she's been clever enough to escape them."

"I'll notify the Connecticut police," said Pen. "This is a small town and, unless she can afford a car, she won't get far. We'll find her."

Isobel shrugged into a loose suede jacket and tucked her hair under a knitted cap. The weather had teased them with a week of mild, sunny days but, this morning, they awoke to a bitter wind and leaden sky that threatened an ominous return of winter. Typical New England spring, she reasoned, remembering the years her early tulips, and sometimes Easter eggs, lay buried under drifts of snow. She turned to Malo.

"Funny," she said. "I feel in the mood for a slice of pizza. Let's take a walk into town."

Isobel and Malo found the Village Pizza Boutique across Main Street from an old brick estate housing the public library. Despite her craving for a sweet, at this time of year, the wrought iron tables outside the ice cream shop across the street looked uninviting. Hearing the rattle of bells, when they entered, a swarthy, angry looking man emerged from the kitchen.

'Yes," he growled, wiping his hands on a sauce stained apron. Then, less rudely, "Sorry, I'm alone. My new girl suddenly collected her money and walked out on me. I pay good and I thought this one really needed the job and would stay." He shrugged. "Should have known. Just another irresponsible kid."

"Could you describe her?"

"Sure." He cocked his head to the side and frowned. "She was pretty, not too tall, light eyes, brownish hair. The hair had that dusty look—like dyed maybe? Nice shape, but that's not why I hired her. I needed the help and she seemed smart."

Isobel guessed his next answer before she asked the question. "Did she say where she was going? Leave an address or phone?"

He seemed too miffed by the girl's desertion to care why they wanted to know and, instead of the 'no' she had expected, he riffled through a jumbled mess of file cards pulled from a drawer under the counter. Instead of Italian, this cook looked so ethnic Greek that Isobel almost expected him to announce Eureka! when he pulled out a card, scribbled the address and phone number on the back of an order slip, and handed it to Isobel.

"That's what she wrote," he said. "Said her name was Alice. Alice Perkins. I didn't check on her. She looked clean and intelligent and I needed a waitress."

The good smells from the kitchen tempted them order a small pie to go and outside, the cold made them hurry the few blocks back to the inn. Because spring had turned fickle, some thoughtful serf had lit the logs in the downstairs common room. They shed their coats and ate their late lunch alone before the fire.

Back upstairs in their room, Malo read out the address and phone number Achilles had written down. Isobel guessed it would be a waste of time, but dialed the number. It rang only twice before a robotic voice informed her that there was no such number, and to please check the listing.

"Just what I expected. No luck." She handed the slip of paper back to Malo who called reception and questioned the address.

"No such street," he said and replaced the receiver. "At least not in this town. I'm afraid our determined young chick has flown the coop."

"And I bet that little hen was our Alice," said Isobel.

NINETEEN

The pizza lay heavy in their stomachs and, despite the dreary day, Malo and Isobel decided that a walk to Fiona's cottage would help. When they arrived, they saw an old-fashioned balloon tire bicycle propped against her porch railing. Two wire panniers on either side of the rear wheel held a least a dozen Easter baskets.

Through the ribbon-wrapped film protecting the treats, they saw the baskets were filled with beautifully painted shapes.

"It looks like Maude got busy again with her cookie baking," said Isobel. "And all personally delivered."

Malo knocked at the door, and without waiting, they let themselves in.

"Fiona," called Isobel. "We've come for tea." In the hall they saw the young waif, Wren, whom they'd met the night of Maude's birthday party, wrap a long scarlet scarf several times around her neck.

"I'm just leaving. Gran had the flu over Christmas, and then shared it. By the time everyone rallied, it was too late to do our annual Christmas cookies so we decided to switch to Easter baskets. Luckily Gran has tons of friends who pitched in to help. Even the widow Frances came over to fill the baskets this week." Wren wrinkled her nose. "I don't like that woman, but she bought dozens for the Women's Exchange to sell for the Art Association scholarship Fund. Have to admit it was a generous donation." She saluted Malo and Isobel, and called over their shoulder as she bicycled off. "Sorry, got to run. Lots more stops. Take care. Nice to see you again."

They found Fiona in the dining room emptying her sweets basket. Instead of Maude's usual Christmas stars, trees and bells, she arranged exquisitely painted bunnies, chicks, and Easter eggs, along with shortbreads and a variety of ethnic cookies, onto a large glass plate.

After their brisk walk from town, they warmed their hands before the living room fire. Fiona said to make themselves at home and Malo offered to brew them a pot of tea. He stopped at the sideboard and added a large dose of whisky to his mug before carrying in the tray.

"You're getting very domestic," said Isobel. "It becomes you. You'll be doing the washing up soon."

"Don't count on it," he said, and took his book, a powdery Pfeffernusse, and his drink to an armchair by the fire.

———

That night, after finishing dinner at the Bell and Whistle with Fiona and Piet as their guests, Malo and Isobel asked Piet to relate exactly what happened that lead to his arrest.

"Unfortunately, because I was found in Jason's studio after he was killed," said Piet, forking up his last bite of Marta's infamous Key lime pie, "I became the first one under suspicion of murder. Those of us renting studio space at the Association have our own keys, and I came in early because Jason called me the night before and insisted we meet there next morning in person. He said he had something he'd rather not discuss over the phone." Piet paused to gather his thoughts.

"He sounded so urgent I made a point to get to the studio early and because I had an awkward load of canvas to carry, let myself in through the basement entrance. The outside door had been locked and I was puzzled to notice Jason's lights shining through his transom, as he would have left the door open if he'd arrived first. When I tapped on his studio door, I got no answer and when I turned the knob, found it unlocked. Nothing unusual. He likes his privacy when working and, as Fiona said, he's known as a loner. I didn't want to barge in on him so waited for him to answer my knock. Upstairs I heard Mrs. Ely, that day's docent, opening the building and switch on the main gallery lights. Jason still didn't answer when I repeated his name, so I let myself in. When I saw his body, I must have yelled loud enough for Mrs. Ely to hear. As you can imagine, it was a terrible sight. Hardly any blood, but that brush sticking out of his eyeball completely unnerved me. I did the natural but most stupid, unthinking thing. I reached down and pulled the brush from his eye."

Jo shuddered. "Piet, how awful."

"The docent," said Piet, "dear Mrs. Ely, is eighty if she's a day, and a stoic old dame. She shut the door on Jason's bloodless but gruesome body and calmly led me upstairs to call 911. Trooper Larry English and his fellow officers arrived within minutes and took charge. In a state of shock, we watched the police go into action with their usual, efficient routine."

"Actually, not so usual," said Fiona. "You said the trooper told you there has not been a homicide in this town for twenty years." Piet gave a rueful shrug. "My lucky day."

"Anyway," he continued, "with bar lights flashing, more squad cars arrived with detectives from the barracks in Eastbrook and the pros contained the crime scene. The techs swarmed over the place, took photos, collected DNA and prints, and began all the scene-of-crime procedures. Our small town has no police department with room for containment of suspects so they drove me down to the barracks in Eastbrook for questioning. Later that morning and, well-known and not being a flight risk, they released me pending further investigation." Piet folded his napkin and leaned back in his chair.

"Back at the Association, yellow tape enclosed the entire building, including the parking lot, to contain all possible evidence. Tire marks, footprints, etc. The ambulance carted off Jason's body to Farmington for an autopsy and the next day the medical examiner's report came back concise and obvious. A sharpened sable #12 had penetrated Faraday's brain through the eye. Having pulled out the brush, my smudged fingerprints were the only ones on the 'weapon'. No other evidence. Penetration through the eyeball is almost bloodless, but causes instant death when it pierces the brain." Piet pressed his eyes and lips together, as if in pain himself. Fiona placed a firm hand on his sleeve and turned to Isobel.

"Naturally," she said, "despite the gruesome circumstances, the police routine and subsequent barriers to normal function, caused an undercurrent of grumbling among Association members. Artistic temperaments tend to flare around here without much provocation. Visiting and staff artist's workshops were cancelled and teaching schedules ignored. Association funding is sparse enough as it is and when all those requests for refunds began and no money coming in from gallery visitor's donations or sales, we fended off dozens of angry phone calls."

Isobel feigned sympathy. Artists, she thought, sometimes possessed too much egotistical *sturm und drang*.

"I understand the board's financial concerns," she said, "but I don't hear much compassion for Jason."

Piet released a long breath.

"He wasn't the most popular fellow," apologized Fiona. "I head that when Trooper English informed the widow Frances of his death, she reacted with genuine horror and insisted she knew of no one who hated her husband that much or capable of such a violent attack. She admitted Jason had spent almost compulsive hours alone in his studio during the past weeks. When the police questioned his fellow artist friends, they agreed that he'd acted moody and depressed over the decline of his talent. Frances, however, said that lately she had noticed a rise in Jason's spirits over a painting he was working on. He refused to let anyone see it, even her, but had promised them something special."

Fiona shrugged. "Like most of us, I think the police believe Frances is guilty. Piet and I suspect she pushed the limits of Jason's conscience and, worried that if he broke down and threatened to confess, she would risk being exposed as his instigator. Unfortunately, there is no conclusive evidence to charge her with murder. Everything about this case is circumstantial, despite the talk of Jason's compulsions and recent solitary melancholy. Frances' plea is for the police to accept the fact that, despite his brief rally, severe depression forced him over the edge." Piet gave her an incredulous look.

"Enough to arrange such a horrific suicide?"

At this, Isobel rolled her eyes—a terrible habit for which she continually scolded her grandchildren. "Well it was certainly dramatic."

"But highly unlikely," insisted Piet. "Stabbing oneself through the eyeball? "Please, we agree that Jason was a strange and reclusive fellow, but not that eccentric."

"I don't know," mused Pen. "It's quick, bloodless, and not as messy as a gun in the mouth. Artists are a weird ilk. Remember, Van Gogh cut off his ear."

"Questionably apocryphal and more bizarre than fatal," commented Isobel.

TWENTY

At breakfast the next morning, after devouring blueberry pancakes and thick slices of maple cured bacon, Isobel decided she needed much less food and more exercise. She ran her finger inside the waistband of her linen slacks. They felt uncomfortably snug. She frowned at Malo across the table.

"I know I promised Fiona we'd help absolve Piet's good name, but it seems the police are stuck with no motive or real evidence to either clear him or charge him with murder. This investigation could go on for weeks."

She stood up. "I think we should spend the day briskly walking about town, then marching through Flo's museum and the local galleries. And, since it's the next best thing to a bookstore, we must browse that wonderful toy store in the shopping area. Absolutely no lunch."

Malo gave her a skeptical glance. "An excellent plan for both of us. However, may I make a small bet that your lunch resolution won't last past noon?"

"Bet taken." They shook hands. "If you recall, I'm a strong woman and possess great willpower." Privately, she had found promises to skip meals easier to make when stuffed.

"Let's start at Cook's gallery. As to our bet—if I win and see something lovely and it's not too expensive, you can pay."

Malo agreed, resigned to lose. "Isobel, most of his artwork is lovely, but seldom inexpensive."

In reply, she patted his arm.

"I know. But think of fine paintings as valued investments. Besides, I've a nagging idea where Jason's Church canvas came from. Fiona knows Talmadge Cook, the owner, and said he might photograph it for me. He has the painting in safekeeping during the investigation and might be more inclined to humor my request if we bought something."

While Malo deciphered this costly logic, Isobel searched the desk drawers for the Shoreline phone book. Unlike Maine's long empty coastal stretches, close built towns lined this state's length of Sound. She thumbed the pages, found Frances Faraday's number, and dialed for an outside line. As she waited, she put her palm over the receiver.

"After our walk, if she is at home, I think I'll press a tea time condolence call on the widow. Express my sympathy and discuss our recent widowhoods, etc. Fiona says local rumor reports Frances is miserable and consumed by both grief and alas," she touched her brow with the back of her hand, "humiliation over Jason's desperate attempt to bolster his reputation by forgery."

"Isobel, you are a bad person," said Malo, smiling.

As they entered the gallery, Talmadge stood in good-bye conversation with an exotic looking couple. The bearded foreign gentleman wore a fur-collared greatcoat reminiscent of a Russian tsar and his buxom companion posed, hand on hip, beside him swathed in an aubergine cape secured at the neck with a carved ruby brooch. The huge stone glittered in the overhead lights and Isobel's thoughts flew again to that wretched diamond cached in the drawer of her Maine desk.

While they waited for Tal to finish his conversation, Isobel collected a brochure from those fanned across the red-lacquered chinoiserie table at the gallery entrance listing titles and prices of the current exhibit. She watched Tal and the couple shake hands and hoped their mutual bonhomie resulted from some lucrative agreement. The bear of a man and his lady bore the assurance of people who, with mere pocket change, could purchase the entire gallery. Probably regulars at posh Newport Inns.

On their way out, the gentleman swept his flat brimmed beret from his head and bowed to Isobel in the Continental manner that reminded her of her first meeting with Malo. She recalled again how his gracious aplomb masked his surprise on finding that the I. Van Dursan he expected to employ as his mercenary was a woman.

When the gallery doors closed behind the couple, Isobel explained their reason for needing a good photograph of Church's work. Talmadge leaned back against his desk and crossed his arms over his chest. "I don't see why not," he agreed. "The Association has entrusted the canvas to me for safekeeping during the investigation and I'm as curious as they about its provenance. If the suspicions circulating among the Association judges prove true, we've got serious concerns over the canvas's rights of sale. I have an excellent camera we use for our cataloging and, if you can wait, I'd be glad to black light it for you. Until the conservators finish their examinations, the painting remains in our safe upstairs. Look around," he gestured. "I think we've put together an especially fine exhibit."

While Tal was upstairs, they made their way around the room, studying the paintings on the gallery walls. Lagging behind her, Malo heard Isobel gasp. She grabbed his arm and pulled him toward a small, gold framed oil of two ripe peaches. Their skins shone reflected in a silver bowl and were so finely painted she could almost feel the fuzz on the fruit. "Could we just ask the price?"

Tal came down from his workroom holding an eight by ten manila envelope that he handed to Isobel.

She thanked him, and Malo pointed to the small canvas on the wall behind her. "I'm afraid to ask, but how much?"

"Ah," Tal smiled. "The painter is a local artist. An eccentric septuagenarian who made a fortune in banking. His marvelous talent with paint is only a hobby. The man's eccentricity is that he insists on meeting a prospective buyer in person before he will sell any of his work." Tal raised his palms. "I know, it sounds crazy, but Eric has all the money he needs and, if he likes you, the painting can be yours for a song."

Malo looked at Isobel who, as promised, had denied herself lunch. "Why not," he said. "And, believe me, Isobel sings beautifully and can be very nice to people when she tries. I'll leave it to you to make the arrangements to meet with your eccentric painter. Call us. We're staying at the Bell and Whistle."

Tal followed them to the doors of the gallery but, before he ushered them out, pointed to the envelope Isobel held clasped to her chest.

"Good luck with that," he said. Then paused and, without explanation, added "and be careful."

TWENTY-ONE

Fiona protested that she needed the afternoon at home alone to work on her neglected writing so she gladly lent Isobel her car to visit Frances. Back at the inn after their walk into town, Isobel listened patiently to Malo fuss and frown over her intent to call on Frances by herself. She understood, from some troublesome past experiences, that his concern over her safety might be justified, and her plan to provoke Frances by displaying the sealed envelope made him particularly unhappy.

Though annoyed at his worry for her safety, such gallant protection touched her heart. This softer side of his personality had charmed her the first time they'd met. As to his opposite face, she must remember that Malo was the Janus man who had dispatched his enemies without regret.

Isobel made soothing noises and gathered up her handbag. She tucked an embroidered hankie suitable for eye-dabbing inside and tucked the taunting manila envelope containing the incriminating photo under her arm. Malo could not resist one final warning.

"Think carefully about what you're getting into," he cautioned. "Remember last year? Like jiggling a spider's web, you have this unfortunate temptation to attract trouble."

"Please stop worrying. I promise to take care of myself." A bit of false bravado, but the statement enforced her stubborn nature. She saw Malo frown and knew this annoying part of her personality was what he found most difficult to accept. He yawned, apologized, conceded defeat, and opted for an afternoon nap. Isobel was relieved to see he also showed signs of fatigue. She didn't feel too lively herself and had to admit that, during their travels, all the rich meals had softened her endurance as well as her waistline.

As she moved to the door, Malo followed and pulled her against him to gently brush his lips across her cheek. She returned his kiss and he took her face between his hands.

"Be careful Isobel, unsettling Frances could be dangerous. Like stabbing at a beehive with a stick. I want you around to enjoy those peaches."

Frances with the late Jason Faraday lived in a nineteenth century cottage, similar to Fiona's, on the main street of the village. She answered Isobel's knock dressed in the same widow's weeds she'd worn at Maude's party, minus the sling-back heels.

"Thank you Frances," Isobel said as her hostess took her coat and scarf. "I wanted to come by and offer my sympathy in person." In return, Frances managed a slight smile but it needed practice and her eyes stayed cold and vacant. "I certainly understand the grief you're going through. I'm a recent widow myself and found accepting my own loss," she paused, "—so devastating."

This was only half true. Isobel was recently widowed, but not at all devastated. In fact, Frits's death two years ago had prompted the start of her new career and the unexpected happiness Malo had brought into her life.

Frances gestured for her guest to follow her into the living room. Isobel hesitated, surprised to see the cottage was decorated with light colors and flowery prints. She had expected somber velvet draperies and dark, heavy furniture, not this bright and inviting room. The woman confused her. Frances certainly proved a dichotomy of personality.

The room's ivory-papered walls were hung with what Isobel assumed were Jason's paintings. She pursed her lips and frowned, disappointed. Though his work showed decent draftsmanship, none of the rather muddy and mundane compositions attracted her eye.

Isobel accepted Frances's polite offer of tea and settled onto a squashy, chintz-covered settee. Her hostess returned too quickly from the kitchen to allow Isobel time for a decent snoop. She must have had the tea things and plate of Maude's Easter cookies ready. As Isobel accepted a delicate Minton cup of jasmine tea, a sinuous, green-eyed Bombay cat leaped up and curled itself onto the cushion beside her.

"Do you mind cats? I can put her out."

"No, not at all," said Isobel and stroked the soft chocolate fur that sensuously undulated under her touch. She missed her own lost cat. Pussums had been lifted off, literally, by an osprey one Maine summer night and, at Frits' vehement "good riddance," she'd not risked another feline attachment. She remembered she had never asked Malo how he felt about cats. Isobel selected a hand painted rabbit and regretted nibbling off its ears. They were almost too exquisite to eat. An awkward silence stretched between the two women. Frances refused to initiate conversation and her silent composure made it obvious she hoped Isobel's dutiful visit would be short.

So it would. Time to get on to business. Isobel finished her tea and casually placed the manila envelope stamped with the Cook Gallery logo on the cushion beside her. She watched Francis follow the motion with her eyes as the cat made a sudden grasp at the string wound clasp with curious paws. Isobel rested her hand on the covering and hoped its contents might equally taunt her hostess.

"Something I want to show Maude," Isobel explained and patted the envelope. She did not plan to make an accusation. Just plant a seed of curiosity. Frances eyed the gesture and sat tensed, like a coiled spring, crushing a macaroon into coconut shreds. Isobel felt a sudden urge to escape from this dour woman who threatened without threats. She looked at her watch, folded the embroidered napkin and murmured some inane words of polite babble about coping with grief. Particularly hard to do, she thought, when the death involved violent murder.

Isobel rose and brushed crumbs from her lap. The startled pet arched its slender back like a caterpillar, jumped down, and daintily cleaned them from the carpet. Tidy, tidy, like its mistress.

TWENTY-TWO

Malo awoke at the insistent ring of the phone. His afternoon sleep had been so deep that, confused and unfocused, he first believed himself home in his own bedroom. Then he remembered he had not slept in his Italian bed for weeks.

"Mr. Malo Bellini?" The caller spoke with ominous authority and Malo recognized the policeman's voice as that of the officer in charge of Jason Faraday's murder. He sat up, instantly alert and his first thoughts were of Isobel. Please, he prayed, may she not be in trouble again.

"Trooper English here, sir. We talked earlier regarding the juvenile runaway from California. Your friend, Mr. Nicolas Penfield, called us. It seems he recognized the girl from Mrs. Van Dursan's description as the waitress employed in a local restaurant." Malo waited. "Yes," continued English, "we find it somewhat a coincidence to find you are also involved in our second ongoing investigation, the Jason Faraday murder at the Art Association."

"Peripherally."

"Peripherally involved," corrected Trooper English. Relieved at hearing no mention of trouble connected with Isobel, Malo let out his breath and forced himself to relax.

"We have found the girl Alice. We are lucky there are not many places a sixteen year old can hide in a small town like ours. We have learned that she has reinvented herself using the stolen identity of a deceased Alice Perkins. We received this information with the help of Mr. Nicholas Penfield and he suggested we call you. We need the help of your friend Mrs. Van Dursan and Mr. Penfield said she could be reached at this number. The girl is currently in custody at our local barracks and," Trooper English cleared his throat, "despite our most careful and considerate questioning, Alice stubbornly refuses to talk to anyone except Mrs. Van Dursan." A tone of chagrin crept into the officer's voice. "I personally recognize the attitude of a sulky teenager. I have two of my own. Sometimes like talking to a brick wall. It seems Mrs. Van Dursan is a person Alice remembers from the inn where they both stayed in Newport and, for some reason trusts. We would find it most helpful if the lady could come to the barracks here in Eastbrook as soon as possible."

Malo ran his hands over his face, wiping away any traces of fatigue.

"Yes, of course I remember Alice. I assume she's the same girl Mrs. Van Dursan and I met while staying in Newport earlier this year. We were both concerned at the time over the girl's relationship with these people she was travelling with. Foley was the name they entered in the hotel register, if I remember, from Hartford, Connecticut. We both thought the entire situation seemed fishy."

"Definitely fishy, sir. And we find it also somewhat fishy that you two are closely involved both investigations. And we find it another coincidence that a person of interest in the Faraday case, Mr. Piet Sonders, is also a friend of yours and Mrs. Van Dursan."

"Trooper English, I can imagine you might find it hard to believe, but this all is coincidence. I employ Mrs. Van Dursan to help me solve these kinds of situations."

Malo suddenly realized he'd made an unprecedented lapse. Too much information. If nothing else, he had learned during his former, unsavory career to keep his mouth shut. "I have Mrs. Van Dursan's mobile number," he said abruptly, wanting to end the conversation. "I'll call her immediately, and I'm sure she'll agree to be at the barracks as soon as possible. I suggest you ask Alice to sit tight and behave. Maybe feed her? I hear food always improves communication with that age group."

"Will do." Trooper English agreed. He sounded weary and Malo wondered if the man with two recalcitrant teens lacked a wife. "You're right about food," the policeman said. "We'll send out for burgers and fries—and a bag of anything in the 'ito' food group that will keep her quiet until you get here. And thank you for your cooperation."

The stress heard in the officer's voice was understandable. He must suddenly cope with a major crime, possible grand larceny, and the kidnapping of a sullen juvenile. All during one week in a town unaccustomed anything much beyond vandalism and an occasional minor felony. Malo dialed Isobel's mobile and, amazed when she answered, related the situation with Alice.

"I'm so relieved they found her safe from the Foleys," she said. "Of course, I'll talk to her." She hesitated. "I've just left the widow Frances."

"Are you all right?"

"Fine," she paused. "We had tea and cookies." Isobel fell silent. He thought her voice sounded taut. "I'll tell you about it later. I'm on my way to Eagles Crest to show Maude Tal's photo of the Church painting. It should only take a few minutes. She'll either recognize it or not. I'll come directly back to the inn and we'll go together and talk some sense into Alice. Call the Trooper and say we'll be at the barracks within the hour."

TWENTY-THREE

Because of the day's gloom and spring's early dusk, Isobel did not notice the car without lights that followed her down Beach Drive to Eagles Crest. She drove along the narrow unlit road, concentrating only on possible solutions to her niece's problems. If what she guessed proved true, Piet would be cleared of suspicion. Then after she spoke to Maude and confirmed Tal's doubts that the painting was not Jason's work, she would pick up Malo and drive down to Eastbrook. She felt sure she could convince Alice to return to California and finish high school. More important, make sure the girl had learned a lesson from running off with the Foleys.

The shore road ran beside a long stretch of rough stonewall. For centuries, New England settlers had hauled the endless boulders, constantly churned to the surface by glacial moraines, to build these dry walls marking property boundaries. Even today, digging a new foundation predicts a major and expensive excavation. She passed a half-dozen lanes, chained off for winter, leading down to empty beach cottages.

The quarter mile of wall along side the road had tumbled in places and, in the gaps, early spring daffodils poked through the stones and shone yellow in the beam of her headlights. Finally, she came to a break and maneuvered Fiona's little car between a pair of stone pineapple-topped pillars. She sighed with relief at seeing lights shining through the windows of a low, gabled gatehouse guarding the entrance to the drive. At least Maude's tenant lived close enough to call on, if needed, at this deserted edge of town. As she drove slowly up the dark curving lane, her fender scraped against an untrimmed yew hedge and she swerved sharply to avoid a wheeled waste bin.

Isobel tried to remember the turns Piet had taken leading up to the main house the night of Maude's birthday party. She had paid no attention. She never did when someone else drove. Her hands gripped the wheel and, in the light from her high beams, gasped when another encounter with a privet hedge barely kept the car from tumbling onto the beach below. She did not intend to return Fiona's car covered with scratches.

As she pulled under the porte cochère, the water tower at the corner of the house, topped with its witch hat roof, loomed tall and pointed. She got out and with the manila envelope under her arm, peered through the lighted kitchen window beside the back entrance. The wind soughed through the firs surrounding the house. Isobel pulled her coat collar up and knocked on the door. No one answered.

She knocked again, harder. Like many others her age, Maude probably didn't hear well. The knob turned under her hand and the door swung open into a stone floored mudroom. Navigating its clutter of gardening tools in the dim light, she tripped over a huge open bag of bird food. Mice, she thought. Probably lots of mice.

Ahead of her, leading into the downstairs hall, a second door stood ajar and she peered into a paneled back foyer. She remembered the dark varnished woodwork from her prowl through the house the night of Maude's party. Light shone from the passage ahead and she followed it through the butler's pantry into the dining room. In the center of a damask-covered table that could easily seat a dozen, a massive vase of antique roses stood above a carpet of fallen petals. At its head, beside a silver dinner fork and linen napkin, lay today's Times crossword. Isobel smiled and controlled the impulse to take the pen beside it and correct an error. She placed the manila envelope containing Tal's photograph of the Church canvas under the folded puzzle. Isobel hoped Maude would find it with the enclosed note asking her to phone her at the inn the next morning.

On her way out, she paused again to peer into the butler's pantry. Like the rest of the house it remained a relic of the past. Glass fronted cabinets held ceiling high shelves of china dinner services and covered serving tureens. Set into the far wall, she saw the open doors of a wide dumbwaiter and recalled the story of Maude's grandchildren's ultimate hidey-hole transport to and from the old cellar kitchen. This outmoded convenience indeed gaped large enough to hold a small child, but she hoped no longer used for a play, as the ropes operating its lift mechanism looked frayed and unsafe.

The atmosphere of the musty old mansion overcame her and she suddenly felt uncomfortable wandering, without excuse, through a stranger's empty house. Isobel gave one last try to rouse someone. This time, if nobody answered, she vowed to leave.

TWENTY-FOUR

Waiting back at the Bell and Whistle, Malo paced their room. He'd tried Isobel's mobile twice but got no answer. She seldom used the thing and had probably left it turned off in the bottom of her handbag. He checked his watch again, then the bedside clock. It had been over an hour since they'd promised to meet here and drive to Eastbrook. Instinct warned him that something had happened. Something serious enough to make Isobel miss their meeting with Alice.

When the phone rang, he snatched up the receiver, almost dropping it. He'd expected to hear Isobel's voice with some lame explanation of getting lost or another misadventure, but the caller was not Isobel.

"Sorry to bother you," said Trooper English. "But we're still waiting here at the barracks and have no facilities to keep Alice overnight. Are you on your way?"

At Eagle's Crest, no one answered Isobel's final shout. She was obviously alone and anxious to get out of Maude's creepy house. Her hand had closed around the mudroom doorknob when she a heard a frantic flapping sound overhead. In the dark passage, she peered uneasily up the steep flight leading to the landing above.

Isobel hesitated. She'd had enough prowling through this house, but what if she was wrong and upstairs, Maude had fallen? Hit her head, broken something? She couldn't possibly leave and drive away not knowing.

The flapping and fluttering sounded again, louder this time and accompanied by the same melodious twitter she had heard coming from Maude's caged birds the night of the party. One of her brightly colored finches must have flown free and was probably battering itself somewhere above in a panic. Now what? She wasn't about to chase some tiny bird around in the dark.

Then came a faint mewling sound. She thought again of those open bags of feed and all those mice. Did they have a cat? They must. Maybe several. She pictured the cat stalking the bird. Like a scene from an old kiddy cartoon. But it might be Maude, not a cat, crying for help. Enough.

She flicked on the light switch at the foot of the back staircase and began to climb. At the first landing she turned and waited. Nervous, in the dim light of a low-wattage bulb, she paused before starting up another flight. She rested silent, hand on the knob of the worn newel post. The dark varnished wainscoting matched the bare stairs that kept turning and rising. Hearing nothing, she climbed on. But at the top of the third floor landing, she stopped, out of breath. Faintly, Isobel called again.

"Hello. Maude? Anyone?"

No answer. But up here the flapping increased and grew louder. Ahead rose four rough-framed steps leading to a platform set below a framed wall panel. She climbed to the top and a little yellow bird flew at her. Its frantic wings beat against her chest and, startled, she clutched at the railing of this precarious perch and almost fell. The finch clung to her coat for a moment and Isobel quickly reached down and cupped it in both hands. Cocooned, the tiny songbird calmed and, having found the source of the clamor, so did Isobel. She looked for something to contain the bird while she carried it back down to its cage. Nothing. Gently, she nestled the little thing into her coat pocket.

She stood and listened for a moment to the house that now only hummed with silence. Outside, a tree branch scratched against the landing window. A creak and shuffle. She stifled her imagination. Just the normal noises of an old house settling?

At knee height, she saw a half-size door set in the curve of wall that she guessed, from where she stood above the kitchen, opened into the conical roof top water tower. Curious about the workings of the odd structure, Isobel gave the panel a tentative push and when it swung open, leaned over the sill. From below, the damp musty odor of gallons and gallons of stored water assailed her. Intent on protecting the struggling bird in her coat pocket, she failed to sense the sudden movement from behind.

Without warning, a hard shove sent Isobel tumbling through the opening. Pulled down by layers of heavy clothes, she thrashed about underwater with the tiny bird trapped in her pocket.

TWENTY-FIVE

By six-thirty, Malo had real reason to worry. Isobel had still not answered her mobile. He knew she'd driven to Maude's after tea with Frances and, rather than chasing around town in the dark, getting lost himself, he should call Trooper English. This meeting with Alice was too important for Isobel to miss, and it was completely unlike her to forget. The impulsive woman was in trouble somewhere and a nasty premonition warned him not to wait any longer to go after her.

Along with Pen and Jo, Malo and Isobel were the Bell and Whistle's only guests for the week, and hearing Malo's predicament, their host immediately grasped the emergency and was happy to lend him her car. Without the GPS, Malo would have never found the unmarked turn-off to Eagles Crest. At the robotic voice's patient prompting, he maneuvered carefully between the stone entrance pillars. As he started up Beach Drive, he had second thoughts about his impulsive pursuit. He was behaving stupidly. Exactly like Isobel and moving alone into a possibly dangerous situation. Malo drove up and stopped behind two cars parked at the top of the unlit drive and recognized the one in front as the compact sedan Fiona had loaned Isobel. The second car could be Maude's or one of her family's. He stood outside and studied the dark-shingled house rising three stories above. He fumbled through his pocket for the card with English's emergency number. The barracks answered immediately.

Malo explained the situation and apologized for his late decision to call. He told the officer of their visit to the gallery and Isobel's plan to stop by and unnerve Frances.

"I tried to discourage her from going alone, but she insisted on driving out to Maude's after she left Frances and have her identify the canvas. She promised to be back at the inn and pick me up within the hour. We planned to drive down together and meet you in Eastbrook to confront Alice. Isobel is too concerned about the girl's difficulties to miss that, so when she didn't show up, I followed her here to Maude's. The car she borrowed is outside on the drive, but the house is dark and I'm sure something's gone wrong."

"Very wise of you to call, sir." Malo could not help hear the admonishment in the trooper's voice. "We'll be there as fast as we can. I can understand Mrs. Van Dursan's reason for wanting the photograph and her suspicions over its provenance," English said, "but why would she risk confronting Mrs. Faraday if she thinks the woman is complicit in her husband's forgery and capable of murder? Even with the plausible excuse of a condolence call."

"That's why I'm calling," said Malo. He inhaled a deep breath. "Mrs. Van Dursan has a penchant for launching herself headlong into dangerous situations." In the dark, Malo unconsciously crossed himself and added softly, "And so far she's been lucky."

English paused for a moment then spoke thoughtfully. "Perhaps Mr. Bellini, you may have something to worry about. Your lady friend and the police are more on the same page than you think."

Malo thought Maude a stalwart antique to live alone in this huge rambling house, but was glad that he'd called the police. At least he had effectively blocked the escape of whoever had parked behind Isobel. He shut his car door quietly, headed toward the lighted kitchen and entered through the half-open door to the mudroom.

Inside, he listened a moment. Silence. He paused at the foot of a steep, flight of stairs leading up to the rooms over the rear wing of the house and felt along the wall for the light switch. He flicked it on. No result. He frowned. Too dangerously unsafe, he reasoned, for them to leave a burnt out bulb in this dark stairway. In the dim light from a high stairwell window, he began to climb. At the top of the first landing he saw a naked bulb screwed loosely into an old fashioned ceramic socket. A tall man, he reached up and twisted and, tightened in its fixture, brought the hall and stairs leading up to the next landing safely into light.

This place is a warren, he thought, and if someone had followed Isobel, they could have hidden and waited for her along any of these dark hallways.

Should he call out and risk alerting her stalker, or just keep searching? Again Malo cursed his stupidity at not remaining outside for the police. He paused on the landing, straining for any sound, but heard only the creaks and settling typical of such an old house. He startled when a gust of wind rattled the loosely caulked panes of the stairwell window.

At least he had blocked her follower with his car. If someone tried to get away after harming Isobel, they'd have to escape on foot. He focused on finding Isobel. He would leave any chasing business to the police. Then he heard a noise that chilled his blood. The faint sound of sloshing water from somewhere overhead.

"The damn water tower," he cursed aloud, and took the last flight of steps two at a time.

———————

"I got the bird out of my pocket," Isobel gasped as Malo reached over the sill to pull her shivering, from the water tank.

He peeled off her coat and held her sodden body against him to stop the shaking.

"It's alive," she assured him, through chattering teeth. "It flew up into the rafters."

By now, English and his partner had arrived in the squad car and the unit's bar strobes emblazoned the drive with its lights. Behind Malo, the two troopers stood on the landing below the opening to the water tower and, once sure that the near-drowned woman was safe and bundled into a blanket, English reholstered his gun and frowned.

"Bird? You were chasing a bird and fell into that tank?"

"No, young man," she said, huddling in Malo's arms. "I was pushed from behind. Almost drowned, but luckily just wet and cold. Get me out of here."

On the drive outside the house, the flasher on the squad car roof cast eerie multi-colored shadows through the surrounding trees and shrubs. Muted crackle and static came from inside the vehicle between bursts of garbled radio voice. Malo wondered why Maude's tenant had not heard the commotion, then realized how isolated they were on this hill above the Sound. And where was Maude?

More important—where was the person who had shoved Isobel into that tank to drown?

As if reading his mind, English sent his partner with his powerful flashlight to search the bushes. Hopeless, thought Malo, considering this vast overgrown property, but probably another of those required police procedures. At least, he thought, there had been no official crime—unless attempted murder was considered a crime—and therefore no scene to cordon off with yards of yellow tape.

"Mrs. Van Dursan," said English, "we assume that whoever was responsible for your incident is either still hiding in the house, which we think unlikely, or after finding they were trapped between our vehicles, got away on foot."

"I'm sure you are right," said Isobel. "However, as for my 'incident,' as you call it, if Malo had not found me when he did, I think I would have soon fallen unconscious from hypothermia and drowned. I shucked my shoes—damn expensive shoes at that—but that tank water was icy."

"Ma'am," English looked sheepish. "Believe me, I use the word incident as an official term and promise that we will treat this matter as a serious attempt on your life. We can trace the car's owner through its plates and quickly identify your attacker." Isobel almost wished he'd said perp.

Trooper English had his phone to his ear during the commotion and, within minutes, another police car with the K-9 handler and his dog, Duke, pulled up before the entrance.

"Your attempted murderer has escaped on foot and Duke's job is to find him. This fellow is one of our town's finest." Duke, a handsome German shepherd, jumped out and, firmly held by his leash with tail thumping and tongue lolling, sat patiently smiling up at them.

"Isobel," said Malo. "You are still shaking. I'll drive us back to the inn and after a hot shower and some dry clothes—and shoes—and we can follow these officers down to Eastbrook." He turned to the trooper. "Will you notify them we're coming and explain to Alice what's happened?"

"And when we get there, I'll make an official statement about my watery dunk, said Isobel, "and we can sit down and have a sensible talk with Alice. I want this night over as soon as possible." She slumped against Malo's shoulder. "I'm sorry gentlemen, but suddenly I'm feeling past my age."

TWENTY-SIX

The rest of the evening went better than Isobel hoped. After being escorted under the rear awning into the lower level of the Eastbrook barracks, a converted old homestead on a rise above the side of the turnpike, she was treated with solicitous attention by the staff. Dry and warm, inside and out, after a mug of steaming and surprisingly good coffee laced with the whisky Malo kept ready in his silver hip flask, she confronted Alice. Out of hearing of the officers, Malo explained that the emergency ration he always carried—like W.C Field's necessity in case of snakebite—was a tribute to his Capone hardened past. She doubted he was joking.

When they arrived, Alice shed her sullen slouch and sat up, eager to hear the details of Isobel's night of gothic perils. The girl seemed thoroughly impressed with the tale of rescue, and seemed ready to listen to Isobel's sympathetic understanding of Alice's unfeasible dream of escape. More mature than her age, Alice's recognized this attempt to find an exciting new life had proved impossible. Isobel convinced the girl that her advice made sense and saw that the girl was smart enough to realize how close she had come to perils of her own by joining up with the Foleys.

English listened, impressed at how easily Isobel commanded Alice's respect with her calm, insistent but unpatronizing manner. The woman managed to persuade the girl to return to her foster parents, whom Alice, losing her sullen attitude, confessed weren't really so bad, and encouraged her to complete high school. By the time Isobel finished, she had encouraged Alice to accept that, if she got her act together, she could raise her grades enough to apply to college.

Alice's face brightened when Isobel suggested she try a drama school. Surprising them all, Alice impulsively leaped to her feet, almost toppling her chair, and gave Isobel a great bear hug. The girl reddened, embarrassed by the burst of emotion, but Isobel hugged her back and promised Alice they would keep in touch.

Within the hour, the police had traced the plates of Frances' abandoned car. Duke, leading their search, found her later that night, collapsed in the bushes along the shore drive, cold, weary and bedraggled. They bundled her into the squad car and led her downstairs to the Eastport barrack's interrogation room. Showing little emotion, Frances confessed her sad story.

She had followed Isobel to Eagle's Crest and, after following her through the house and pushing her into the tank, had not expected to find herself trapped between two cars and need to escape on foot. By the time she stumbled away down the dark, twisting drive, she'd become completely disoriented. Somewhere in her flight along Beach Drive, she lost a shoe and fallen, twisting her ankle. Cold and in pain, the sweep of police lights caught her lying crumpled in a ditch where she surrendered, the huge dog panting above her, without protest. Her miserable future was far from what she'd planned. Arraigned and convicted, she realized she would likely be sentenced to life imprisonment without parole for not only murder, but also grand larceny, and attempted fraud.

The night before they returned to Maine, Malo and Isobel, along with Jo and Pen, treated Fiona and Piet to a celebratory farewell dinner at the Bell and Whistle. Around the table before the wide picture window in an alcove of the inn's dining room, they toasted the return of Piet's reputation and the award of prize money that made their tickets to Italy a reality.

Outside on this warm spring evening, cherry and pear trees bloomed pink and white and the grass shone with that sharp, brilliant green that lasts briefly before the soft weedier shades command summer. As a result of the local garden club's ambitious efforts, most of the town's open spaces bloomed with thousands of yellow and white daffodils. Isobel looked wistfully at the mellow scene and realized that, back home by this time tomorrow, from her windows she would see only the frosted landscape of Maine's lingering winter.

"In retrospect," said Isobel, recalling the past week's events, "you have to believe that Frances' blind faith in her husband's vanity predicted her downfall."

"I guess," said Piet, sadly. "Over the weeks before his death, I watched him fall apart and barely recognized the conflicted and moody man he'd become—so often at odds with himself. All of us have barren spells and are frustrated by our sudden lapse of talent." Piet looked genuinely miserable. "I wonder if I could have helped him? Got him free of Frances's tenacious grip?" He tried a feeble smile. "I have to admit I miss his company. His studio next to mine is still unused, maybe some curse of bad luck—artists can be superstitious—and somehow awfully empty." Jo touched his arm and tried to raise his spirits.

"The members must be glad that the business of the association has returned to normal," she said. "The big name gurus are back teaching their classes. The gallery is open and visitors with their money are coming in."

"Yes," said Fiona with a wicked grin, "and gossip over the scandal will keep member's mouths busy for weeks."

"Ah yes, and perhaps a few of those vipers soothed," added Pen.

"You're both right. Some good came of it all," said Piet, "The look on Maude's face and her pleasure at finding the old Church painting he gave her mother all those years ago. Though the sentimental value probably means more to her than any monetary sum, with Tal's help, she could reap a tidy sum if she chooses to sell it."

"Ironically, Maude was out jogging underwater at her weekly aerobics class at the local Y while Isobel almost drowned in her attic. And sorely peeved to have missed all the action," added Fiona.

Pen faced Isobel. "Now that's a good idea, Mrs. Van D. Next time why not swim off some of your extra energy in a much safer and supervised pool?"

"Excellent plan," agreed Malo.

They all laughed when Isobel lifted her palms in surrender.

"But in the end, it seems Frances managed to manipulate Jason only so far before he rebelled," Isobel said seriously. She looked at Piet. "As you guessed, I think the poor man became more and more upset and when he couldn't deal with the guilt, must have threatened to

---

165

confess. After all her efforts, Frances couldn't chance that."

"And then Wren," said Fiona, "that sweet young granddaughter of Maude's, told the police she remembered the day Frances came over to help pack the baskets. The woman must have left the house with the painting hidden under a layer of the cookies she planned to donate to the Women's Exchange. When the police questioned Wren, she said she caught Frances wandering through the house on the excuse of looking for the loo. She must have discovered the painting hanging in one of the rooms full of unused furniture and because of her experience with dealers, recognized its value."

"Wandering around those empty rooms the night of Maude's party," said Isobel, "among all that discarded furniture, I remember seeing a small square, lighter in color than the surrounding wallpaper and, now that I've seen the painting, about the right size."

No one spoke. The others stared at their plates while Malo sipped from his glass of merlot and gave Isobel a suggestive look.

Fiona pointed her fork at her aunt. "Hmm," she murmured. "I suppose, like Frances, you too were looking for the loo?"

Pen raised his glass toward Isobel in a toast.

"Time I think, Mrs. Van D., to get back to Maine."

TWENTY-SEVEN

The next day, on their return to Elmore Harbor, Isobel saw that her home in Maine, true to the groundhog's prophecy, had resisted any hint of spring.

Finally at dusk, after a long day on the road, they bumped along the lane to her cottage. The gravel drive had runnelled by freeze and thaw over winter and Malo cautiously navigated the low-slung rental through the ruts. He pulled up beside Isobel's red car, switched off the engine and, for a time, they sat and listened to its cooling ticks. Isobel stared over the brown front lawn sloping down to the expanse of water beyond.

"To think that on the other side of that mean-looking ocean lies warm and sunny Spain," she said."

"Or," answered Malo, turning his head to the west and shading his eyes against the streaks of crimson sunset blazing above the inner harbor, "far across that more benign distance, awaits Sasquatch and the great Olympic Peninsula."

"Oh Malo. Are you going to sulk until we get back west?" He pulled her against him. "No, of course not," he said. The giant yeti will wait. After all, he's been roaming around out there in your mossy mist for centuries."

With effort, Isobel pushed open her passenger door and set one foot on the ground. "I'm sorry I made us rush back here," she said. "I meant what I said and intend to keep my promise to get us back on that peninsula." She nodded toward the house. "But not until I cope with what's in that package inside. The history of that severed hand remains too much a puzzle and I can't leave again until I solve it. Why did someone kill and mutilated the woman who wore that ring last and then leave the hand with the diamond behind?" She shook her head. "It doesn't make sense." Malo had come to recognize her frown and stubborn tone of voice guaranteed she would not budge without an answer. He hoped it did not require a return to Newport. They both needed a rest from travel, even first class.

Easing his legs out and to the ground, Malo wearily went to heft their luggage from the boot and trudge with it up the porch steps. Isobel followed and he waited behind her as she fumbled over the door lintel for the key. Malo cleared his throat at her idea of security and Isobel assured him that crime is a minor issue in this small harbor.

"Not much has changed here over fifty years, and locking our cars and houses is not yet a habit." She added, "I regret that my visit to Fiona ruined Trooper English's boast of 'no murders in his town since ninety-eight.' I don't know how I feel about the recent signing into law ending Connecticut's death penalty. He said it would guarantee that Frances Faraday, if convicted, escape lethal injection but spend the rest of her life suffering Dante's last circle. At the taxpayer's expense, of course," she added crossly. "A year's incarceration costs more than most college tuitions."

On the drive home from Connecticut, Isobel and Malo had argued the morality of the states's decision. She told him of pictures she'd seen showing the deplorable conditions in most of our federal prisons and they both agreed they would opt to die rather than spend the final days of their lives enduring such living hell. Though committed to her new and privileged life with Malo—and enjoying its material compensations—she honestly believed her devious machinations to rid society of its most despicable sorts avoided incurring huge debts on innocent taxpayers. She smiled ruefully. At least this fragile, high-minded philosophy eased her conscience.

Isobel pushed open the front door, replaced the key above the lintel, and waited while Malo shouldered through with their bags. She sensed one of his black Irish moods coming on and remembered his little problem with temper. In spite of her impatience, it was not a wise idea to provoke him by mentioning the package. What he needed was a large whisky sipped before a roaring fire. She kept containers of fish chowder in the freezer and, while it thawed, fried up chunks of thick bacon to top it.

His mood mollified and appetite satisfied, an hour later, they began a contagion of yawns and agreed to call it a night. Malo banked the fire, carried their dinner trays to the kitchen, and left the dishes in the sink.

"Leave them, they'll wait," said Isobel. She silently regretted not checking the desk drawer for that package and lagged behind him as they mounted the stairs. On the second floor landing, Malo took her arm.

"I know what's on your mind, but let's give it a rest, literally," he said. "Like Scarlet, we'll deal with it, and the dishes, in the morning." He put his arm around her waist. "Isobel, believe me, if I had the strength, I'd sweep you into my arms like Rhett." They both laughed.

TWENTY-EIGHT

The next morning when Isobel opened her eyes and looked out at a grey, damp dawn, she didn't feel like Scarlet. Nor did her garden look anything like a Tara spring in Georgia. Downstairs, she stood peering through the kitchen window at the dismal landscape when Malo appeared for breakfast. His mood had improved with a good night's sleep and rose further when she set before him a bowl of Irish oatmeal topped with blueberries and cinnamon sugar. She remembered the sparse crop she'd picked from last summer's low bush patch; maybe it was time to burn it over.

After breakfast, they agreed their first priority was to return the rental car to Rockland. Food being her second concern, Isobel would follow him in her Subaru and together they'd suffer a tedious restocking trip to the market. Exhumed by coffee, she reached for pencil and paper. Making grocery lists, any list, was her favorite pastime—eating, her second. Or maybe vice-versa. She was well into organizing columns of necessary staples the ringing phone jarred her concentration.

"Hello there," a woman's throaty voice boomed over the line. "Have I reached Isobel Van Dursan?"

Isobel recognized the voice, but could not place where she'd recently heard that hearty timbre.

"You have," she said, warily, and looked across the table at Malo. Having finished breakfast but lacking the morning paper, she recognized his impatience to get going.

"Good, I'm so glad. Remember me? It's Amber. From the Newport Historical Society. Well, you'll never believe it, but I missed the front top step coming to work last week and fell and broke my ankle. The doc said to stay off it as much as possible, but I am so bored sitting here at this 'genuine claw ball, carved shell kneehole frontispiece desk' all day I could die. If I have to describe the history of one more Newport antique to one more polyester antique, I'll be sick."

Isobel covered the mouthpiece and made pointy fingers at the receiver. Amber—Newport—she mouthed. Malo frowned, confused. Isobel continued to listen, equally puzzled at this diatribe from this person she barely knew. Amber rambled on.

"Latham," she said—"you remember my cohort Latham? You really gave him a laugh. Though he's not usually patient with people and he's had to run the tour groups alone while I've been incarcerated here fussing with paperwork and organizing our fusty files. Dear Latham is a good soul and has dealt kindly with my sour mood. He appreciates how tedious it is for me to just sit—I'm a mover and shaker—he tries to cheer me up and then we remembered your interest in past unsolved murders." Amber took a breath and enunciated her next words. "Especially those that occurred during our gilded, wicked age." Amber blustered on, giving Isobel no chance to interrupt.

"Well, to get to the point, while changing the display cases yesterday, I came upon that old photograph of the lady at the Breakers dinner party, remember, the one you and your friend found so interesting? The young woman wearing that huge diamond ring and sporting the fancy ostrich headband?" Isobel clutched the phone, her marketing list forgotten.

"Amber, of course I remember you and Latham. I'm sorry. I never got your last names. To tell the truth, your call must be one of those mysterious degrees of separation coincidences. Malo and I have not stopped thinking about that woman in the photograph since our visit to Newport."

"Yes," Amber said. "I remembered that it sparked your curiosity and while poking through our records, I discovered a strange story behind that old photograph. Anyway, to the point of my call, I found your name and this number in our visitor's registry and I took the liberty of calling. Not because of the picture—that photo looked like any other of Newport's summer fetes—but later, going through our old records, I recalled your inquiry, and found an interesting reference to a bizarre murder that took place that same year. An unresolved crime, no less— just up your alley." Amber gave a loud, hearty laugh and Isobel saw Malo wince. "Tell me, my dear, if I'm being a bother?"

"No, not at all," assured Isobel. "We've just returned to Maine after several weeks away, and I'm still fascinated by that woman. In fact, the going's on during Newport's entire glamorous era. I think that what you're referring to, today's police would call a cold case. Can we discuss it over the phone?" Isobel heard Amber's regretful sigh, followed by an awkward pause.

"Actually," the docent said, "there is a lot of stuff here I'd like you to see. The problem is I can't remove it from the Society building. Our antiquated, but strict, rules are the same as most libraries."

"I understand," said Isobel. "Always an issue with reference material."

"Exactly," said Amber. "I could photocopy what we found important and send it to you, but it's a complicated story and I'd rather explain it in person."

Isobel hesitated and looked warily at Malo. "I suppose we could drive down," she said. "But we've been away for several weeks and are travel weary." She ignored Malo's piercing scowl. "How would you and Latham feel about taking a little vacation from all your boredom? Are you well enough to drive up and visit us for a weekend in Maine?"

She was unsure about the relationship between Amber and the lanky, dapper Latham. What exactly was a cohort?

"If your friend agrees to drive, because of your ankle," she added. "It's not a long trip and we can put you up in country comfort."

"Oh my dear, that sounds just ducky." Amber's enthusiasm at the invitation echoed across the room and Malo grasped his head in his hands. "A trip down east is exactly what we need to escape my mental rut. If you can stand us, we can make it a long weekend. I have a list of volunteer docents who can cover for us at the Society. Most important, I promise we are self-entertaining." Isobel stifled a laugh as she tried to imagine what that meant.

"You and Latham plan on it," she said. "Today is Thursday. Why not come as soon as you can get away? Give us a call and let know when to expect you." She read out directions and replaced the receiver. Malo just stared at her.

"Do you realize you have arranged to spend our first weekend home in weeks with strangers" he said. "You don't even know the woman's last name."

Isobel shrugged. At the moment, Amber's surname bothered her less than the need to reorganize her marketing list.

"Do you suppose they're allergic to lobster?"

Malo drummed his fingers. "While you finish your grocery list," he said, "I'll go look in your desk for the bauble causing all this fuss. I'm glad we avoided the issue last night, but with good cause," he added. "We needed a night's sleep and clear heads before deciding what to do with the contents of that package."

Though Isobel had also enjoyed a solid sleep, the night's rest had provided no plan. Despite Malo's opposition, maybe Amber's opportune call would help with that problem. While Malo rooted through her desk, she checked the big freezer in the pantry and found a half dozen packages of her neighbor's free-range chickens. She added to her list the fresh ingredients needed for her delicious *coq au vin*. Isobel missed her small flock of hens. She remembered how they would rush onto the porch at the smell of baking cookies and peck at the screen for a hand out. She gave up her stint at raising poultry after one bloody night's invasion by a family of foxes. The local remedy for this offense was shooting the killer and nailing his body above the henhouse door. This gruesome threat to his fellow marauders was not her thing. She frowned and tapped her pencil on the list.

What if Amber and Latham were vegetarians? Or worse, ovo-vegans. Not sure of that sect's regimen, she decided to take them across the harbor to the Westwind Inn the first night and see what they ordered. Then she remembered the Inn only did breakfasts for their overnight guests this early in the season. Oh for the good old days before these special diets when you ate whatever your hostess served. Well, too bad. They would eat her mushroom and lobster Marsala with buttermilk biscuits and love it or leave it.

"Isobel, come here quickly." The unusual tone of Malo's call from the front hall alarmed her. She put down her pencil. Please, she thought, not a body hanging in the closet. No, they would have found that last night when they had hung up their coats.

"Isobel," he called again.

This time, the urgency in his voice hurried her from the kitchen. Malo stood in front of the open desk drawer. "You said Jo left the package in your desk?" He had pulled out the drawers and tossed their contents aside. "Well, my dear, I've looked through them all and there's nothing here."

TWENTY-NINE

Isobel dialed Jo's cell number at the Greenberry Mountain Resort in the hills of Virginia and waited anxiously for her niece to answer.

"Jo?" she said, relieved. "I'm so glad I've found you!"

"Hi, Aunt Isobel. You have, and this place is warm and wonderful. A beautiful southern spring. Pen's had his fill of golf and we're off to play tennis. You would love the perks here. Too much good food and lots of the special pampering you find at places like this. I'm afraid I'm becoming spoiled by the rich nomad's life. Good to hear you're home safe. What's up?"

Isobel relaxed, relieved to have caught her niece in their room. She needed to ask a question better not left on a message machine.

"Malo and I arrived back last night and it's far from spring here. In fact, still pretty dreary. We're both tired but," she paused, "okay."

"Okay?" asked Jo. "What does okay mean?"

"Just that," before Jo could pin her down, she went on. "Remember that little errand I asked you to do for me the day we left for Bainbridge?"

"You mean the package I picked up at the post office? Of course. I did as you said and stowed it in the drawer of that big desk in the front hall."

"Well, the package is gone," said Isobel. "I called to make sure you left it where you said before I make inquiries. We don't want to call the sheriff in Rockland and raise a fuss about a break-in if it's somewhere in the house and we've somehow not found it."

"Oh my, I'm so sorry. Was it something valuable? I absolutely assure you I put the package, unopened, just as it came from the post office, in the middle desk drawer. Exactly as you said. You can't have missed it."

After a moment's silence, Isobel spoke softly, as if to herself. "Then someone really did enter the house while we were gone. We were too tired to deal with it last night, and Malo only found it missing this morning. We made a thorough search of the place before I called you. There were no obvious signs of breaking and entering when we arrived last evening. No doors jimmied or broken windows. The house looked as undisturbed as the day we left." She added with chagrin. "I'm afraid Malo had every right to scold me. Whoever broke in obviously found the house key I leave on the ledge above the front door." She gave a feeble laugh. "I told him that, at least, there is no damage to repair."

"Isobel," said Jo, sounding equally chagrined. "Whatever was in that package?"

"I'm afraid that's a long story and I need more information. I promise to call you back and explain as soon as I have some answers. Friends we met in Newport are arriving for the weekend and may shed some light on the problem."

"I'm sorry if you've been robbed. It all sounds very strange," said Jo. "I'm only glad you're home safe. Call me when you find out what happened to the mystery package."

Malo came into the kitchen as Isobel replaced the receiver and told him the gist of her conversation with Jo.

"The question is," he said seriously, "if the thief came after the ring, how did he know you sent it to yourself here in Maine?" Isobel nibbled her lip.

"There must be some connection with Newport," she said. "And for mailing it to myself, rather than carry it around for the rest of our stay, he must have guessed it an obvious and logical plan." She ran her hands through her hair. "The only people who could possibly be involved are the Foleys, Alice, or Amber and her cohort Latham— her word not mine."

"I've no idea how any of them could have witnessed your find on the beach," said Malo. "You say you were alone on the afternoon of your walk and sure no one saw you pick it up. And if those docents were a part of some scheme, why would they risk coming to visit us here? In a way," he allowed—obviously pleased with his idea—"the theft of the damned thing might be the solution to our problem. Like Frits and your cat, I too say good riddance." He brightened. "I suggest that the hand and ring be gone and forgotten. Maybe it is cursed like the doomed history of those infamous diamonds that brought generations of misery and misfortune to their owners."

The look he received from Isobel conveyed exactly what she thought of his suggestion.

THIRTY

Malo heard the sound of tires crunching on gravel as the car bumped down the rutted drive minutes before it appeared around the screen of firs. If most of the roads leading to the houses along the harbor could be called unimproved, the road down to Isobel's cottage would be classified as extremely unimproved.

He had been dreading the arrival of the Newport docents, but when he saw their motorcar, his jaw dropped. Possibly Latham was a man of his own tastes after all. This wondrous vehicle they had driven to Maine was the only type antique of which he approved.

The sleek 1954 British Racing Green XK120 rag-top Jaguar pulled to a stop in the drive and Malo stood enraptured, listening to the gentle tick of its cooling engine long after Amber turned off the ignition. She pushed her oversize dark glasses above her forehead and grinned up at him.

"Are we welcome or are we not? And don't you just adore my lovely motor car?"

Malo remained speechless until he managed to rouse from his awe and call out.

"Isobel, Come here and meet our guests."

Isobel appeared at the door and stopped, amazed, on the porch. "My goodness!" She came down and rested a gentle hand on the tan leather upholstery at the open window. "Amber, I thought you'd be in a leg cast? Did you drive all the way?"

"No, I allowed dear Latham to navigate the turnpikes. But only because of my condition," she frowned. "I usually don't trust anyone behind my wheel." She patted the burled wood dash. "I don't regret my indulgence as this beauty is, so far, my only major extravagance."

Malo silently calculated, from the advertisements he had fancied in antique car journals, that her indulgence was major indeed. About one-twenty-five K, he guessed. And if I am very nice to this odd woman, he thought, maybe she'll let me take it for a drive.

"But your ankle," said Isobel, "I imagined you would be more immobile."

"Actually," said Amber, "I saw the doc before we left and he said it had healed much faster than expected and strapped it into this canvas zip wrap contraption. Don't you find that medicine has much improved its doodads since we lugged around those cumbersome plaster casts? When the ankle swells and gets painful in the evening, I loosen the wrap, take a few tokes of my medicinal MJ before bed and sleep like a baby." She frowned. "You don't have a problem with that do you?" She gestured around her. "I'll just slip out into the woods and let the puffs dissipate among these pines."

"No, definitely not an issue with us," said Malo, still dazed by the patina of the motor's wax finish. "Let me bring your bags in and then I suggest we leave the Jag down in the boat barn." He had to fight the urge to caress the machine's glossy bonnet. He nodded over at

Isobel's mud splashed car. "Maine's spring weather can be unpredictably harsh."

Before they went inside, Malo eyed the horizon and rubbed his palms together. "As you can see, the sun's dropped over the yardarm, and fortunately, only the more classy, yachtier parts of America place limits on cocktail time."

"Good God," said Latham. "There is never any good reason to delay drinking. I just hope you some decent olives as I brought us a gallon of excellent Dutch gin." He held up a heavy carrier bag. "I guarantee we'll finish this off as dear Amber has quite a tale to tell."

Pleasantly numbed by Latham's excellent martinis and followed by a dinner of Isobel's *coq au vin* they relaxed in the living room's flickering shadows, lit only by the fire's dying remains.

Earlier, alone in the kitchen while clearing plates, Malo and Isobel hoped that neither docent was involved in the missing ring situation. Instead of the awkward houseguests they had dreaded having to entertain for the weekend, Amber and Latham were entertaining them.

Isobel was relieved to see Amber maneuver briskly with the aid of two elaborately carved canes. After dinner, the docent declared she was feeling no pain and, if they were ready, eager to begin her tale before leaving to sneak into the woods for her 'sleep aid'.

Latham shook back a gold linked cuff and peered at his watch. "That is, if you're not too tired after cooking and serving us that marvelous meal?"

"Not at all," Malo and Isobel denied in unison; laughing in embarrassment at their enthusiasm.

"In fact," said Isobel, "we may find Amber's story more pertinent than you think. Help us solve some disturbing problems." She saw Amber's quick glance at Latham and wondered if Malo had also caught their silent exchange.

"To begin with," said Latham, "Amber's discovery first caught our interest because of my passion for vintage photography. Rather like her fondness for fancy motor cars." He arched a brow. "And I must confess that, what with outfitting the darkroom and price of equipment involved, my own little hobby has become an expensive indulgence. Over the years, I have collected some rare old cameras and now manage a small private gallery in downtown Newport specializing in late nineteenth century photography. I brought you a copy of the photograph of the young lady who caught your interest the day you visited the society." He opened the string tied portfolio on the table before them and gently removed the reproduction from between its tissue cover sheets. Latham angled it toward her and Isobel bent over the scene.

"This was taken mid-century at a garden party opening at Marble House. We couldn't remove the original photo, as Amber said, being the property of the Society. As you can see, these nouveau millionaires found their high jinks vastly entertaining. Unfortunately, many of those tax-free idle rich were a wildly irresponsible lot with way too much money to indulge in their self-amusements. This was taken to celebrate one of their notorious gala events," he said, "and typical of their summer extravaganzas. From the date on the back, I found Mrs. Vanderbilt had hosted this fete and the picture taken by one of the photographers hired for the party. He was an apprentice of Voigtländer—the man who, along with Zeiss, became famous for his lenses and one of the best camera makers ever." Latham paused after his speech and blushed. "I am lucky to own one."

Amber burst in. "Talk about an expensive indulgence!" Unable to curb her excitement, she pointed to the woman in the photograph. "However, we must forgive him because we think the young lady in Latham's photo, taken by this gent Voightländer, is wearing that piece of jewelry you found so disturbing." Amber touched a red lacquered nail to the woman's forehead sporting an ostrich plumed headache band and giggled. "Now that's a fashion accessory I particularly admire."

Isobel imagined that, if anyone, Amber could carry off the dated headpiece with style.

"Get on with it dearie," Latham said, "before these people fall asleep."

Isobel was not about to fall asleep and chafed with impatience while Latham settled Amber's ankle on a cushioned footstool and nestled her into the cushions.

"Now, my dears," she began, "for the story behind the photograph, let me transport you back to Newport's Gilded Age." With dramatic gestures and diction, Amber evoked the mid-nineteenth century with all its lavish conspicuous consumption and squandered tax-free fortunes. This woman's family," she indicated the picture, "had acquired as much cash and material pomp as possible, and decides to add a little flair to the family line by mating the daughter with some European royalty."

Latham leaned toward the hearth and from Malo's decanter of warmed VSOP, replenished their snifters.

"Believe me," he said, "at that time there were plenty of impoverished titled families abroad with cash poor scions just waiting for the likes of an American heiress. Dog faced or presentable." Both Amber and Isobel winced. "Sorry ladies," he apologized, "blame the brandy." He raised his glass. "No sexist offence meant to either of you beauties. Get on with the story Amber."

"That poor girl," she continued, "and I stress *poor* only because she had the misfortune of being under the thumb of an overly ambitious mother. As you can see, the young woman in the photo was more than attractive; she was a beauty who could have married any of the rich Americans intent on courting her. But like Austen's Mrs. Bennet, this zealous mother dearest played the society game typical of that time, and set her eye on an English lord for her only daughter."

"Unfortunately," interrupted Latham, "Dear mother made a bad choice and picked a royal loser. The chosen peer appeared publically charming but seen more often as a mean womanizer, years her senior, with a reputation for fortune-destroying gambling."

"However," Amber raised a finger, "the daughter inherited her mother's iron will and, with romantic intentions of her own, proved a match for her mother. She had fallen in love with a decent American fellow, not lacking for cash himself. Gossip raged when the daughter threatened to elope and mother locked her in her room with a guard at the door."

"Good grief," said Isobel. "It sounds right out of an atrocious Victorian novel."

"Believe me, it gets worse," said Latham. "When her daughter resisted the English prince and insisted on wedding her American lover, mother considered having him murdered."

Malo gave Isobel a wicked smile. "And we thought the Mafia devious. So what happened?"

"Your word devious applies," said Amber. "Fortunately talked out of homicide, mother conceived other tricks. She suddenly fell 'deathbed ill.' The laudanum-assisted acting she portrayed was so real that the frightened daughter succumbed to mother's apparent last wish. Months of planning followed and the lavish transoceanic wedding arrangements were said to rival those of any genuine princess."

Latham bent towards them. "And then, guess what?"

Isobel raised an eye. "I bet that mother made a miraculous recovery and rose from her deathbed in time for the ceremony."

"Exactly."

"But where does the ring fit in?" she asked.

"Ah, that's where the story turns tragic. The ring on the girl's hand in that picture is the engagement diamond, passed down the matriarch line, his lordship, the cad, managed to salvage from the remains of his family's fortune. Not a huge stone, but of excellent quality and mounted in that unusual setting."

Isobel barely contained her curiosity. "This diamond ring," she asked warily. "What happened to it?"

"Yes, well that's where the sordid part of the story begins," said Amber. Malo yawned audibly and Isobel glared at him. Amber suddenly grimaced and sat up. She lowered her leg to the rug and, testing its weight on the injured ankle, gave a yelp of pain.

"Oh dear, I'm afraid I've run out of steam. Can we finish the tale in the morning? I think it's time to slip out for my nighty-night puff on the porch."

THIRTY-ONE

Through a long restless night, Isobel's dreams troubled her and she swam towards morning through a warm and murky ocean. Long streams of hair wound languidly in the currents surrounding her body. Blinded by its coils across her face, she brushed too close to a coral wall and felt a thick strand catch in a crevice. She fought to pull free and swim to the surface, but the more she struggled to escape, the tighter the shroud of hair held her trapped. Drowning, gasping for air and finally unable to breathe, a hand grasped her shoulder.

"Isobel! Wake up." She tried to cry out but, in that way of nightmares, her throat closed and rendered her mute. She wrestled for her life against the arms trying to suffocate her but with no more strength, fell limp and collapsed.

Isobel remembered the bird in her pocket as Malo cradled her against him to quiet her panic.

"Shh, shh," he hushed in her ear. As Isobel's gasps subsided, he gently sat and rocked her until she came fully awake.

"I'm sorry," she whispered against his chest. "What a horrible nightmare." She pulled away and ran her hands through her hair, reassured by its familiar short bob. "Did I wake our guests?"

They listened, but there was no sound from the downstairs guest room. The pre-dawn house remained quiet except for the clank and hiss of steam awakening the iron radiators. Despite everyone's fuel-efficient suggestions on ways to modernize the cottage heating system, Isobel considered them charming eyesores and, as long as they functioned well enough to heat the barn of the place, insisted they stay. There was no returning to sleep, so she dressed and headed downstairs to start breakfast.

The aromas of waffles and frying sausages brought Malo, followed by the thunk of Amber's cane along the hallway, into the kitchen. They entered the warm room, kept heated in winter by the wood-stoked end burner, and Isobel noted Malo's eyes surveying the ruffled neckline of their guest's generous bosom thrusting above her negligee. They had agreed, at that first meeting in Newport that Amber, as well as her name, admirably fit the criteria for the cover of a lusty bodice ripper romance. Definitely a full-bodied woman.

"Sit," said Isobel, indicating the seat across from Malo. "Help yourself." She had set the table with a carafe of coffee, a bowl of fruit and large pitcher of fresh orange juice. "Sleep okay?"

"Like a baby," said Amber. "And the ankle feels much better, thank you. Latham's on his way and does he love real waffles! Not those packaged frozen ones with those fruit specks that are probably dead flies."

Latham entered the kitchen wearing a checked lumberjack shirt tucked into well-worn jeans and a rawhide belt sporting an ornate silver buckle. His appearance suggested a Ralph Lauren photo op, and completely transformed him from his dapper, pin-striped, pocket-square image.

"Dude," said Amber, peeling a banana, "you are indeed a country macho vision this morning."

When he saw the breakfast Isobel had made, he smiled and pointed to the jug of maple syrup warming on the end burner. "By the time I finish off yet another excellent meal," he announced, "I'll be fit to restock your woodpile." He rubbed his hands together. "You wait and see. I'm a demon with an axe and chainsaw."

Malo poured himself more coffee and shook his head. "You put me to shame," he said to Latham, "but I'll take my wood delivered and stacked in neat cords—by someone else."

By the time they finished breakfast, the sun had risen above the ocean, but masked fog-paled and cool. Out on the deck, the chairs were beaded with moisture. Too early in the season, they decided, to drink their morning coffee outside.

"Latham, please feel free to attack the woodpile," said Isobel. We stack it below under the porch overhang. "Work up an appetite as later we're going over for a lobster roll lunch at the dock pound. Malo can stoke up the fire in the living room while I clean up. Then Amber, I insist you continue last night's cliffhanger."

Their guest's polite offers to help with cleanup were refused. Malo rekindled last night's fire and, when Isobel came in from the kitchen, she helped Amber settle her well-upholstered self on the sofa with the strapped ankle cushioned on pillows. Amber pulled an odd square of knitting from a carpetbag the size of an elephant's privates and Isobel waited patiently while she counted stitches.

"What are you making?" she asked, watching her guest's needles click rapidly across a multi-striped piece that was too small for a blanket and too big for a quilting patch. Amber held up the work and dangled the bobbins that held the wool making up the pattern.

"Potholders," the docent declared.

Isobel could not think of a polite reply. "How nice," was all she managed.

"Buy some cheap wool," explained Amber, "knit up some foot size squares, throw them in hot water and they felt up to just the right size and weight. They're all I have enough attention for. Never could decipher patterns with sleeves and necklines. Within these squares, little mistakes don't matter. I also do scarves. But for those I use good wool and just knit away, back and forth, until it's long enough or I get bored."

The fire sent out welcome heat and with the background click of her needles, Amber returned them to Newport and the cursed diamond ring.

"The extravagant wedding arranged to be held at Vanderbilt's Marble House, went off with grand society pomp on a lovely summer afternoon. Except for the miserable bride, the affair proceeded just as her mother had planned during the months she lay on her faux deathbed surrounded by a retinue of social advisors. The day of the nuptials, the stoic bride and her groom were curiously watched by Newport's 'four hundred'—the precious number of guests able to fit in the ballroom—and most of those invited were well aware of the production's elaborate behind-scenes machinations. To her mother's relief, and the couple's credit, they managed an adequate display of affection during the reception following the ceremony."

"The bride and groom, along with their retinue, were photographed under showers of rice and confetti and left by steamship the next day—luckily not one of that era destined for disaster—and spent the months of their honeymoon traveling the capitals of Europe. At mother's expense, of course."

"History destined that trouble waited in the wind and, with the pall of war brewing over Europe, the marriage did not go well for the couple when they returned to America in late fall. While they were gone, Mother had redecorated a wing of the mansion for them including, with unlikely expectations, a nursery. During the following months and through the winter holidays, not-too-subtle rumors circulated among their clique over the new husband's wandering attentions. By the New Year, the bride's friends made it known to her that he had renewed his reputation as a gambling philanderer. Even with her mother's strict reins on the family purse, he managed to incur debts too embarrassing to ignore."

Amber shifted her leg on the cushions and continued her story. "For his bride, wearing the wedding band was offensive enough, but the elaborate engagement diamond became a constant reminder of his infidelities and, when possible to appear without it, she would toss it into her vanity drawer. Rumor had it that the final straw came when she returned home early from some errand and, horrified, found her maid, reputed to be her husband's latest and most convenient dalliance, posing in her mistress's gowns before the wardrobe mirrors. Draped over the bed and chaise, were designer ball gowns, negligees, and sets of her most intimate garments. When the wife entered the dressing room, the maid froze, mid-posture, before the full-length glass. The vanity drawers gaped open and when the girl's hand flew to her mouth, it displayed the hated engagement ring. The maid wrenched the ring from her finger and tossed it on the floor. Servants said they watched in awed amusement as, dressed only in her shift, the girl fled screaming through the house. She was never heard from again."

Malo rested his arms on his thighs and pressed his palms together. "Amber, some of these dramatics must rely on conjecture. Where did you find this account?"

Amber chucked her knitting aside. "Actually, I've romanticized some," she admitted. "It's my nature to improve on the truth, but the story is basically as I've recounted from reading her diaries."

"Believe us," added Latham, "ladies of that day kept private diaries and when unearthed, forged the scandals of an era that were as thoroughly chronicled as today's. Juicy gossip recounting celebrity misfortune never lacks for publicity and as popular then as the headlines emblazoned across our modern tabloids. Illicit sex and lost fortunes will always sell papers. The more lurid the better."

"Too true," said Amber. "But as far as our lady of the ring, she finally decided she had enough public humiliation. By now, even her mother, embarrassed by the nasty gossip among their society, sympathized and agreed to weather the disgrace of divorce."

"Off with the peer!" announced Latham.

"My God," said Isobel. "Then what?"

"Actually," said Amber," things improved. But only for the lady. No such luck for the odious cad." Amber tightened the straps of her ankle wrap and tested her foot on the floor. She winced as it took her weight. "Maybe time for a morning puff?"

"Better not." Latham checked his watch. "It's a little early. Let me fetch you one of your tranquility pills." He left the room.

"Tranquility pill?" asked Malo.

"Vicodin," she answered.

A toke of marijuana or the more potent narcotic? Did it matter? Malo wondered. He had seen lethal results from abuse of both drugs during in his regrettable past. Amber didn't look the type to succumb to addiction.

Latham returned and doled out a small white tablet that Amber washed down with the dregs of her coffee.

"During this time," she resumed her story, "the American who remained her true love patiently waited out the scandalous year of her marriage. His fortitude convinced mother of his decency plus the fact of his substantial fortune—his family had the foresight to invest in these promising new railroads—made her concede defeat. After the divorce and the dust of scandal settled, he gallantly rescued her from the sordid affair and they were married in a quiet civil ceremony."

Latham snapped his fingers and finished Amber's tale. "And they lived happily ever after." Isobel formed a church and steeple with her fingers, turned them inside out, and wiggled their tips.

"Just too romantic to be true," she said.

"I didn't bring copies of the society papers that chronicled it all, but they remain on record," said Latham. "Despite the couple's attempt at privacy, the fairy-tale ending to their saga, the gossip surrounding the lovers was as relentlessly covered by those day's paparazzi as the lurid details of her first marriage. It seems the tabloids can manage to appreciate a rare break from their usual reams of prurient journalism to report a happy happy. Especially one involving Newport's whacky society folk and an honestly made fortune."

"I'm glad it worked out for the lady," said Isobel.

Amber nodded her approval. "All along that girl held my sympathy for having the gumption to survive her iron maiden parent. One forgets how few rights and what little power women had during that century. Men reigned over all aspects of their lives." She held up a fist. "Until they began to rebel. I've seen pictures at the Historical Society of those stalwart Newport women who managed to keep their huge fortunes out of their husband's hands. They were some of the first to march the streets as staunch suffragettes. Even the *grand dame* Consuelo Vanderbilt, probably out of boredom, paraded for the Women's Movement."

Isobel caught Malo's eye and wondered if he too questioned the final destiny of the missing piece of jewelry. Was it really the same ring she'd found washed up on the beach in Newport? Along with Amber's report of its early history and the setting's unusual design, she thought it must be. So who stole it and where was it now? Too many unanswered questions.

"You said her first husband, the odious peer, didn't fare as well? Did the press keep track of him too?" she asked.

"They did, and his story resembles an even worse novel," said Amber. "As so often in real life, his final days were more brutal than any fiction. The unfortunate—apt word that—man got what he deserved and ended up possessing nothing but his mangy title and the rejected ring he rescued from the marriage floor."

Isobel smiled.

"It sounds like our cad, love that word, it so suits the time, had the sense not to gamble it away," said Amber. "He must have recognized his fragile future and managed to save it as collateral. Accounts report that the decline in his health began earlier with bouts of 'consumption' he contracted during his years at university and, coupled with a lifetime of debilitating habits, now recurred more frequent and severe. He continued to seek women with money, but they wisely avoided his attentions and, with no friends left willing to tolerate his sponging, drifted further into beggary. By his fifties, photos caught him looking twenty years older and reduced to living in a seamen's hotel. It's rumored this waterfront hostel discreetly functioned as a brothel and he made arrangements with its manager, aka Madam, to look after him. During his last days he got sicker and weaker and they drank together, gambled for pennies and, when he could no longer leave his bed, she fed him what little he could swallow. In return for her nursing, he signed papers promising her possession of the ring when he died."

Amber sank back against the cushions and Isobel saw her eyes soften as the narcotic took effect. She couldn't bear it if the woman dozed off. She had to hear how the hand with its ring managed to end up on that Newport Beach. She turned to Latham.

"So the story ends in a harbor-front brothel?" Latham winked at her and grinned.

"Not exactly," he said. "And the papers never referred to the place as a brothel. Prudent journalism even by those day's tabloids. These residential hotels, as we call them, still exist in most seaside towns, convenient to transient freighter crews and dockworkers. Most of them operate as legitimate wharf side taverns and rooming houses. Our Newport Madam became more respectable over the years and lived well—in all senses of the word—into her nineties. They say she never took the ring off and insisted on being buried with it on her finger." Isobel started to protest but Latham held up his hand.

"Wait, there's another chapter to this drama—the final act. It seems that when the mortician came to spruce up the old lady's body for burial, he found the ring missing. Fortunately, the funeral home had an honest reputation and quickly exonerated from any suspicion of theft. The police correctly suspected that one of Madam's employees—personal companion, escort, or whatever they call them now—had stolen it. It seems the stupid whore thought it was just a fancy piece of costume jewelry. Too gaudy to suspect its real value. That's when the case got even uglier and the greedy thief unlucky. One night, about a year ago, he pulled a knife on the woman he'd chosen as his evening's companion and, despite her protest that the ring was only costume jewelry, he must have threatened to kill her when she stupidly refused his demand to give it up.

One of the victim's friends told the police the sailor had arrived drunk and gotten rough. But she said the couple did not make enough noise to cause her to interfere. As in most of these establishments, the working girls look after each other. When questioned by the police, she told then he must have tried to wrench the ring off but, because of her friend's severe rheumatism, didn't take time to soap the swollen finger and couldn't get it over the enlarged joint. The next morning they entered the room and found the girl lying in a pool of blood—her hand severed at the wrist."

THIRTY-TWO

Isobel calculated the time line in her head.

"So the handless body ended up in Newport Harbor not that long ago. Over a hundred years after the story began."

"Then the murder occurred less than a year ago," said Latham. "However, the police reported that although the woman's mutilated body was washed ashore and identified by her friend, neither the hand or ring was recovered." Malo regarded his shoes and shook his head. Isobel refused to look at any of them.

"The history of this Newport ring sounds like one of those tales of curses attached to some of the more famous stones," she said. "Look at the misfortunes reputed to have struck down their owners with violent disasters and debilitating illnesses." Malo looked unconvinced.

"Don't you wonder if those stories of cursed stones were only self fulfilling prophecies?" he asked. "More likely a series of unfortunate accidents, even death wishes—if you believe in them? Queen Victoria owned the Koh-i-Nor—the famous Mountain of Light—and lived a long and fulfilling life. Maybe our thief decided his chances of being caught disposing of a severed hand and being linked to the body that might soon be washed ashore not be worth the risk? Especially if authorities identified the ring by its unusual setting when he tried to sell it? If the police connected him to the murdered girl he'd been seen with that night, he'd be questioned as the most logical suspect. If the fellow had any sense, he'd decide it not worth the chance of spending his life in prison for a piece of costume jewelry. He'd be safer if he tossed it into the harbor. The same as he'd done with the body of the cheap little tart from whom he stolen it."

Isobel had to agree. It made sense. Malo stretched.

"I'm in need of a walk," he announced. Amber had dozed off, snoring lightly, and Isobel covered her with a soft throw from the back of the couch. Latham stood up and flexed his arms.

"Enough old history, he announced. "We all need some fresh air and exercise. Malo, show me that woodpile."

After the men went outside, Isobel checked that Amber still slept and left her snoring softly. Unlike Latham, she had not had enough old history. She climbed the stairs to her bedroom and, seated at her desk in the alcove overlooking the ocean, selected a blue five by eight index card from the stack in her file box. Isobel's motto when she needed to organize her thoughts: make a list.

She tapped her pen against her teeth and began her outline:

1. Where is the ring?
2. Who could have taken it?

Isobel stared out the window as if the ruffled waters of the harbor could provide answers. She frowned at the card in front of her. Her jottings looked like notes for an early Nancy Drew. "The Case of the Missing Ring." But she was not Carolyn Keene and lacked even a single clue. Much less a frock or a snappy blue roadster.

"Stop," she spoke aloud and threw down the pen. At least the nagging truth that the hand she had found could not have remained intact washing around in the sea for a hundred years. She didn't need a medical degree to know that those bones, unless encased in artic ice, would have long ago disintegrated.

The docents' story and its time line now made her find on the beach possible. Isobel studied her meager entry. Where was the thief who had so easily found her cottage, entered and known where to find the ring without disturbing anything? Her mind remained blank. Good old Nancy had her pal Georgie and that docile boyfriend Ned. Maybe she needed Malo to play the 'what if' game. He would help her decide if the time had come to take Amber and Latham into their confidence. The docents had proven a clever pair and unearthed all that century old gossip. She weighed her chin in her hand. Could their arrival here the day after the robbery be a bit too suspicious?

Isobel had no reason to doubt their story and, as Latham said, the facts could be checked. To contrive all that evidence would take time and mastermind plotting. If the stone was real and the girl who stole it from the old Madam murdered, had the pair come to prove her guilty of theft? Could Isobel risk that the docents might report her to the Newport police when they found she had kept it? They had known the docents only a few days and intuition told her not to worry. Remembering her guest's nighttime tokes, a serious flaunting of the law, neither Amber nor Latham seemed concerned with legalities.

And legally, who was the ring's rightful owner? This called for a new list. She selected a yellow card.

1. The name of the dead Madam?
   a. Her heirs, if any?

2. The peer's English family?
   a. Must the ring be returned to original owners?

3. The bride as owner? (cannot imagine she'd want anything to do with it)
4. Isobel.
   a. Owner by right of salvage?
   b. Check out the law.

She stared at the outline on the yellow card and decided the only thing useful about it was that her high school English teacher might have approved. She tossed it aside and tapped her fingers on the desktop, impatient at having accomplished absolutely nothing. What did it matter. The ring was gone.

THIRTY-THREE

Malo knocked on Isobel's door, pushed it open and slumped, sweaty and red in the face, into the rocking chair beside her desk.

"You look exhausted," she said, alarmed at his high color.

"When do you think they will leave?" He raised his arms then dropped them in mock despair. "That Latham is way too full of energy for his age. I thought I was fit, but could barely keep up with the splitting and loading the damn logs into the wheelbarrow as fast as he sawed them into lengths."

"You are fit," she assured him. "Go take a shower. It's past noon and, when you've cooled down and rested, we can take them over to the Dock and feed them one of Sue's lobster rolls. A cold beer, a basket of her crispy *pommes frites?* After we have sated them with all that salt and cholesterol ambrosia, I suggest we tell them about the theft of my package and ask for their help." She retrieved the yellow card from the floor and handed to him. "I thought we might call it 'The Case of the Severed Hand'." He looked at the index card and made a piteous sound. She bit her lip. "As you can see, I am out of ideas.

Our guests are smart, if eccentric characters and, if I remember, Amber actually quoted the great one. I saw a light come into her eye as she said: 'The games afoot'."

Malo stared at her as if she'd gone mad. Perhaps she had.

"I'm sorry," she held up her palms, "but I'm afraid this entire business is driving me crazy."

"Isobel, I'm going to ask Amber to give you a couple of her tranquility pills. There has been no let up of disasters since we left Newport." He examined her outline and shook his head. "I understand how lists help you feel organized, but I think the first thing to do is track down whoever broke in to your cottage and stole the ring. Without any evidence to support a break-in," he said, sailing her outline into the wastebasket, "none of this matters."

"Actually, that might not be so hard," said Isobel. "People in a village this small notice strangers, and especially this time of year when the town is empty of summer people. It's worth asking around. A local would notice a new face wandering around town. There is only one restaurant open during the winter and it keeps fishermen's hours—six to six. Jen's B and B down in Martinsville is the nearest place to spend the night."

The best person to ask about strangers is Doris over at the post office. She would be curious—actually much too curious—as to why I sent a package to myself. I think some of us wonder if our dear postmistress steams open folk's mail. Doris is a well-meaning soul and fount of kindness, but sometimes, the woman knows everyone's business before they do. If our thief chose to hang around outside the post office watching for the person who picked up my package . . ." Malo finished her thought.

"Then he could have followed Jo down here and broken in after she left." Isobel got to her feet.

"I'll go clean up in the kitchen. You rouse Amber and see if she's up for a drive over to Sue's. The post office closes from twelve to two year 'round. We can drop in and have a chat with Doris after lunch." Malo perked up.

"Maybe Amber will let me drive us over in her car?" When Isobel pointed out there was no room in the Jag for four people, he looked wistfully down at the boathouse garage and agreed.

At noon, they turned off the main road through town and drove down the lane to Sue's Dock. Isobel was disappointed to see no red and white lobster flag hanging outside the entrance.

"She's closed. I can't believe it," said Malo. "I had my heart set on one of her lemon butter lobster rolls."

"Well I can," said Isobel. "Summer's a long way off. It's still too cold to eat outside on the deck. She keeps the fuel pumps open all year to sell diesel to local lobster boats and the occasional paid boat movers. The pound fish tanks operate, but it's too early in the season to open the kitchen." She spoke over her shoulder to the docents. "I see lights on upstairs. Wait here in the car. Sue lives all year over the restaurant and she's an old friend. If she's home, I bet she'll come down and steam us some lunch. It's not fancy inside, not a real restaurant, just bench tables, but there's a huge wood stove that heats the place. It won't hurt to try, and I'd rather pick up a pizza or crab rolls at Denise's and go back and eat at home than drive a half hour into Rockland."

They waited in the car while Isobel knocked at the storm door. She pressed her cheek to its glass panel and saw lights on above the fish tanks in the main room downstairs. She stood back and peered up at the second floor windows. A curtain flipped aside and Sue's face broke into a grin when she recognized Isobel. The bottom half of the casement screeched up and Sue's head poked out.

"Deah, I didn't know you were back," she shouted. "Wait, I'll be down in a sec. Door's open. Come on in and we'll catch up. You home to stay for a while? News around town says you've been up to more crazy travels. Isobel, how is it you attract trouble as easy as a fly tempts a spider?" Above her, the panes rattled loose in their mullions as Sue let the frame drop onto the sill.

Within minutes they were seated around the old iron stove holding their hands out to the warmth of the end burner. Isobel introduced her houseguests, and watched as Sue took in Amber and Latham. She raised her eyebrows that exactly matched the ginger halo of hair. Isobel guessed she was not used to folks more exotic than herself.

At the end of the room, the lobster tanks bubbled oxygen into the water and they watched them inside through glass walls. The critters either huddled in somnolent piles or crawled around and over themselves. Isobel found that staring at captive live lobsters with their beady bug eyes and feelers waving at her, like a hypnotist's swinging pendent, had a soothing, mesmerizing effect. Sue's voice jolted her back to attention.

"Glad you all came by. Too early and not worth opening the kitchen shack for retail business 'til the lobstermen start running their lines," Sue said. "I keep some live critters ready for the locals and keep the stove and sinks going all year for my own heating and cooking. It won't take but a minute to get the pot steaming and fix us some lunch. Isobel, you can melt up some butter and squeeze in some lemons." She nodded at Malo. "No fuss, simple, and, if I remember, the way you like 'em. I brought back slaw salad and a package of soft split rolls from last night's potluck supper down at the Grange Hall." She patted Isobel's arm, "and no one got poisoned this time." She laughed, referring to the fateful dinner two years ago. "None of that deadly aconite salad on the menu." She pointed to the counter sideboard. "Help yourself. There's beer or soda in the fridge and hot coffee and kettle of water ready for tea on the stove."

Amber stamped her cane on the floorboards and emitted a groan of pleasure.

"Sounds excellent," said Latham. He followed Sue to a wooden table in front of the windows overlooking the dock and helped her cover it with a layer of newspaper.

"It's the easiest way to enjoy this delicious but messy meal," she explained. At each setting she placed an absorbent tea towel and beside it, a hefty stone from a pile the children had collected from the beach. While the lobsters steamed, Sue poked through the refrigerator and found a bowl of cabbage, apple and carrot slaw. She warmed the rolls on the end burner while Malo flipped the wire cap corking a stone bottle of the local brewed beer.

The weathered walls of the fish house remained bare framed as the day it was built and offered no lures to summer tourists. No painted buoys draped with netting or hokey fishing gear hung from the rafters. In fact, to Latham's delight, between the studs, he saw that the walls were covered with faded, water spotted photographs.

On the drive into town, they had driven past the town graveyard leading down to the ocean. An acre or more of rough mowed grass sprouted with tilted, lichen etched stones that remained tenderly cared for by generations of their families.

Isobel averted her eyes as Sue plunged the lobsters head first into the boiling water. The scrabble of their claws against the side of the blue enamel pot and the hiss that she imagined as lobster death throes bothered her. She'd heard that lobster hugger cooks kept them in the freezer to anesthetize their sensibilities while the pot came to a boil. Sue obviously had no time for that nonsense.

While they drank beer and waited for the lobsters to redden, Latham got up to study the old photos tacked on the walls. Mottled, sepia tinted faces from the past of young and old, but all somber-faced fishermen, stared back at him. They stood along side or at the rail of their boats. Families of the village's workingmen and women; most of them long ago lost below the deep green fathoms of Penobscot Bay. Latham promised himself he'd return with his favorite camera before they left and spend time alone at the cemetery.

Malo carried the platters of steaming creatures to the table and they settled on the bench seats across from each other. Amber sat at the open end and Latham carefully propped her ankle on an empty lobster creel.

"First thing," insisted Sue, "everyone roll up your sleeves and take off your watches. Otherwise, you'll be sniffing at your wrist all next day."

"Second thing," added Isobel, "eating lobster is a serious operation. You can't dissect out every edible bit and talk at the same time." Quiet descended as Sue brought a hefty stone down on her lobster's large claw, crushing it just enough to pull the meat from its shell and dip the succulent morsel into her cup of lemon butter. She twisted the lobster's tail from its body and drained the water from the carapace into the bowl set in the center of the table. She carefully spooned out the green tomalley liver to savor along with the sweet knuckles of body meat picked out as a final treat.

Without talk, they set to work on their meal and when they had done it justice, including every sweet bite drawn with their teeth from the legs, Isobel looked across at Sue and spoke seriously.

"I have to confess that we've come for more than a social call and your delicious lunch. Malo and I need to ask your help with a little problem." Sue laughed.

"Well deah, why am I not surprised? From the sounds of it, you're recent exploits have turned Elmore Harbor into a regular Cabot Cove." Isobel appreciated the irony behind Sue's words. Since she began working for Malo, the harbor had witnessed more than its fair share of mayhem. Latham and Amber glanced across the table at each other, pushed back their plates, and wiped their glistening chins.

"So tell us what beside Sue's tasty lunch brought us here?" said Amber. Isobel's tea had gone cold but she drained her mug and began.

"The night we arrived home from Connecticut, I found I'd been robbed."

THIRTY-FOUR

"Robbed?" Sue looked shocked. "You're serious? Nothing like that has happened around here for ages. It's still too early for tourists, and it can't be any of our regular snowbirds. Those fragile souls that can't take our winter have only begun unfolding their tiny wings and flying home to open their cottages. Most every day now a few more arrive back."

"That's why I'm asking," said Isobel. "Have you seen or heard of some one you don't recognize hanging around town?" Sue ran her hand through her fiery frizz of hair.

"We're a small community," she answered thoughtfully, "and as you know, we tend to keep an eye on each other. More than necessary, sometimes. You can be sure a stranger in town, especially this time of year, would be noticed and talked about."

Latham fidgeted. "Ladies, enough about snowbirds and strangers, please Isobel, what was stolen?"

"And when did it happen?" asked Amber. Her eyes darkened. "You've not mentioned a word about this break in since we arrived, and my dear, how could you? You know by now that Latham and I adore solving mysteries. Who stole what from you and when?" She nudged Latham.

"Tell her. Are we not ready to help our new friends get on with the game?" Malo tried hard not to look at Isobel.

"It's a long story," Isobel said. "It started weeks ago and all because of my birthday escape." She rested her elbows on the table. "I refuse to call myself a snowbird, but this year I reached one of those nasty milestone anniversaries that felt more like a millstone. Apologies to Coleridge and his Mariner, but all of the sudden my age dragged me down like an albatross and I had to get away. I just couldn't bear another obligatory Van Dursan celebration." She saw concern on their faces and tried to explain.

"It's become one of those family rites that, on each of our birthdays, the Van Dursan clan feels obligated to gather around the fire pit on my lawn and celebrate. Summer occasions are fine, but on mine, usually a bitter February day, for some reason we obey the command to huddle bravely and pretend to enjoy ourselves until even the most stalwart are forced inside by the cold. Rescued by the warmth of my house, we endure the traditional buffet picnic. The extended dining room table is laden with all my daughter-in-law Raybelle's comfort foods dredged from her south of the Mason Dixon line roots. The quivering molded salads, pimento cheese dip, and bowls of odd pickled vegetables. Most of us avoid her cakes topped with rings of pineapple, their centers filled with maraschino cherries or those swathed in shredded coconut. Plates of fried okra, cheese grits, and those rock-hard beaten biscuits supporting pieces of salty cured ham. Oh yes, and least we forget, no lack of pecan pies. Not always a northern delight."

"Actually," said Sue, "By the end of summer, I don't want to cook another lobster and I'd take a piece of gooey pecan pie over blueberry anything." Isobel had to laugh.

"Good god," said Malo. "No wonder Raybelle's boys went west to become chefs."

"I'm sorry and I apologize," said Isobel. "My complaints over her menu were unfair. Raybelle's suppers are tasty and her traditional southern dishes as good as any fish chowder, but our family has expanded. These frequent birthdays, often fueled by too much Kentucky bourbon, have become the butt of mean jokes. I'll end my diatribe with the final straw that sent me to Newport this winter. After supper last year, with much clapping hoopla, they wheeled out my birthday cake. A thickly frosted chocolate red velvet layer cake lit with one tactful candle. No one remembers that I don't care for either cake or chocolate."

"Ungrateful woman," whispered Malo. "It sounds delicious." Isobel shrugged.

"Well, you've spoiled me with our taste of adventure and this year, on impulse, I just escaped. Deserted the whole crew and booked a suite at a faux Newport castle turned inn. The place is famous for its luxurious rooms and fine cuisine and I planned to indulge myself for an entire weekend. I wanted to start this next decade with a new tradition. Pamper myself, wherever I choose, in the style I now expect as a result of Malo's employ."

"Well deserved, my dear, and long may it continue."

"The day I arrived in Newport the weather turned mean, but not as cold as Maine, and my suite had a cozy gas fire that burned and flickered like virtual wood. All it lacked was a crackling sound track. By afternoon, the rain had stopped and I went out for a walk on the beach below the inn. I'd arrived too early in the year for tourists, or the sailor's influx of spring boat riggers, and I enjoyed my walk alone. When I was thoroughly soaked from sea spray, I turned back to the hotel. That's when I came upon a half-buried piece of salvage washed up by the storm." Isobel paused and saw Latham and Amber's exchanged glances. Both seemed to guess where her story was going.

"I did not want to waste my short vacation dealing with provenance issues, so back in my room, I wrapped my bizarre treasure in a hand towel and hid it away in the wardrobe. I was determined not to let it spoil my day. Later, downstairs over tea, I forced the find from my mind when the best of all birthday gifts arrived. Malo had tracked me down and flew from Europe to join me in Newport for the weekend." She nodded at the docents. "When I showed him my gift from the sea, he agreed that it might be valuable and I decided to mail it to myself here in the harbor so as not have to worry about it for the rest of the weekend.

That night we had a lovely dinner, no cake, and the next day rented a car and, on our sightseeing traipse around town, met you two at the Historical Society." Sue interrupted.

"Good grief Isobel. Provenance of what?" Malo said nothing. He got up and quietly collected the bowl of lobster shells to carry outside and toss over the railing. He was halfway across the room when a crashing knock pushed open the front door. Two fishermen, whom Isobel recognized as local EMT volunteers from the firehouse, burst into the room.

"Sue deah, sorry to bother you. We know you're off duty this weekend, but there's been an accident and we think there'd best be a woman to help." Sue immediately rose to her feet.

"Of course. What's happened? Who's hurt?"

"It's Anna's daughter, Jen. She's been attacked at her bed and breakfast down Martinsville way."

Isobel felt her stomach tighten. Anna, one of her oldest friends, had died after losing a long bout with emphysema. She and Sue had taken turns reading to her during those final days. They had sat beside the padded rocker where Anna's shrunken body remained a prisoner by the lifeline attached to her oxygen bottle. Isobel still regretted that, until her death, her friend had blamed herself for selling Isobel the dry ice that had nearly killed her.

Anna's two daughters—twins named Jen and Jan grew up as the town's classic example of good and evil. Jen, the sweet and popular sister, remained single, though not from lack of suitors. Everyone assumed her fierce distrust of men came from watching her father's callous treatment of their mother. After Anna died, Jen wasted little time before she turned their rambling old farmhouse into a successful bed and breakfast. She was a good cook and popular for serving guests a gut filling 'full English breakfast' that lasted the day. Jen's energy and good will were endless and she would literally give you the shirt off her back if you needed one.

Like Janus, the two faced god her sister Jan was born mean eyed and remained so. The two girls were identical at birth, but Jan, from childhood, set out to prove herself as opposite in temperament from her twin as possible. They had the same corn silk hair and azure eyes, but early on, Jan's prettiness became hard-edged and her sharp tongue too quick to cut. No one called her out right evil, but somehow when trouble occurred, folks found her either at its center or its cause.

The girl's father up and disappeared before their fifth birthday and left them nothing but a legacy of skimping.

For Anna, his memory recalled only pain. The years after he deserted them, she did her best to raise the girls alone, but she was as frail in spirit as in body and couldn't and didn't cope.

The twins were in their teens when their mother's lungs began to fail. Jen cared for her as best as she could but the day after they buried Anna, Jan packed a duffle and disappeared as fast as her father. Good riddance, friends muttered. However, like the proverbial black sheep and always unexpected, Jan would turn up on her sister's doorstep. Either she needed short-time shelter from some current nemesis or, with good reason, pleaded for a loan of cash.

Isobel pulled her thoughts from the past and introduced True Smith, the older EMT, who stood staring at Amber and Latham. He didn't offer to shake hands with them and she saw the relief in Amber's eyes stared back. Like Isobel, she too was repulsed by his veneer of body tattoos. Snakes and spiders covered his throat and descended below the neck of his shirt. In ten years, she thought he might regret that they resembled an advanced case of leprosy.

"Sorry to interrupt your lunch folks," apologized Carey, True's partner, crushing his cap in his hands. "Jen, down the road, was pretty viciously attacked and," he nodded at Isobel, "we heard you had come here for lunch." He cleared his throat nervously. "Her story seems to involve you." Sue grasped Careys's arm, her voice urgent.

"Please. What's happened?"

"She's okay. Tim, he's our postman," he explained to the docents, "had a delivery that Jen needed to sign on and recognized her SUV parked in the drive. When no one answered his knocking, he got upset. He tried the door and it opened and he went inside and hollered. No answer, but when he heard this thudding noise overhead, he hollered louder and hustled upstairs."

"The ruckus came from one of the second floor guest baths. Tim broke open the bathroom door and there sat Jen, huddled in the tub, hands tied to the handicap rail. Said her attacker left the shower doing a slow drip and enough slack in the line so she could reach her mouth to water. Tim said the piece of line he'd used to tie her wrists to the rail had one of those fancy knots only a sailor would know. He cut her free then called us down at the firehouse."

"When we got there, Jen was in the kind of state you'd expect. More embarrassed and angry than hurt. Told us she'd been tied up in the tub since Tuesday night. She'd had a big dinner and with plenty of water, three days without food wouldn't kill her." Carey pulled his Red Sox cap from his head and brushed his hand across its grimy brim.

"Tim waited there with her 'til we came," he said. "Made sure she was okay," he assured Sue. "Jen said the man had one of those stocking things pulled over his head with only slits cut for eyes. Never saw his face but says she'd know him again by his stocky size and cocky attitude. Said he talked like a flatlander." True spoke up. "She wouldn't let us take her into Pen-Bay for a check up. You know Jen; she's a pretty stubborn lady. Insisted the guy only slapped her about and, aside from some bruises, insisted there was nothing to check up."

"She won't budge from her house, but we both think it's a good idea if one of you ladies come down and spend the night with her," said True. "Despite all her protesting, she seemed kind'a shaky. We're pretty sure the man won't come back, probably got what he wanted from her, but we don't like leaving her alone. We thought right off to ask you. Being such good friends through her mother's lung sickness and all their family troubles."

"Why did this man attack her?" asked Sue. "You said he got what he wanted, but it's ridiculous that someone would break in to rob her. The place is a typical old Maine farmhouse. When she set up for business, she's fancied it up by building that cute chalet hen house and painted the horse barn. She made it nice and comfortable for guests. I've been inside and the bedrooms are big with none of those crochet doilies and pots of dried flowers—all that dresser top clutter people hate." Isobel spoke up.

"Every gardener in town is jealous of Jen's beautiful summer garden, but there is nothing valuable enough inside the place worth menacing her for." Both men shook their heads.

"He wasn't going to rob her," said True. "Jen told us he promised not to hurt her if she co-operated and insisted he only wanted information. Said he'd driven through the village and on down to the dead end at the Port Clyde ferry. This early in the year, all the galleries and shops are closed tighter than a nun's knees—pardon me ladies. Says he turned around and, driving back by her place into town, saw the light on over the vacancy sign. The trusting woman let him in before she realized that, his face down and hidden under his hoodie, he wore this stocking mask."

"She said he pushed her into a chair and right away started with the questions about Isobel. Did she know a Mrs. Isobel Van Dursan? That's all he wanted and promised to leave her unhurt if she'd tell him where you lived. Then he pulled out this wicked looking fishing knife and it frightened her so that she told him right off what he wanted. Said that after she gave him directions to your place, he grabbed her up, put the knife to her back, and forced her upstairs. In the bathroom, she was terrified he'd take her clothes off, maybe mess with her, you know?" True blushed and looked at his partner. "But he didn't. Only made her sit with her clothes on in the tub and tied her to the handicap rail. Jen broke down on us then, all her anger spent, so we made her tea and promised we'd bring someone back to stay with her the night. If you can't, we'll find someone else."

"I'm on my way." Sue turned to Isobel and her guests. "Can you cope with this mess for me?" She didn't need to ask. Amber apologized for her lack of mobility, but the others had already begun clearing away the remains of their lunch.

"We'll leave it ship-shape," promised Isobel. "And call me at home as soon as Jen's settled. I'm sorry it happened this way, but the man's attack on her clears up some questions about my own break in."

THIRTY-FIVE

Back at Isobel's cottage, Amber's patience gave out. She stomped around the living room with her cane while Malo attempted to revive the fire. Latham watched him prod at the embers without effect, then reached for the fire iron and arranged new logs gathered from his morning's efforts.

"May I?" he asked. The men stood back and watched the smoldering coals burst, with an explosion of sparks, into flames.

Amber settled herself on the couch.

"So, it seems," she said, "the masked bandit of Elmore Harbor then broke in to your house and made off with your mystery package. That's solved one part of the 'who' question. Now tell us what treasure is worth enough to cause this person to go to such trouble to retrieve it?" In a voice full of irony, she answered herself. "Can we assume the package contained the cursed ring you found on the beach? Now we understand why you were eager for our visit." She picked up her knitting and began casting on stitches. "Am I right?"

"Yes, "admitted Isobel. "The morning after we returned from Connecticut, your call asking for the weekend escape came as a gift."

They listened while Isobel told her story that began back in February with her walk on the Newport Beach and the discovery of the hand with its grizzly bonus. She told them briefly of their trip to Seattle and Tom's difficulties with the Chinese Mafia and the events that took them to Connecticut ending with their arrival in Maine and the vain search for the missing ring.

"Before calling the sheriff, I phoned Jo and she insisted she'd picked it up from the village Post Office, and adamant she'd left it in the drawer of the front hall desk. Jo is extremely levelheaded and, of course, she had left the ring in the desk. Someone broke in and took it." Malo turned from warming his backside before the fire. He faced Isobel and thrust his hands in his trouser pockets.

"Perhaps a lesson learned by leaving your house key above the front door and so convenient to thieves. Perhaps next time under the door mat or a flower pot?" She scowled at him.

"Well, at least admit that he didn't have to break any windows or smash down the door." Malo started to interrupt but, before he could get on with his righteousness, she changed the subject. "I hope you understand," she continued, "that before Amber and Latham arrived and told us the history behind that old photograph, I found it impossible to believe that those fragile bones holding the ring, survived their toss in the sea for over a century." Amber put down the growing knitted square. Her pain must have eased, as she no longer grimaced with each shift of her leg.

"It seems that our combined stories might explain the ring's journey so far," she said. "Our next step is to identify the man behind the stocking mask and find where he and the stone are now."

"I hate to dampen your reasoning," said Latham, "but don't you think it's time to decide whether or not to call in the authorities?" The fire popped and a green log hissed steam. Isobel looked at Malo and, as if reading her questioning eyes, shook his head. Perhaps they should wait before revealing their complicity.

"Ah, the authorities," said Amber. "You have gotten yourself into an interesting situation. Should you call your local sheriff and report a robbery from your cottage in the Harbor?" She cleared her throat and wiggled her fingers in an iffy gesture. "If so, I'd forget mentioning the bones and stick with the stolen ring. Or do you tell the whole truth and inform the Newport police of your discovery on the beach?" Isobel looked unhappy. "Because, if you call the Newport authorities," continued Amber, "there is the problem of explaining why you have waited almost two months to do so? It's a tricky ethical issue and a decision only you can make."

"Our difficulty exactly," said Malo. Isobel chewed at her lip.

"Whatever you decide," said Latham with a supportive pat on her knee, "we'll consider it none of our business." Amber nodded her agreement. Isobel looked relieved.

"I'd rather do a little more investigating on our own before getting entangled in any procedural red tape," she said. Malo sat back and crossed his arms.

"Unfortunately Isobel, whatever you decide, illegal meddling has never stopped you before."

"Ah, a woman after my own heart," said Amber, and resumed her knitting. Isobel looked at her watch. Already late afternoon and the light in the room had dimmed. She switched on the table lamp behind Amber and directed its light on the soft, azure piece of wool lengthening in her guest's lap. This was no potholder. At her questioning look, Amber said, "got bored with those dinky squares, decided to knit you a nice cashmere scarf. I find it a challenge to turn a piece of string into something useful." Isobel was touched and bent to feel the fleecy blue wool.

"Thank you so much. That's an expensive piece of string and you have chosen my favorite color." She wondered if most of the suitcase Amber brought had been filled with yarn. The light outside softened and Malo went to stand before the bay window overlooking the harbor. Fog rolled in, like waves over the ocean, and within minutes, everything beyond arm's length lay shrouded in a dense veil of grey. Since he'd arrived in Maine, Malo had been fascinated by its changes in weather. Every morning he tapped the glass front barometer and tuned in NOAA for the day's forecast.

"Unless he's gotten a good ways inland, our thief won't get far in this," he said. "At last check, the weather station reports that this system is stationary and the entire coast could be socked in for days."

The thief had not gotten anywhere. Not far down the road, he lay with his hands behind his head on the motel's mattress that had conformed to too many bodies and cursed the combination of bad luck and poor judgment that had stranded him in this backwater. By now, he and the diamond should have been back in Newport. He propped his head on one arm and sucked on his cigarette. The springs pinged when he moved, and he swore the mattress rested on wire coils.

He had not needed to close the window blind. The air outside hung a curtain of its own. He blew a stream of smoke toward the ceiling, angry at being more helpless to escape this place than from any doldrums he'd waited out on a ship at sea. The only sound came from the regular muffled moan of the Muscle Ridge foghorn and the distant clang of an offshore bell.

The smoke from his habit fouled the room but did little to defeat the pine-scented deodorizer. Its acrid reek had made his eyes water when he'd first turned the key and pushed open the door. He had seen that his car was the only one parked before the string of eight cottages and guessed that the I Pine For You Ocean View Motel now had seven vacancies. And with good reason. Maybe these cottages held some charm in summer, but on this dismal day the place seemed a dump. He smiled and mentally amended the down east rhyme its name brought to mind—'and you'll balsam too'. He had.

He brushed at and smeared the inch of ash that fell on his shirt. Naturally, there was no ashtray on the bedside table. He squinted up at the forty-watt reading light and swore. This cheap attempt at economy hotelkeepers use as an excuse for saving energy irritated him. Do they expect their guests to read in bed by Braille?

The bedsprings creaked as he hoisted up on one elbow and took out the ring from a concealed zip pocket inside his belt. He slid it on his pinkie finger and realized, when it stopped at his first knuckle, that it had been sized for a woman. When he'd first opened the package and saw the boney skeleton, he couldn't believe she'd kept the whole hand. After examining the gruesome thing for only a minute, he snapped the brittle bone and striped off the ring. He had pulled to a stop at the nearest dumpster and tossed in the disgusting bones along with its wrapping.

The stranger got up and went into the cubicle of a bathroom where he folded the ring in a tissue and tucked it back in his belt's zip pocket. As safe a hiding place as any while he waited out the weather. He reminded himself that, before leaving for Maine, he had signed on for six months as an engineer's mate aboard the tanker *Eastern Story*, due to leave Providence in two weeks. He resented the precious time wasted while stuck in this isolated harbor. He had to return to the city and turn the diamond into cash before he sailed.

His stomach growled and he shook out his last cigarette, crumpled the empty pack, and tossed it into the basket across the room. "Score!" he yelled with satisfaction as it landed dead center. Inhaling, he curbed his hunger by recalling the lunch in Newport where this treasure hunt began. Unlike this morning, hungry and mired by fog in this motel, he reflected on that sunny afternoon as one of fate's golden moments. That February day had brought him a stroke of luck. Later in the spring and jammed with tourists, he might not have been seated in the popular waterside fish house, but early in the year, it remained one of the good restaurants open. He'd eaten enough drive-thru junk food and felt he owed himself a decent meal. The pretty young waitress placed his lunch in front of him and, suddenly ravenous, he bent over his food and concentrated on stuffing himself. His belly satisfied, he sat back, took a long pull on his beer and pushed aside his plate. He needed to get outside for a cigarette and signaled the girl for the check. He stood up and about to leave when the conversation at the next table began to register. He slowly folded himself back into the booth, pretended to drink from his empty beer, and hunched forward to better focus on the couple's words.

He fought off his craving for nicotine and strained to overhear. At first, the woman's words made no sense. She and the attractive man opposite leaned toward each other across the table, absorbed by some argument over what to do with a diamond ring. He shifted slightly in his seat to listen more closely and what he heard intrigued him.

The couple's server had stood waiting nearby and when she handed them the bill, he saw the startled girl didn't believe it for one minute, when the woman smiled up at her and explained they were discussing the script for a screenplay.

Outside the fish house, he slowed his pace to let the couple he followed stroll ahead before stopping to light a cigarette. He carefully shielded his face with his palm. He had walked to the restaurant from his dockside rooming house and knew that if the pair he had overheard had come by car, there was no way to follow. He stopped to inhale a deep drag of smoke and saw they paid no attention to the non-descript seaman trailing behind. They entered the parking area along side the restaurant and he watched from the street as the gentleman bent to unlock the passenger door of the only car in the lot. Another bit of luck. This was no anonymous sedan.

He envied them the sleek foreign sports model and, though unable to guess its maker, recognized it as fast and expensive. He trusted his memory and etched the plate numbers into his brain, along with a mental photograph of the animal hood ornament and the swooping lines of its low-slung body. A custom car like that should be easy to trace. The door closed with an expensive thunk after he handed in the lady. The sailor envied the throaty roar of its mufflers as it moved through the gear changes and disappeared down the street. This machine was a rich man's toy and their discussion of diamonds he had overheard at lunch might likely be true.

That morning, he had signed on for six months at sea as a merchantman on a vessel leaving the Providence shipyards in three weeks. Being a curious fellow, he now intended to make good use of them.

THIRTY-SIX

His cottage rental at the *Pine Tree* had no phone but what did he expect for fifty bucks a night? He felt lucky that the landlady took pity on him and offered him a unit until the weather cleared. She'd explained that they only rented out the cottages during the summer as housekeeping units. They disconnected the phones and TVs in winter, but said he could use the office phone in an emergency. She stressed emergency, and handed him towels and a wafer of soap. The woman nattered on explaining how they don't drain the pipes in this one unit, and assured him he'd have plenty of heat and hot water.

Back in the room, he debated standing under a long, hot shower, but suddenly exhausted, dropped onto the bed and decided the effort to wash too much trouble. He curled on his side, pulled the thin spread to his chin, and let the moan of the foghorn lull him to sleep. An hour later, he awoke groggy and with a furry foul taste in his mouth. He sat up, pulled himself to his feet and went into the closet sized bathroom where he almost backed into the shower to close the door. His throat felt scratchy and his mean mood had made him ignore the 'no smoking' request propped on the dresser. Cancer? He made another useless resolution to quit, then decided why bother. He had no family. Not one person left who would know or care if he lived or died. Probably more likely to die from an accident at sea.

He brushed his teeth then returned to the room and sprawled on the rumpled bed. The only sound was the incessant, distant moan of the foghorn. His empty stomach rumbled again and he realized his diet of cigarettes and coffee was not doing the job. He needed a solid meal. A thick juicy burger and some greasy, salty fries. Okay, maybe a big green salad.

He shrugged on his jacket and trudged down the path to the owner's quarters. He knocked on the door with a sign that read office, but no one answered. He turned the knob and pushed the door open. Inside, a printed card on the reception counter instructed him to ring bell for service. He did and waited until the chatty old lady who had let him the room came through a door. His stomach rumbled again at the tempting smells she brought with her from the kitchen.

"Can I help you, young man, is everything okay?" She wiped her hands on her apron and he inhaled the spicy scents of curry and something Asian. These international aromas that wafted in with her appearance further fueled his hunger and tempted him to invite himself for dinner.

"Everything's fine," he assured her and felt even more guilty at ignoring the no-smoking request. He silently promised to air out his room before he left.

"I really need a hot meal," he said. For an unreal moment he hoped she might invite him to stay. Not a chance. "Is there anywhere to eat around here close enough to walk to? I'm from away, as you Mainer's say, and don't trust myself to drive in this fog."

"I understand. And young man, count yourself lucky to have gotten this far. We're used to whiteouts along this peninsula, but the roads are narrow and twisty and dangerous if you don't know the way. It may sound strange to city folk, but the safest thing is for you to leave your car here and follow the center road line into the village on foot." She gestured out the window at the impenetrable white mist. "Don't need to worry about traffic today. In less than a mile you'll come on the General Store. You can find almost anything you need there, including wine and beer. If you're hungry, Denise can nuke you up a pizza slice, or one of those frozen dinners, maybe heat up a bowl of her homemade soup." She folded her arms across her narrow chest.

"Or if you want and she's feeling friendly, she might ask her lazy, no-good son to drive you down to Jen's B and B, Martinsville way. The boy moonlights as a taxi hire and could drive you there blindfolded." She saw him flinch at the thought and raised her hands in apology. "Oh, he's not that bad," she assured, "but Jen's his cousin and a total opposite type of person." She lifted her brows, "lot's of close cousins around here. Jen's a good soul and even if you don't spend the night, she likes to cook and, being slow times, might make you a real meal." Then she frowned and pulled at the bib of her apron. "Though maybe not today. Jen's had a nasty spot of trouble and might not be up to guests."

He set out for the village center feeling like Dorothy heading toward Oz, except the road he followed was tar, not yellow brick. The manager of the Pine Scented motel was right about 'traffic'. Not one car passed him coming or going and, surrounded by dense, white mist, he kept placing one foot carefully in front of the other down the middle of the road and trusted that eventually he'd come upon this General Store. His major worry was not fog, but her mention of the bed and breakfast in Martinsville where he had set on the woman he now knew as the paragon of goodness, Jen. And why was he walking straight into the town that probably had a mounted vigilante in wait for him?

Hunger and his nicotine addiction drove him toward the disembodied lights of the storefront that suddenly loomed out of the fog. The jangle of bells, as he pushed open the door, startled the woman on the stool behind the checkout counter. She swung her legs to the floor and stood up in surprise.

"Well I never," she exclaimed. "You're the first person to come in today and a stranger at that. Where *did* you come from?" Then he saw her blush, regretting her rudeness. "No matter," she smiled, "how can I do you for?" He pulled off his cap.

"I'm stuck in the motel down the road, waiting out the fog, and the owner sent me here on foot. Actually followed the white line into town. I'm hungry and she said you have a microwave and might heat me up some kind of meal?"

"I think I can do that. What would you fancy?" The place smelled of cooking and she reeled off the options.

"Any or all of the above," he said. "I'm starving."

The woman laughed and went to the rear of the store where she set to work slicing him a large wedge of pizza and heating a bowl of ham and pea soup from an electric hotpot. He saw her look him over while she worked and decide he wasn't a threat. Despite the talk of Jen's attack by the stranger she didn't seem uneasy. Then he remembered the motel keeper's mention of her grown son upstairs and pictured some muscled gorilla clomping downstairs if she yelled for help. While she heated his dinner, he went to the cold case and chose a Bud from the shelf. He looked around for a place to sit but saw no chairs other than the stool behind the cash register.

"Is there somewhere I can sit and eat here? By the time I walk it back to the motel, it will be cold." She pointed at his beer and to the church key opener hanging by a string on the wall.

"In summer, folks eat at the picnic tables outside." She gestured out the window at the narrow platform overlooking the parking spaces. "Let's agree it's not the day for sitting out. If you don't mind, just go through that door there and bring in one of those plastic chairs from the stack." He did, and she carried a tray with his bowl of soup, a plate of pizza, and a handful of paper napkins to a place she had cleared at the front counter. He thanked her and ravenous, folded a wedge of hot cheesy pie into his mouth. It smelled of oregano, cheeses and tomatoes and tasted fresh made with none of the cardboard texture of frozen pizza. The soup was as good, with thick chunks of ham, but he paused with his spoon halfway to his mouth. Maybe he'd make a mistake in eating here. What if she got curious and started asking questions? If they got chatty, she might link him to the attacker down at the bed and breakfast where he'd demanded the Van Dursan woman's address. He'd been stupid to risk eating here in a small village like this. His stomach knotted. He had to get moving and take a chance driving in a whiteout.

"Heard any weather report as to when this fog might lift?" he asked. She shrugged. The bells above the door jangled as an attractive older woman entered the store. The storeowner held up her arms in recognition.

"Good afternoon, Denise," said the older woman.

"Isobel, I might have known you'd manage to get out. You're the second person today" she nodded at the stranger, "to cross my threshold. Practically a stampede." They laughed and Denise nodded toward the stranger who stood up and wiped his mouth. "This is a visitor stranded over at the Pine Tree," she said. He touched his cap.

"This kind lady offered me a hot meal while I wait out the weather," he explained. Isobel pursed her lips and looked from Denise to the stranger.

"Elmore Harbor is an out of the way spot," she said. "Sort of on your way to nowhere until summer. What brought you to our village in March? There's nothing open and it's too early in the season for lobsters. The fishermen won't start running their lines for a another week or so."

"Didn't come for lobsters, ma'am," he said, a little puzzled by her spate of blunt curiosity. "Took the wrong way off Route One on my way to Rockland and didn't realize the turn off led to a dead end peninsula. By the time I figured I'd made a mistake and should turn back, the fog rolled in too thick to drive. I came upon the motel up the road and the owner took pity and rented me a unit." He was talking too much but this woman Isobel's gaze held him in a steely grip that sucked words from him like filings to a magnet.

"So you walked here from the Pine Tree?"

"That I did ma'am. Did just as the owner said and followed the white line down the center of the road.

It wasn't that far and worth it." He looked at his empty plate. "This lady makes a real tasty pizza."

"You're lucky. Denise here is our local Dom De Lucas's. You should come back in the summer and sample her fruit pies. Crust melts in your mouth."

"If I ever get down this way again, I promise to do that." He had to get out of here or he'd unload his life history on this nosy woman. He pulled out his wallet and added a generous tip to the modest price of the meal.

The only heat in the store radiated from a space heater on the floor behind the checkout counter and he'd not bothered to take off his jacket while he ate. He tipped his cap to the two women and after the door jangled behind him, started back down the center of the road the way he'd come feeling chased by demons. Out of habit, he felt in the pocket for his cigarettes and stopped and swore when he remembered he'd not bought any. No matter, he'd rather suffer nicotine withdrawal than go back and face those two.

THIRTY-SEVEN

Isobel and Denise looked at each other.

"What do you think?" asked Isobel. "Could he be the man that broke in to my house and is now stuck here in the fog?" Already the whole of Elmore Harbor knew of Jen's attack down in Martinsville and Isobel's missing thief. Curiosity as to what the stranger made off with remained the current gossip and speculation.

"Much as I'd like," said Isobel, "there is no cause for the sheriff to pick that man up for questioning. Unless Jen identifies him as the one who tied her up, everything is circumstantial. We have only suspicions about a stranger in town, who may or may not be the man who threatened her and robbed me." Denise counted the man's money and stashed it in the till. She raised her brows at the twenty-dollar tip.

"If we call the sheriff and make a fuss, the story will be written up under Police Notes in the next *Free Trader* and, if it's all for naught, won't exactly boost our Harbor's reputation for hospitality," said Isobel. She rubbed her brow with her fingers. "It's just that I can't imagine anyone headed into Rockland would make the mistake and turn onto Route 136. It's a well marked right lane turn that dead ends at Port Clyde." She shook the question away and pulled a marketing list from her pocket.

"Almost forgot why I came here. The nearly blind trip into town made it quite a challenge not to run off the road, but my larder is bare and we've hungry houseguests."

"So I hear," said Denise. "Sue, over at the Dock, came by for groceries before the fog set in and said you have two unusual folks visiting. Museum people from Newport, Rhode Island? On their way into town, the lady and gent filled up at our pumps outside and came in to ask directions to your cottage. I remember the lady well as she had some kind of injury and drove an eye-popping sports car." Isobel smiled, amused, because by the time Amber and Latham left, the village would know more about both docents than her guests could imagine. Along with the joy and banes of a small town—its care and concern whenever needed—you accept a great lack of privacy. Isobel would never complain. Last year, that kind of special concern by a neighbor had saved her life.

She untangled an antique wire shopping cart and started along the aisles. After checking everything she needed off her list, she added bottles of wine and, surprise, a pricey imported Dutch gin for Latham. Where did Denise find this stuff? Finally, as her personal indulgence, Isobel went to the cold storage room and picked three tight sprays of Oriental Lilies from a bucket in the flower case. In the warmth of her house the buds would slowly open, releasing a sweet scent that would fill the cottage for days. Denise folded the lilies in tissue and packed the groceries into her canvas carryall.

"Isobel, I don't want to interfere and cause trouble, but I can't help thinking we should do *something* about this fellow? It's only an instinct—you of all people understand that. Maybe we can bring Jen over to the Pine Tree and find a way for her to get a look at him? She told the EMT boys from the fire station she'd recognize him if ever she saw him again."

"Denise, I share your instincts and don't worry. As soon as I get home and unload these groceries, Malo and I will figure out a way to drop by the Pine Tree and get a look at his plates before this fog lifts and he gets away."

Back at the cottage, Malo peered anxiously from the kitchen window, waiting for the sound of Isobel's return. At the crunch of tires on the gravel drive, he rushed out the door and down the porch steps. The minute she got out of her car, she saw his frowning face flushed with anger. He shook his Italian fist at the swirls of white engulfing them.

"Why did you go out in this weather alone? I never heard you leave. You could have run off the road or into a tree. Lie in some ditch bleeding to death until the fog lifts. Too much like last year. Did you think to take your mobile?"

"Hush, calm down. The trees haven't moved in forty years and I didn't run off the road. I'm sorry, and I appreciate your concern but I'm used to going and coming on my own. My cell is always in the glove box, and I promise I'll be more careful to charge it. Please be a gallant and help me tote in the groceries." She tucked the sheaf of Carmen-striped lilies in the crook of her arm and carried them into the pantry. Before arranging them in her favorite vase, she blunted the ends of their stems and snipped off the anthers from each blossom to prevent the red pollen staining the furniture. She was adding the enclosed packet of bloom keeper to the water when Amber hobbled into the kitchen.

"Let me help put the groceries away," she said. "I feel so useless and Latham and I are sorry the fog has caused us to abuse your hospitality."

"Don't be silly, we wouldn't risk your driving in this weather. Besides, we've enjoyed your stay." Malo, still irked, started unloading the bags of groceries. Puzzled, he held out a warty and hairy brown knob.

"What is it?"

"Celeriac. It's a vegetable for my *remolade.*" He frowned at the ugly object. "Hope it tastes better than it looks." Amber took the root from his hand and shooed him from the kitchen. Before he left, Isobel held up a hand to stop him. "Wait, I have a bit of news." She told the docents of meeting the stranger at the market and Denise's story of his being stranded down the road at the Pine Tree. "I'd like to get Jen over there to have a look at him before he leaves. As soon as I walked in, he scarfed down his meal and left in a hurry. I wouldn't be surprised if he's our man and took a chance with blind driving and bolted." Latham beamed at them.

"We may be too late to stop your thief, but I've just heard the weather and NOAA says the fog will lift by morning. One more night and we will be out of your hair." Isobel cut the string from a sheet of newsprint and unwrapped a large slice of swordfish.

"Put that in the fridge Amber, if you please. I watched Denise cut it off a fresh caught fish the size of a whale. It's tonight's dinner and, broiled with dill and lemon, should melt in our mouths." She handed Latham the bottle of gin. "This is for all your help and, if I can, ask one more favor."

"Of course, and thank you so much," he held up the bottle. "Forget tulips, this genever elixir is Holland's finest export", he said with reverence. "Whatever can I do for you?"

"I just explained to Amber and Malo what I learned at the market. I think perhaps our thief is stranded at a motel down the road and we need to get his license number before he gets away. Jen said she would recognize him if she saw him again." Isobel paused. "But on second thought, maybe that's too risky. I feel guilty enough over involving so many innocent people in my problem. Also, now that he's seen me, he might have made the connection with the ring and assume I will call the sheriff. Amber's ankle is not steady enough to chase villains, but he's never laid eyes on you, Latham. Would you drive by the motel and get a look at his license? Denise said he's the only one staying there."

Malo came into the kitchen and Isobel saw his temper improve when he saw Latham cradling the bottle of Damrak. "Ah, martini time," Malo said. "Ladies, I overheard you and I think a wiser plan is for Latham and I to drive there together." He grinned at Amber. "Before our thief 'gets out of Dodge,' as you Americans say." She muttered a rude sound and handed him the jar of olives from the fridge. He thanked her politely. "Not to mention, my dear Isobel, that if you're right and he is your thief, you are the one in danger."

"I agree," said Latham, and after hearing the account of your recent tangling with villains, it sounds like, so far this year, you've survived a dicey track record. Within months, you have managed to win out over Mafia smugglers and escaped a murderous art forger. Let's not tempt a hand-severing, jewel thief." Amber let out a roar of delight.

"I love it Isobel, tangle away! To me, your life sounds an unending source of pulp fiction despite how often these zealous attacks get you in trouble." Isobel waited for her to add that they must get on with the game. Amber placed the gin bottle and martini glasses in the freezer and looked at her watch, a fuchsia plastic device with a dial that, instead of numbers, showed signs of the zodiac. She pointed at Malo and Latham. "Our drinks ritual will wait until you return."

The beer and pizza had made him drowsy and, back at the Pine Tree, the stranger struggled awake and propped himself on one elbow. He blinked at the sun now streaming through the open blinds. The fog had lifted while he napped and he knew it was time to get out. Quickly he collected his few belongings and stuffed them into a canvas duffle. He had paid his bill in cash when he arrived and, leaving the room key on top of a ten-dollar bill, was in his car and on the road out of town within minutes. His euphoria vanished when the dashboard's blinking gas pump's icon warned him to stop and fill the tank. He wanted no more delays until he and the diamond were safely back in Providence.

Ahead, on the left he smiled when he saw the sign. *'Piggy's Gas and Grub'*. He slowed and pulled in beside the single self-serve pump. Nerves and eagerness to get away had robbed him of hunger and, though tempted by the large lettered sign in the window that read 'fresh roasted turkey sandwiches,' he decided not to risk going inside and being seen by more curious town folk. If he got hungry, he'd stop at a plaza down the turnpike and stock up on junk food. While he stood and listened to the gallons rumble into the tank, he forced himself to calm down and consider his predicament. Too many people in that harbor he'd left behind could identify him and link him to the theft and have the cops on his tail within the hour. He frowned and decided that damn woman Isobel was a serious threat and, like the whore who had begun all his trouble, had to be dealt with. He inserted his card into the slot that paid for the gas and collected his receipt. He hesitated for only a moment before deliberately turning the car around and head back down the road to the harbor.

At the turnoff to Neck Road, he drove slowly, not expecting such luck. The red sports car he'd seen parked in the drive of the Van Dursan woman's cottage the night he'd collected the ring was parked at the side of the road. Just beyond her car, at the edge of the road, stood a white wooden signpost lettered Roaring Spout with a painted arrow pointing into the woods. He stopped and scanned the pine forest beyond. The track didn't look like it would lead anywhere near the ocean, but land geography was not his strong point. He drove ahead and, a few yards beyond, pulled into a lane where his car would be hidden from the road.

The wind had risen and, as he cut the engine and pushed open the car door, its force slammed it back against the thin skin of his shin. He cursed at the pain and rubbed his ankle. He felt blood trickle down inside his pant leg and fumbled in his pocket for a tissue. While he mopped at the mess, he saw that storm doors boarded the entrance of the house at the end of the driveway and guessed it closed up for the winter.

THIRTY-EIGHT

NOAA was wrong. They did not have to wait until the next morning for the fog to lift. As Malo and Latham pulled onto the road into town, they saw the wind sway the top branches of the pines and melt away the fog as fast as it had rolled in. Streamers of sun filtered down through the tree boughs from a sky suddenly turned the deep blue of aconite.

Following Isobel's directions, the men had no trouble finding the Pine Tree motel. They drove the road through town, passed the abandoned quarry, and pulled in to the forecourt of the motel owner's quarters. The entrance sign at the row of cottages read 'Closed For The Winter'. They got out and Malo knocked on the office door. To their surprise, it opened immediately and a small, dark haired woman, who must have been watching from behind a curtain, regarded them over wire-rimmed glasses.

"I've been expecting you," she announced, wiping her hands on her apron. "You must be Mr. Bellini, Isobel's friend. She called me and said you'd be by. Good thing. Wouldn't have answered your knock otherwise. Not after what happened to my friend Jen down in Martinsville." She nodded over her shoulder. "Come in."

Malo suppressed a grin. His year spent with Isobel in this out of the way harbor, reminded him of his past life in the Irish hamlet where his mother was born, lived a long life and died. Long before telephones, news in that isolated village traveled like ripples across a pond, elaborating and recording the endless chain of gossip that gave substance to their days.

The men followed her into what could only be described as an old-fashioned parlor. Velour covered chairs guarded each side of the fireplace; their arms protected by crocheted antimacassars. An upright piano topped with a fringed Mexican serape was covered with framed photographs of what seemed like an entire orphanage of children.

"Set yourself," she said. Latham perched on the piano stool that no doubt stored reams more of the sheet music displayed on the piano's scrolled stand. Good God, when had anyone last bought sheet music? He wished Amber could have been with them and seen this room. She would immediately gather everyone around the keyboard and lead them in a chorus of *"Oh, Susannah"*. The small bulky television held no position of honor in this room and he bet that this woman owned no digital devices.

Malo suddenly felt stifled. This fusty room smelled of old people and brought back too many memories from a past he would rather forget.

"You missed him," she announced. "The stranger you're looking for. He took off less than an hour ago. Told me he'd take a chance that it might clear up as he drove further inland."

The afternoon sun filtered through the lace-curtained window and she squinted at the men against its patterns of light. "He guessed right about the clearing weather and

I had no reason to stop him from leaving. I checked his room and he left the unit tidy and his key on the dresser. I never heard him drive off."

"When he signed in," asked Latham, "did you take down his license number? Rental cars have identifying tags and we can trace him through the agency if we need to."

She scowled and shook her head. "You some sort of authority? Can't help you. Didn't deal with any signing in. Explained that we're closed for the season, but we're church people and I considered it the duty of a Good Samaritan to give him a room under these conditions—this thick pea souper came on quick. What'd the young man do anyway? Despite what you suggest, he looked a decent sort, and when he offered me generous money for my trouble, I gave him the key to the only unit we keep open in winter. She pointed to the photographs that covered every flat surface. "For when friends and family come to visit."

Latham shrugged at Malo, both disappointed to have missed him by minutes, but neither of them offered her further information or the reason for their inquiries. They thanked her. As she started to close the door, Malo turned and raised a hand.

"One more question. Could you describe his appearance? Jen, your friend who we think he attacked, told the EMT fellows who found her that she could identify him if she saw him again, even though he wore a stocking mask covering his face. She said he was short and muscular, and for sure, she'd recognize his cocky attitude." She nodded.

"He's your man."

When they returned, they found Amber sitting outside on the deck, basking in the limpid spring sun.

"We missed him by minutes," said Malo. "He took off just before we arrived. The owner didn't bother to get his plate number, but she described him. We should phone Jen and, if she agrees it's him, call the sheriff." He looked around. "Where's Isobel?" Amber hesitated and looked at him warily.

"The minute the sun came out and she stopped worrying about you two running off the road or into a tree or lying unconscious in a ditch, she grabbed up a walking stick and strode off down the road. Announced she felt caged by cabin fever and needed some fresh air." They ignored her sarcasm about ditches and looked up at the swaying branches of the fir trees. "Though the way this wind's come up," Amber added, "she'll have a chilly walk." Malo leaned his palms against the deck railing and stared out at the ocean. Rolling waves, crested with whitecaps, raced down the harbor.

"Did she say where she was headed?"

"Indeed," answered Amber. "She said there's a clearing high on a cliff above the outer ocean called Roaring Spout, and during a sou'easterly like this, it's a spectacular place to watch the surf crash against the rocks. Said the spray bursts high enough to wet your face. It sounds wonderfully dramatic and I hate not being agile enough to go with her, but this damn ankle is not up to a hike through the woods."

"She's often talked about the Spout, but I've never been there," mused Malo. Latham looked confused.

"Something about the name rings a bell." He snapped his fingers. "I remember. I saw it on a roadside signpost driving down Neck Road on our way here. From the road, it looked pretty rough, more like a foot track than drivable." Malo jiggled Isobel's car keys in his hand. "Latham, you stay here and keep Amber company," he said. "I'll drive up the road, park at the turn off to this overlook and follow the path to the top on foot. I'm sure Isobel's fine, but she's been touchy lately about interfering with her independence and I'd rather stay out of sight. I don't want her to think I'm chasing her." Latham glanced at Amber and saw her smother a smile. "We understand completely."

THIRTY-NINE

The stranger thought it wise to have left his car off the road. The rough trail he followed from the signpost at the edge of the road wound though the woods and around glades of orange-banded trees marked to be saved from the bulldozer. Among the machine's ridged tracks, cleared and staked areas showed where construction would continue when the weather warmed enough to pour footings. Where the woods thinned, the rutted tracks of the dozer skirted groves of deciduous, catkin-tasseled aspens, white paper birch, and wild apple trees, kept protected by a thwarting undergrowth of brambles. Those saved trees would remain an oasis of color come spring. But this early none had leafed out and their bare braches allowed the wind to roar through the pines overhead. Twice he hesitated when the trail forked and he had to choose blindly which path to follow. He was no Natty Bumppo and, lacking a knife to scar notches, he relied on memory to find his way back.

The soil lay hard-packed beneath his feet and if the woman had hiked ahead, she'd left no evidence. His eyes wandered and he tripped over a rotting log that tumbled and crumbled to reveal a seething cache of some pale hibernating larvae. He bent to look more closely and, fascinated by the wiggling mass, noticed a round indentation in the dirt. He raised his eyes and saw the holes followed a regular line, as if made by the tip of a walking stick. How convenient, he thought. Like finding a trail of breadcrumbs.

The ground rose slowly as he climbed and his shortness of breath and pounding heart forced him to stop. He listened for some sound of crashing surf. If this awesome Spout lay ahead, its roar was muted by the soughing of wind in the trees. The trail beneath him steepened as it narrowed. His eyes were intent on the ground when the stick's indentations suddenly disappeared.

He had no choice but to continue upward but when he stopped to clutch at a sudden stitch in his side, realized that if he came upon the woman, he'd be trapped on this narrow path with nowhere to hide. His fingers ran along the belt at his waist and felt the lump of the diamond secure in its lining. He had made no plan and carried no weapon. The motto taught among thieves he had known was that, when conceiving a crime, the simpler the better. Kiss.

Back at Denise's market he had noticed that Isobel was a slight woman and, even if they struggled, at the top of this climb, he was sure he could use his strength and weight to advantage. He straightened as the stitch passed but, still winded, waited and considered his lack of plan. Perhaps not so simple if his luck failed and she proved some Lisbeth Salander clone and possessed an arsenal of self-defense skills. He shrugged off this remote possibility and decided to take the chance that, underneath that frumpy L.L. Bean jacket, she wore no black belt in karate.

Confident he could overcome her physically, he assessed the rest of the odds in his favor. From this Roaring Spout cliff-top, he saw no lobster boats running their lines out to observe him and too early in the season for the hardiest of offshore sailors to be cruising Down East. He respected the power of the ocean from his years spent at sea and would rely on its force as his greatest advantage. The woman's body, pounded by the surf among the granite boulders below, would be unrecognizable by the time the currents washed her ashore down the coast. If she surfaced after weeks, maybe never, he would be long gone on a far distant ocean.

Her stalker was right in that Isobel possessed no arcane martial arts, but as Malo had implied earlier, her acute hearing could detect a fart in a gale. Isobel had been aware for some time of someone following her. At first she assumed it was Malo. He had annoyed her lately by his over-concern for her safety. She stopped to lean on her walking stick and listened. From long hours spent reading to Anna during her battle with emphysema, she recognized the sound of labored breathing from somewhere behind her.

Good heavens, was she being paranoid? Any one of her neighbors might have felt the same urge to hike up here to watch the storm's display. She tried to recall whose damaged lungs might be suffering from the climb, but could not think of any friends who still smoked. It definitely was not Malo. He reminded her constantly how much he abhorred the filthy habit and waved away the air at any whiff of smoke.

To her advantage, Isobel had thought it wise to wear her old hiking jacket that blended into the underbrush like a hunter's camouflage. She decided to keep still and wait for him on the small ledge tucked below the opening where it widened onto the cliff head. Generations of Neck children had used this cozy aerie as their secret retreat. It still remains a favorite picnic spot for the ambitious, sloping safely away from the edge and level enough to spread a blanket. What activity beside picnics went on up here between the town's teenagers was something parents tried to ignore.

At the moment, Isobel did not feel either cozy or safe. An unpleasant spasm tightened her stomach and she felt the throb of pulse in her temples. Besides, she couldn't bear it if Malo proved right and, after her protests that she could watch out for her self, had carelessly allowed someone to threaten her life. No need to fuel another of his lectures on caution. She remembered the burly man who had looked up from his pizza when she'd entered the market and eyed her so warily. She dismissed the thought of him stalking her because the weather had cleared and, if he'd had any sense, he'd have left by now.

Isobel lifted the flap of her jacket pocket and ferreted inside among the gritty jumble of lip balms—her winter makeup—plastic baggies, her trusty red knife, and a wad of tissues. She carried the plastic bags for any worthy specimen she might come upon, and the Swiss knife to pluck it. The tissue crumples were for the constant dabbing at her allergy-plagued eyes. Not a lot of weaponry. She must look into that mace spray Jo said she must not leave home without. Did you need a license to carry a Taser?

Behind her, she heard the thud of a stumble followed by a man's muffled curse. She froze motionless as a statue. During a lull in the wind, the woods around her fell silent. She heard the rasp of a match and, followed by a labored exhalation, smelled the sharp odor of smoke. Isobel wrinkled her nose when the harsh reek of tobacco overpowered the sweet resinous smell of pine. Masked by the sound of wheezing, she felt safe to move behind a screen of brush hiding the ledge below the cliff head. Heart pounding, she held her breath and waited; sure he could hear the throb in her chest.

FORTY

Malo pulled off the road in Isobel's red car and parked beside the Roaring Spout signpost. He sat for a moment behind the wheel, angry when he remembered how he'd endured this same situation only a few weeks ago. That dark afternoon, he'd parked on the drive in front of Maude's turreted house overlooking Long Island Sound and, on this stormy afternoon, here he sat again, chasing after Isobel. He got out and locked the door, relieved that this time no other car blocked his way and no water tank waited ahead to drown her. He pulled down his wool cap to cover his ears and recalled Amber's description of the view from this precipitous headland. Would Isobel's headstrong decision to climb alone to its top claim a far worse end than a dunk in a water tank?

Malo was unaware that, ahead of him, the thief had followed Isobel to the top and had heaved himself onto the clearing at the cliff's edge. The stranger stood high above the ocean, deafened by the din of the surf and breathless from the effort of the climb. His throat felt sore and he tossed his cigarette into the sea and swore it would be his last smoke.

He studied the trees and brush surrounding the lookout but saw no sign of the woman he had so laboriously followed up this damn mountain. Winded, he rested, waiting for the pain in his chest to ease, when a spray of surf burst high from the ocean below and obscured his vision. Blinded, his eyes stinging with salt water, he stepped back from the crumbling brim and wiped his face with his sleeve. When his vision cleared, and even though soaked by spray, he had to admit that this cliff top rivaled the elation he'd felt while standing at a vessel's forepeak during storms at sea. A seagull screamed and soared in the air overhead and a magnificent sense of pleasure overwhelmed him.

The thief never saw her. He never heard a sound. One minute he stood poised, vibrant and alive, awed by the ocean's spectacular havoc and the next felt a sharp thrust in the center of his back that sent him, like Icarus, falling onto the rocks below.

FORTY-ONE

Malo stopped on the path below the cliff top and sighed with relief when he saw Isobel leaning on her stick and staring out at the angry ocean. She stood precariously near the edge, but he forced himself to keep quiet. During a pause in the surf's violence, it did not surprise him when she turned and motioned him to come stand beside her.

"Worth the climb, don't you think?" she asked.

Malo glanced at the overhang and merely nodded in assent. Dramatic heights, especially unguarded, made him queasy, and he reached forward to take a firm hold of her arm.

"Wonderful," he lied and gently urged her back from the edge. The sky had faded from blue to a pale overcast, and the gusts of wind that had wet them with bursts of icy spray, now felt more harsh than exhilarating. Malo zipped his jacket to the neck. "Let's go home," he urged, "we'll build us a fire, and have that martini Latham's been waiting for." Isobel took hold of his hand but, before turning to follow, she gave one last glance over her shoulder at the surf churning and foaming among the granite boulders below.

The path leading back down to the road was too narrow to walk together and, until they reached the open track below, Isobel strode in front at a pace that made Malo scramble to follow. She did not slow to rest or speak and, when they came upon the car parked by the side of Neck road, she still remained silent. When he opened the door and helped her into the passenger seat, he felt her entire body shaking.

"What's wrong?"

"He came after me," she said. "Followed me up there; the thief who stole the ring. I'm sure it was him." Malo reached across the seat and cupped her hands between his. They were icy cold and he turned on the ignition and set the heater control on high. They waited silently while the fan hummed its warmth through the car. She had stood alone when he reached her and he could guess what had unnerved her. Until the shock wore off, he understood her reluctance to talk.

"Let's go home," she said. "I need a long soak in a hot bath and one of Latham's martinis—maybe two. After they've done their job and, in front of that fire you promised, I'll tell you what happened."

Amber and Latham rallied as the perfect houseguests. Malo hustled a numbed and distracted Isobel up to her bath. Amber started to speak, but when he raised a hand at their frowns of concern, he saw they recognized her distress and postponed their questions.

Upstairs, Isobel lay back with her head cushioned against the slope of her claw foot tub and indulged in a miasma of scented steam. Downstairs, Latham added wood to the fire while Amber set out a buffet supper from leftovers she'd found in the fridge. The fresh fish bought the day before would keep.

By the time Isobel came down, the glasses and silver shaker were frosted and waiting to be filled with Latham's Dutch gin.

"First things first," he said after Amber settled a relaxed and rosy Isobel on the sofa in a reversal of roles. With her feet up, wrapped in a silk dressing gown and smelling of expensive bath crystals, she accepted a generous martini. Latham handed the others their glasses and they toasted each other's health, content to sit and gaze at the fire while its warmth and the alcohol did their work. Isobel apologized for the lack of crudities, but Amber insisted that the pimento stuffed olives flavoring their drinks qualified as a vegetable canapé.

"So," said Latham, "I take it your walk in the woods proved successful?" Isobel looked amazingly revived and Malo, though he remained irked by her stubborn lack of good sense, could not hide his relief at her resilience.

"I can only imagine that our thief had second thoughts after I walked in on him at Denise's." She looked at Malo and returned his warning look. "I know. I know it was foolish, but I really enjoyed giving him the evil eye. He bolted his meal and left the store in such a hurry that, after he drove off from the motel, must have decided I remained too much a liability. That he'd better play it safe and take a chance on returning to track me down and get rid of me." She ignored Malo's look of dismay and held up her palm to ward off a new volley of recriminations.

"Don't bother to tell me. Under the circumstances, I made a lapse in judgment to hike up there alone. I acted rashly and, with your constant reminders, am well aware that my zealous behavior is a recurrent problem." Malo held his tongue. "Again, today I was lucky but let me say that perhaps your angry concern is more distress from self-blame than my recklessness. This time Malo, please believe me when I insist that you are in no way responsible. My decision to dispose of this thief was not the usual business assignment between us so forget the guilt. When I heard him come up behind me at the top of that cliff, I knew he intended to kill me. I acted on impulse and reversed the plan but did it of my own will." She smiled, "I expect no perks for the job."

They had finished dinner by the time she ended her story, and Latham held a brandy snifter toward the fire and rolled it between his palms.

"I feel I can speak for Amber and think we both agree," he said diplomatically, "that, during this year alone Isobel, you have gained enough points to win a merit badge for fortuitous—what do you call them—disposals?" Malo looked at him wryly and directed muttered words at his shoes.

The combined warmth of the fire and Latham's potent gin finally proved too much for them. They needed no excuse when Malo announced that Isobel, despite her protests, had weathered enough of this day and insisted they all go to bed. When phone rang, Isobel made a feeble attempt to move from the couch, but Amber was the only one who managed to rouse herself. Malo held up his hand and motioned her back to her seat.

"Do not touch it," he said firmly, pointing to the instrument. "That is someone calling to plague us."

"Too harsh," said Amber. "Not knowing who called would drive Isobel crazy." Her eyes sparkled in the firelight. "And possibly, for a change, it might be good news. You stay," she pointed to Isobel as if commanding a dog. "If necessary, I promise to take a message." Without aid of her cane, she crossed the room and lifted the receiver.

"Mrs. Van Dursan?" The background noise and a mechanical airport voice announcing arrivals and departures made the caller's question barely audible. "Is this Isobel? I'm trying to reach Mr. Malo Bellini. I'm sorry if I'm calling too late, but my flight from Europe was delayed and I'd like to speak with him if he's there."

Amber put her hand over the receiver.

"It's a man with a charming accent asking for Malo Bellini. From the racket, it sounds like he's calling from a busy airport." She held out the phone. "Are you here or not?"

"Good God, yes." Malo crossed the room and grabbed the receiver from her hand. He recognized his son's questioning hellos competing with the *telefonino's* crackle in his ear.

"*Pronto* Michello. *Di dove sei?* Where are you?"

"At Logan Airport in Boston and it's a mob scene. Bad weather, all the fog, delayed so many the flights. I'd like to get out of here and if this area code 207 I'm calling is in Maine, I'll try to make some connection and join you. Life these past weeks has been a zoo dealing with *mamma* and I need some R and R." Warning bells sounded in Malo's ears.

"What's happened to your mother?" There was a lengthy silence on the line.

"That's a long story," said Michello. "I'll tell you when I see you. Are you in Elmore Harbor?"

"Yes, of course," said Malo. He smiled and his son could hear it in his voice.

"Ah, papa, I made a good guess, *si*? You are with *la bella* Isobella?"

"Yes, is that a problem for you?"

"No, papa, your private affairs are your own. You know you never allowed me to interfere with your business—personal or that of your other *familia.*" Malo took a long breath. Aside from the nature of his work, Malo's major regret was the distance he'd been forced to keep from his son during his *capo* years with the Mafia. He found it remarkable that he and Michello remained, if not close, at least friends. Leaving his son in a succession of strict boarding schools and vacations shuffled between the Irish aunts were poor substitutes for an absent father. His negligence fueled Malo's eternal penance of Catholic guilt. To this day, these same aged and pious aunts never ceased to remind or forgive him his failings. But both his and the boy's life had suffered even worse turmoil caused by his wife. She had been the weak half of an arranged marriage and he barely knew the veiled young woman before he met her at the altar. The boy's mother remained a stranger to both he and their son and still drifted in and out of her self-absorbed *melata del mente.* With effort, he pulled his mind from his regrets of the past.

"I promise, *mi figlio,*" he spoke firmly, "that aspect of my business is finished as I promised are my dealings with certain former associates."

"If you say *mi padre,* but it doesn't sound so. From what I hear, you and Bella are having another busy year?"

"Ah, but that, Michello, is an entirely different kind of business." He heard the ironic tone of his son's reply.

"Of course, papa." "Isobel and I have dealt with some unpleasant people lately, completely unrelated to what you call my other 'family,' and during that time, I must admit we have become more comfortable together." That wasn't entirely true, as he did not consider the operations of the Chinese Triad scavenging the Northwest harbors part of his realm. There was a pause on the line, but before his son could draw him into further discussion, he changed the subject. "So, tell me, what has brought you across from across the ocean at this mean time of year?"

"Papa, to be frank, I can't stop thinking about Jo and want to renew my relationship—what a chilly word—with Isobel's niece. Is she with you in Maine or gone back to work in New York?" Malo slumped onto a chair beside the desk. He was too tired to deal with this delicate complication over the phone at this hour. His anxiety over Isobel's close call only hours ago must have disturbed him more that he realized.

"Yes, well Jo also has had a busy year." He didn't mention with whom. He knew it was a nebulous answer but was all he could manage. "We can talk about it when you get here." He looked at his watch. "If you've flown from home, you are jet hours behind and I'm sure equally tired. It's too late to come tonight. Isobel has had an eventful day and we are all exhausted. There is a local airport here in Owl's Head with connections from Boston. Spend the night somewhere nearby and fly here in the morning. Give us a call on your *telefonino* and we will pick you up when you arrive in Thomaston."

"Sounds good, papa. *Ciao* and *dormi bene, si vede al matino.*" Malo let the receiver fall onto the cradle and moved slowly to drop down beside Isobel on the sofa. He doubted he'd sleep well, but it would good to see his son in the morning.

"I apologize my dear," he said wearily. "This time I'm afraid it's my family come to plague us." She smiled and ran her hand down the unshaven roughness of his cheek.

"I'm sorry," she said. "It sounds as if there is more difficulty with your *signora*? I would love to quote Tom," she said, "but I'm afraid you would do the abominable thing and roll your eyes. Don't worry. How do I say 'no problem' in Italian?" He didn't bother to answer.

"I don't speak Italian," said Amber, "but isn't your wife the woman who tried to kill Isobel? If you have enough room and the patience, Latham and I would love to meet this most charming sounding young man."

"We could call Jen and see if she has room at her infamous rooming house in Martinsville," said Latham. "Give you privacy here with your son. From what we overheard, it sounds like there is a family *problemo.*"

FORTY-TWO

"I'm sure Jen would have room for you but you're welcome to stay on here," said Isobel. "We have plenty of space upstairs for Michello and loads of blankets. Sheets are probably musty, but your ankle seems better and we can share the housekeeping." Latham stood in front of the waning fire and rubbed his palms together.

"We don't mind dust or must. I'll get more gin and Amber's a whiz in the kitchen." To clinch a winning bribe, Amber smiled broadly at Malo.

"Tomorrow morning, I trust you to drive my motor to the Owl's Head airport to pick up your son." Isobel tilted her head and winked at Amber. From the look on his face, they both knew it a done deal.

The next morning Isobel, Latham and Amber sat and waited with their breakfast coffee outside on the deck and, feet up and heads back, soaked in the pallid spring sun. Isobel checked her watch again. They had been gone far longer than necessary to drive to the airport and back. Even allowing for a late arrival. But she had called Owls Head before they left and reassured that, as the weather had cleared, Michello's plane from Boston was on time. She had even the brief, wild thought that Malo might have abducted Amber's motorcar. She discarded that irrational idea when the crunch of tires on gravel announced their return. The three rose to welcome them. His son, as dark haired and handsome as Isobel remembered, strode up the stairs and, after she introduced him to Amber, he kissed her guest's hand with continental aplomb. Isobel drew Malo aside.

"Where have you been? We called before you left and they said his plane was on time. I am sorry to say, but I actually worried that you and Michello might have taken off in Amber's car." She thought he looked sheepish before he turned to gaze at the Jaguar he'd left parked in the drive.

"Isobel, I admit I came close. I drove through South Thomaston on our way back and passed a foreign car dealership. I'm afraid I could not resist going inside and make some inquiries."

"Inquiries?" It was all she could ask before his son and the docents interrupted them and he escaped upstairs.

Earlier that morning she and Amber had aired out and made up an upstairs bedroom overlooking the harbor for Michello. After he settled in and returned downstairs with his father, Latham poured them lunchtime bloody marys. By the time they'd eaten the last of the grilled swordfish and finished the meal with pie a la mode made from last summer's frozen blueberries, everyone felt relaxed and content.

She and Malo decided to wait until later to delve into the details of Isobel's near escape the day before. Michello could hear those details after he and his father had a chance to discuss their own dilemma. She could see the pleasure he felt at reuniting with his son. It made yesterday's unpleasant hike seem a remote kind of fantasy. Malo's more immediate concern was to cope with this latest situation. His wife's newest imposition upon their life and its effect on Michello could not be swept aside. Latham, Amber and Isobel tactfully moved into the kitchen to clean up while the Bellinis went out on the deck. Malo sat and faced his son, braced to hear the worst.

"So now tell me what has happened to your mother?" Michello leaned forward to rest his arms on his thighs and stared at his father.

"Papa, she's escaped again and you know what? I don't care. We spend a fortune to keep her in that fancy 'asylum' and it's up to them to find her and bring her back. I've had enough and, I'm sorry, but I have no more feelings for her. All my life she's ignored me, been nothing to me but this weird behaving alien." He shrugged. "So, I left."

Malo felt saddened by his son's confession. His mother's behavior was not Michello's fault and he, not his son, was the one who should be burdened with this responsibility.

"You did the right thing," he said. "Don't worry. I promise to find and take care of your mother. Try to relax and enjoy yourself. This quiet harbor is a good place to unwind and recover your good humor." Michello let out his breath with almost childlike relief. Malo thought how, at least one constant in his son's life had been his faith in papa's ability to 'fix things.'

"Thank you, papa. That's what I expected you'd say. And, as I said, the real reason I came here was to find Jo and have some fun for a change."

Isobel came out with a tray holding a carafe of coffee and mugs.

"So," she said, passing sugar and milk while Michello poured coffee. "How are things with the Signora?"

"That will be taken care of," said Malo. "It is not your worry. What Michello asks is that we track down Jo." Isobel looked at him and then at his son. Oh my, she thought, the alpha male contest is on.

While they drank their coffee, hundreds of miles south Jo sipped at a tall rum Collins. Her tanned body glistened with sunscreen and she smelled like a coconut. The wicker chaise where she lay overlooked the serene blue length of an infinity pool and acres of manicured golf greens stretched beyond. Pen had left early to play the course with a fellow golfer he'd met at dinner the night before and Jo assured him she preferred to lay back and soak up the perfect day alone. Before leaving their rooms that morning for the short walk to the pool, she had debated whether or not to drop her cell phone into her tote. Like her aunt, she'd become a firm believer that most bad news came by phone and, after the past season with Isobel, she could do without hearing more. But when the familiar theme from *Jeopardy* erupted from the bag at her feet, curiosity got the better of her. She fumbled for the phone and checked the caller ID.

Sure enough, the green digital 207 area code flashed on the screen. Despite an urge to toss the device in the pool, she took a fortifying pull through the straw poking from her drink and pressed the answer icon.

"Jo?" Her aunt's voice in her ear sounded calm and collected and held none of the urgency that might signal some new calamity.

"Aunt Isobel. What's up?" Jo held her breath. No matter what new disaster, she and Pen were enjoying themselves too much to leave this idyllic haven and return to New England's chill. Easy-going, non-demanding Pen had proved the ideal companion on this current stretch of indulgence. From the beginning of their time together, she refused to call it a 'relationship', she had resolved not to ask him where the money came from that supported these expensive vacations. She would delay opening that Pandora's box until necessary. If ever a commitment seemed imminent, they would take time to discuss these practicalities.

"Good news, Jo," said Isobel, jarring her back to the present. "We have a surprise houseguest who's asking for you. Have you made any plans to return?"

Jo rattled the ice in her drink. With a sinking feeling and, despite instant relief that it was not some new family crisis, intuition told her exactly who had arrived in the harbor.

"Michello Bellini," she said. She almost laughed at Isobel's intake of breath.

"Well, yes. How did you know?"

"Aunt Isobel. It wasn't hard to guess. He's the only one that came to mind and, I confess, despite the short time we spent together, I often think of him. He is an intriguing man." She paused, "So different from Pen."

"I don't want to pry into your private life," said Isobel, "but I assume you and Pen are somewhere warm—together?"

"We certainly are and, as you would approve, enjoying life on that luxurious level you promised when you signed me on as your sidekick." She almost said accomplice but bit her tongue.

"I'm glad," said Isobel. "Shall I tell Michello you are away for a time? Although," she paused. "I'd hate to see his face if I gave him that news. Would you at least call here and talk to him? I don't want to act the intermediary after he's flown all this way." Jo, muddled by sun and rum, needed time to think. They had been lolling about here over a week and she found herself a little bored by too much idle pampering. She actually missed her work and the energy of the city. In a few weeks, Manhattan would erupt into vibrant spring with daffodils and early blooming trees lining the avenues. She hoped that Pen might have had enough golf and knew him too impatient for beach sitting.

"Aunt Isobel. I must be mad. When I saw the call came from you, I made up my mind nothing less than disaster would return me to Maine. Now, hearing your voice, some magical attraction has changed my mind." Hearing Isobel's relief, they ended their call. She hung up and finished her drink. She must, when completely sober, think this one through. On the path back to the hotel, she looked back at the shimmering pool that beckoned for one last warm swim, but decided against it. She missed the salty tang of the ocean.

FORTY-THREE

Pen came into their suite and flopped down beside her on the bed. The misery on his face told all.

"Had a bad round?"

"I'm giving up golf." He pulled his cap down over his eyes. "Must have been the balls." She held up her cell phone.

"I had a call from Isobel." He bolted up but she pushed him back down. "No, everything's fine. She just wondered when we're coming home."

"What did you tell her?"

"From the lift and question in his voice, she guessed that maybe, he too, was tired of vacation. Later, as they walked along the tree-lined path to the dining room's veranda for a late lunch, they agreed that it was time to leave.

Later, on the flight home she looked across at Pen, sprawled asleep in his seat, and decided Michello's presence when they arrived in the Harbor would be an interesting surprise.

Isobel met them at the airport in Owl's Head and, on the ride out to the harbor, neither she nor Jo mentioned the elephant waiting at the cottage.

Their meeting was indeed a surprise for both men and, although good manners prevented verbal hostility, Isobel and Jo felt the aura of bristle between them. Malo, aware of the tension, glanced nervously at his watch. Definitely a good time for Latham to concoct something to lubricate the awkwardness.

Whatever they drank, plus the two bottles of claret that accompanied the garlicky rib roast, by the end of dinner that evening, everyone had mellowed. At ten, Pen pointed to the clock, yawned, possessed Jo's hand and headed toward the stairs.

"Excuse us," he said. "We've schlepped on and off planes and taxis since dawn and I'm beat." He looked pointedly at Jo. "Ready for bed?" Isobel shrugged helplessly at her niece from behind Malo and his son. Jo smiled up at Pen but, before following him upstairs, removed her hand from his grasp, crossed the room and gave Michello a kiss.

"Good to see you again."

Made in the USA
Middletown, DE
06 July 2021